# THE KNIGHT ON THE BRIDGE

William Watson, novelist, playwright and journalist, was born in Scotland. Of his first novel Isabel Quigly said, "He writes glitteringly funny stuff that seems to move on the pages of *Better than One* as if juggled by a skilful, paranoiac compositor . . . he turns out to have not just a way with words but a mind worth meeting." *The Last of the Templars* the present novel's predessor was described by Martin Seymour-Smith as "a highly impressive and unusual historical novel . . . no mere historical entertainment but a study of inner life, of great beauty and wisdom, and containing much poetry and grim enchantment. It deserves treatment as a major achievement".

William Watson, writing as J K Mayo, is also the creator of the Harry Seddall thrillers.

D0680927

*William Watson*

# THE KNIGHT
# ON THE BRIDGE

THE HARVILL PRESS
LONDON

First published by Chatto & Windus in 1982

This edition published 1996
by The Harvill Press
84 Thornhill Road
London N1 1RD

9 8 7 6 5 4 3 2 1

Copyright © William Watson, 1982

William Watson asserts the moral right to be
identified as the author of this work

A CIP catalogue record for this title
is available from the British Library

ISBN 1 86046 140 9

Printed and bound in Great Britain by
Butler & Tanner, Frome and London

For
CATHERINE

# CONTENTS

## PART I. THE DREAM

## PART II. WAKING

# CONTENTS

*Part I*

# THE DREAM

## Chapter 1

# THE MADMAN

THE Minervois was a desert. It hung under the sky as if it had been thrown up there, scorned by earth and spurned by Heaven. "Who would blame them?" the madman cried aloud.

He stood on a stone plain that stretched to the horizon. From his feet to that far edge of the plateau was a world made of stone, an adamantine floor covered with boulders, heaps of splintered rock and banks of pebbles. Bushes flourished close to the ground, some as high as a man's knee, a few to the hip, and here and there had grown a tree, of walnut or yew or olive: but even in their flower and with the butterflies upon them, these follies of nature did not mask the desolate character of the place. Here was a wasteland, an end of the earth.

The man who had shouted was tall and leaned a little down. It was if he had been made too high for commerce with other men and had begun to grow back towards them; so that even solitary as he was in this wilderness, his bones must stoop. The hair was short and tangled, pale as lint. The brow was solemn but his mouth smiled high even in its rest. Between them were a long nose that carried enough flesh to declare tempers of its own, and eyes that gave back the wild sky-blue of noon.

He came on a clump of flowers where butterflies hung and poised in the air, feeding. "Where are my bees?" he said. "Thirty of you, all at work, and not a sign of my bees." When he stopped there the butterflies shifted about on the chicory flowers but three or four of them were all that flew away. There was a continuous coming and going to and from the bush. Some that went lit on other blooms nearby; most flew off in the air and into nowhere; and the newcomers came from nowhere. They might have been made of air or sky, come to frolic round the clear blue flowers, and they returned themselves to the sky. Under this thought, or fancy, the man frowned. Even so, frowning, the sides of his mouth stayed high and the business in his eyes kept up its bright stare; he seemed therefore always on the point of breaking into a laugh or into grief. He saw a bee that slept drunken on the ground in the moving shade of the butterflies. He put it on his hand.

He went to a wild olive, one of the full-grown trees that were so few on this bare place. Now that it had won into its prime the olive was prosperous with leaf and the man went into its rich shadow, coaxing his height among the branches. The bee slept on his hand. When he had placed himself and was still he heard the sound in the tree: the light wind that crossed the plateau in silence, which made no stir out there by the butterflies, but in the tree harped quiet and unceasing. The wind came from the north, from the farthest mountains: on a clear day the mountains filled the distance beyond the edges of this uplifted plain every way a man looked: every way but the way he had come. His hand made a fist and the bee fell.

When he found it again the bee was on the move, trudging drowsily into a black hole which the creation, doubtless, had left in a pile of rock. To the bee, had it been capable of such realisations, the place would have been a great cavern. The man put in his arm and took out the bee just before it was lost in the darkness.

"You fool," he said to the bee where it wandered round in his cupped hands. "I will take you back to the hive. Look at the butterflies, how they flourish on the bright flowers, in the sun." He closed his hands all about the bee so that no light would get in. It tickled on his skin. "Yet you stumble there in the darkness like a man in a black cave." Surfeited with wisdom as with chicory, the bee stung his tender palm and began to die.

"Even in the sunlight!" the man yelled to the ground where the bee had fallen, and drew the sting from his hand.

He turned his back on the bee and the butterflies and set off across the gigantic shingle towards a place where the ground dropped away and the tops of two square towers showed. He stooped more than usual as he walked, crouching over the stung hand and peering at it to see how furious the poison was. He stepped at length off the waste of stone, onto grass and red earth, and began to descend.

The way before him was a steep ridge that swelled onto a hump of grassland like a hog's back. At the far end of this meadow rose two towers, the nearer one big enough for the keep of a castle. The view beyond the towers was framed in at first with crags and cliffs, screes and rockslides, from which the stark mountain tops heaved and pitched as if they slept with evil dreams. Yet the wildness in this fierce landscape made of the pass that cut its way down to the land below, showing as it went glimpses of green, first grass then vine, and far off patches of ripe corn, the gateway to a kindlier world.

The hay was off the meadow and goats were pastured on the grass. The old woman who minded them stood with her chin on her hands, the hands folded on top of a stick and her elbows out wide. She stood as straight as the stick and all the top of her, head, shoulders and elbows, lay in the shade of that wide-brimmed hat of leather. It was like his own hat from Moorish Spain. It was that hat. He went close: he saw black and red aged to one colour, that was his own hat on the head of this old serf woman.

His hand went out to take it, but withdrew. He had bewildered himself all morning with unanswered questions. This fresh whim of an inscrutable universe, to set his own hat here suddenly beside his path, the lord's hat on the serf's crown, was one paradox too many. A rage as red and sudden as a baby's flushed over the face he laid to the old woman. He spoke, however, in a whisper.

"My Spanish hat," he said. He blew the words through his teeth. "How do you have my hat?"

He stood nose to nose against her. She had not moved. Nothing stirred in her narrow eyes. They gazed on the face before her own as if it might be no more than a piece of the day that had stopped on its way past. He stayed where he was, tilted, leaning on silence to make her speak, until the sinews that had strung him there like a puppet went loose, and the heat left his face. Deserted by his temper, he slumped back on his heels.

He walked away. Nothing at all about the old woman had remarked that he was there. He turned to see her again. She had not moved, and still looked across the glaze of wild flowers on the meadow, where her goats slept out the midday heat, to the stone face of the mountain.

He took the goat-path home. The meadow ended and the way fell into a little ravine that cut across the hilltop. When it emerged from this, the path turned along the side of the hill and brought him to the foot of his great tower, the one he had built to be the castle keep. Below him a wood of stunted oaks struggled up the slope, and from its topmost trees, which showed over the shoulder of mountainside ahead of him, a voice sounded.

"Go on, cowards," it said. "Oh, you cowards!"

This was his wife.

## Chapter 2

## BONNE AND THE BEES

WHEN he stepped round the hill a laugh jumped up in him, and he bit on his knuckles to quell it. At the edge of the wood was a dead tree, a leaning stump where honey-bees nested. Two men stood near it. One of them was Vigorce, the hired captain of his tiny garrison: an odd figure, half-armoured as if taken by surprise, but with a cloth on his head under his iron cap, like a veil. This fell completely round him to the waist, where the skirts of his old mail coat appeared. He was armed with a switch of long grass, and whisking this weapon before his face, while at the same time inquiring behind him with his heels, he began to come backwards up the hill. Vigorce was quitting the field. On it, he left his comrade-in-arms encompassed by a host of raging bees.

Bonne had sensed that her husband was near. As she turned, the laugh that was in his mouth cheated him and came out: he had forgotten it was there. She stayed looking at him across her shoulder. Her eyes portrayed the mishap of this inept meeting, and reflected the tale of like misfortune from other days and through other years.

He thought of how it might be for her, to look up at him from within that fate-defying beauty; how it might be to stand squinting uphill at him and into the sun, into his endless smile.

"Really, Caesar," she said, as if she had overheard him say something absurd, and turned away.

This put her face to face with the man Vigorce, fresh from his shameful retreat. He arrived laughing. He took off his iron helmet and freed himself of the cheesecloth draped over his head. He brushed a few dead and crippled bees off it and threw it down with the helmet on top. He was not tall. He was a broad-made man; his head and face were oversized. The head was black curls greying, and the face went from a wide brow to a bluntly pointed chin, with big mouth and nose. The eyes were brown and deep, and wild-hearted. He still held the grass brush in his hand. He flourished it cheerfully.

"Poor Solomon!" he said.

Bonne snatched the grass from him. "Coward!" she yelled into his laughing teeth. She hit him in the mouth with the grass; about the head. He was helpless from the laughter of this new attack. He gave ground before her temper and fell on the steep hillside and rolled a little and lay there, laughing and laughing.

She shouted down the hill to the wretched man who stood in the cloud of bees. "Solomon, blow on it! Blow the smoke at the bees!"

Solomon had a shovel on which something burned smokily, without flame. He held it before his face in both hands and, doubtless, blew. The smoke flew about. The man's veil puffed out and then fell onto his face again as if he had sucked in air. He had taken the cheesecloth into his mouth and begun to choke. In these straits he let the shovel, with its reeking cargo, too close to his face. He stood choking on the cheesecloth and coughing in the smoke, and began to issue small and pitiful cries.

Vigorce sat up and surveyed the stricken field.

Bonne looked at the sky. "What a fool," she said. "One a coward and the other a fool. What hope is there in that?"

"What is on the shovel?" her husband asked.

"Dung is on the shovel," she said. "The smoke of it pacifies the bees."

Solomon sank to his knees, still faithful to the shovel. The bees sank with him.

Vigorce scratched his scalp thoroughly and wiped his face with his hands, and then shook his head like a dog. "They will kill him if he stays there," he said. "They are African bees."

Bonne bent over him and shrieked onto the top of his head, "Rubbish! Rubbish! They are just bees!"

She grabbed the cheesecloth that lay on the ground and the helmet rolled off it, away down the hill. She began to wind the cloth round her head, but as she set off her husband grabbed her by the shoulders and brought her back.

"Bonne," he said, "The man will die." He shouted down the hill. "Solomon, Solomon! Run away! Run away! Leave the shovel and run away!"

Solomon laid down carefully the shovel, an oddly level-headed act. He got to his feet and pulled the cheesecloth from his mouth. He gave an indistinct cry and rushed into the wood, where they heard him crashing among the little oak trees and yelling. Doves pelted up out of the leaves. The frenzy of the bees abated and they collected about the tree-stump, and some returned to the nest.

"I had some thought about bees, today," the tall man said. It was simply meant, a thing to restore them from excitement to a rhythm with the day, and he winced at Vigorce with the top part of his face, cheeks and eyebrows and forehead, not benevolent or placating, but saying, We humans, eh? Then he put into the space among the three of them his bee-stung hand. "I was stung myself," he declared. "See!"

Bonne as if acknowledging that by being stung on this day, the day of the foiled attempt on the honey in the hollow tree, he had committed an act of public relevance, gave despite herself a nod; but bit her lips together.

Vigorce said, "Where?"

The two men, looking at the hand, only after some difficulty found a palely crimsoned zone on the line of destiny, the merest ring of a white patch within which the skin showed strawberry pink. The victim pressed it, and it did not hurt. He asked Vigorce, "You came off unscathed?"

"Bah!" Vigorce said, boasting. "Not a mark!"

Bonne said, "What was the thought you had about bees, Caesar?"

Her hair was the red of copper, and her eyes were the colour of dark gold. They were not the colour of a nut, or a plum, or a tree in autumn leaf, but of gold alone. When she was full of life they shone, gold in firelight. Meanwhile, not shining, still they were gold. They waited for an answer.

"Ah!" Caesar said. "The bees, the bees!"

The eyes watched, catlike in silence. They watched him as if they had set, rather than sought the answer to, a riddle.

"Yes," Bonne said. "What was it about the bees?"

Under the press of questions such as these he never failed to meet those eyes. The bees: what was it he had thought about the bees? The answer itself was of no moment, since all she wanted of him was a gift from his private thought. These solemn challenges of hers would take him by surprise. Within our hearts, questions so earnest seemed to say, sources of happiness might spring. Now therefore refusing, as was his way, such well-remembered menaces of joy, he gazed onto the surface of her look and let pass all memory of bees.

Soon her eyes of gold, Bonne's unshining eyes, that had been for an instant marvellous with tatters of old hope, turned blind on him and a little later, closed.

He put her hand on his arm and said, "Vigorce, come and eat with us."

The soldier had gone down the hill after his iron cap and stood with it in his hand, looking up at them, unfriendly to their manner of being together. "I must see to my man," he said, and started down for the wood.

Bonne opened her eyes. She looked south to the world beyond and far below. "I will not eat," she said. Her hand lay still on his arm. "I shall sit here a little, to rest."

Caesar said, "Why? Have you eaten already?"

"No, but I am not hungry. I will eat tonight."

He took her hand from his arm. "Very well," he said. "This is not much of a place to sit. Over here is better, sit here."

He sat her downhill from a blackberry bush which had put its first edge of afternoon shade onto the grass. It was a flat place, and he laid on it the discarded bits of cheesecloth bundled into a meagre cushion. The bush had been picked almost clear of its berries, for summer was ending.

In her green housekeeping dress, with its white linen coif to keep the sun from her head, she settled there with her arms round her knees and her back straight as a rod. He walked two steps uphill and turned to say a word of leave-taking. A plume of copper hair fell outside the white linen and lay back along the side of Bonne's head. He did not speak, after all, but went on up the hillside.

# Chapter 3

## AMANIEU

THERE was a stranger in his hall.

"Company!" the tall man said. "Good!"

He waited by the door, and the figure inside the room came forward to the light. The visitor was in his early manhood, and had an unpleasant look of being not completely formed. His head was too small. It had black hair cut almost to bristles, deep hollows behind the forehead, and ears that fanned out to the side to a degree rare among humans. The face showed a pale skin smeared with yellow. Black eyes threw out a look that was both direct and insultingly watchful, a look sudden but still, that at once flourished and hid an interest, indefinably too eager, in its originator's fellow-man. The mouth was overlong. In the top lip ran a constant activity as if it kept a life of its own. Now, saying nothing, movement went along it like the flick travelling down a whiplash: or like a dream troubling a snake. The body was lank, round-shouldered, uneven, long in the arms, and at its joints variously splayed, angular and lumpish. In short, all that could be said for this creature, at first sight, was that his shirt was silk and his riding-boots, though creamed over with dust, would have comforted a prince.

The tall man made a sound like reassuring laughter. He cuffed the apparition on the back and shook its arm and urged it inside again. "Do you know how welcome you are? But for you I should eat alone."

The room was square and high, pinched in at the top like a bell. Their feet resounded on the stones. With his hand on the boy's arm the tall man guided them through dimness. Small windows made patches of brilliant blue in the walls and a far glim of sky came from the roof, which peaked in a hole to let out winter smoke. The place took most of its light through the doorway, and at the back of the room they stood until their eyes grew used to shadow.

"My name is Amanieu of Noé," the guest said.

"I am Caesar Grailly," the host responded. "Sit there. The truth is," he said, "we eat very plain here." The table where they sat offered sausage and cheese, olives and chick-peas. "I eat the same meal every midday." He sniffed deeply. "What's this? We don't have this every day. That's a fishy smell."

This was a dish of porridgy appearance that smelled to Heaven, of fish and garlic at least. "I brought it," Amanieu said. "It is what I have been eating on the road. I told your kitchen woman to serve it." There was a taste of effrontery in this remark, and the young man licked his lips and listened to what he had just said. "It's extremely good," he assured his host, "delicious, and it will have gone off by tomorrow."

Caesar stuck a piece of bread in the fish and ate it. "You're right," he said. "What a tang!" He pushed sausage towards his guest. "Tonight we shall have a feast of many courses: roast hart, beef, wild boar, quail, bear's brains, countless jellies and sweet confections, and wines," swilling, "of such extraordinary strength that they do not take their flavour from the pot. This is our own wine," he said, "and feeble stuff, feeble. The fact is, my lad, that I am destitute."

"I saw signs." The boy's unflinching teeth made mincemeat of the tough and gritty sausage. He spat out bone and gristle. "I wondered. I saw your new towers, but the rest of it seems a poor man's place." Insolence! Or was it simply a thick skin that let him speak like this? "Since you are so poor, what about all this building? You do *seem* to be building a castle."

Caesar Grailly sighed and the sigh lurched into an uncharted deep, like a flooding tide that drops down a sinkhole in the rocks. "I have been building a castle," he said. "I was building a castle. I had almost achieved my castle—!" His hand turned on its wrist, the fingers shaped air, and together they showed a cornucopia of hope spilling onto the ground.

"So?" the boy asked impatiently. "What went wrong?"

"The war ended."

"Ah!" the boy said.

"What d'you mean, 'ah'?"

The boy laughed. It was a sour and sarcastic laugh and despite his youth, strangely authentic, as if he had been spitting bile since the cradle. "You're a bit out of the world here, aren't you? The peace has ruined things for everyone, down there."

"Unfortunately," Caesar said, "not quite everyone. All of a sudden, builders are in great demand. Forty years of knocking everything to rubble means a good few years of putting it all up again. A month ago my mason and his men worked cheerfully for bed and board, and on credit. Now they are down in the plains of Languedoc, being paid in money; growing rich." He wiped the last of the fish paste out of the bowl with a piece of bread and chewed this slowly. "I daresay they feast like princes now, meat every day."

"No," Amanieu said, "not meat every day." He leaned closer to his host through the dimness, unmasking the smile with which the worldly-wise instruct the innocent. "No one eats meat down there. Once in a blue moon you'll get a bite of horseflesh. Down there no one eats every day. If you eat anything on four days out of the seven, that's a good week. It's famine down there. It's been war there for forty years, you know that. Listen! This last bit of war has been six years long, and I went to it two years ago. Well, there's nothing to tell you what grew there when there was peace: you don't know if it was orchards or crops or vineyards. It's all burnt buildings and burnt land and bones. In this last war the black vulture and the griffon came up from Spain. They had scented carrion over the mountains. I'm not lying!" Caesar had made a sign to turn away all this news. "I'll tell you worse!" His smile now was the portrayal of a snigger. "We ate each other down there."

Caesar gripped his head with both hands. He wiped his face with one hand, and he slapped the other over and over on the table top. He thought of something to say but what came first was a belch, a gust of fish and garlic that left his mind vacant. Afterwards he was not sure if he spoke to the boy out loud, or if the words he uttered stayed within him. "I know you," he said, silently or otherwise, to the boy. "You guzzle and grab at life. You get experience you can't stomach and make others share the weight of it." He stood up. He walked up and down in the dark, and saw now and then the black eyes shine with intelligence and comprehension; though afterwards he was almost sure he had not spoken aloud. "You need victims. There are a few men whose souls hear what you say, and when you find one you know him. Now you have found me. You're like a pig that knows when there's a truffle below the earth." He laughed, a short, dry crack of laughter, which later he knew for certain had made a sound. "I am to be your victim, the truffle!"

# Chapter 4

## UNSPEAKING SOULS

THEN, sitting on the floor with his back leaned against the wall, he chewed his knee, and it was the boy who now walked back and forth in the gloom, crossing and recrossing the path of light from the door. Listening to Amanieu rattle on with his history of himself, which was uncoloured by anything to show that the narrator had just heard a scarifying diagnosis of his own nature, Caesar understood that, sure enough, he had failed to make his remarks out loud.

This sprang from no Delphic reticence on Caesar's part: rather, it represented the worst of his misfortunes. This was, that though he believed himself to own (as he had silently told Amanieu) a soul unusually sensitive to what the souls of others attempted to say, and which could decipher those hidden messages that often strive unsuccessfully to emerge from the inmost parts of a human spirit; nevertheless, when it came to making a response, to effecting that reciprocity without which so singular a perception might almost be accounted worthless, he was speechless. He found what to say, it is true: he spoke words in answer. He failed, however, to speak them aloud.

He contained, it seemed, a spiritual intuition able to bridge the space that separates the inmost beings of men, one from another; and he could recognise what came to him across that bridge. When, however, it was a matter of sending back news of his own—why, then the mechanisms of his voice were disobedient to his will. He would watch in vain to see his messengers pass outward across the bridge, carrying his soul's reply to what its spiritual ear had from other souls elicited; and he would realise, each time the words he wished to speak went from him without sound—each time afresh—that no one but he (no soul but his) had the least inkling of his numinous correspondence.

It was an extraordinary event, each time it happened, like a rare conjunction of the stars. He would feel on his face, and see in the face across from his, nothing beyond the contemplations of ordinary mortals. Yet deep within his soul, like the resonation of a harmonic, he would hear the vibrant echo rise in response to a note issuing from the soul that stood, or sat, next to his own. There for one moment they would be, unique among mankind, on the very eve of sharing that Divine dialogue of truths known otherwise only to souls in Heaven: and it was at such supreme moments, when he was about to open discourse of unexampled purity; when he had found the words that would fly immaculate along the marvellous plane between his soul and another's—had found words unleavened by such corporeal dross as sin, the passions, or weakness of the mind—that he would be struck dumb.

Then came the descent into the abyss. Icarus-like, from the thresholds of exaltation, he fell down, down and down to be broken (once again) on the rocks of frustration, impotence and the bitter question: Why?

As he rehearsed the three answers to this question, he would stand sometimes for minutes, sometimes for hours, with his hair on end, his eyes rolling and starting in their sockets, and on his face the mask of Sisyphus. His first answer was, that there must be an imperfection in himself which, though his soul could hear the utterance of other souls, prevented his own soul from replying in kind: a secret enemy within. His second, was that it had been the inspiration of the Creator to invent man as a machine, not only for lodging souls, but for keeping them incommunicado; so that the spiritual or soul-to-soul debate to which Caesar aspired was beyond the human design, and his aspiration to it, impious. Heaven, therefore, intervened and silenced him.

The third answer was, in a sense, the least superstitious of the three, and it was to this explanation he always returned, for it meant that there was still hope of bringing his unusual gift to its fulfilment.

By this account his faculty of hearing the voice of another soul was an exceptional endowment; it distinguished him from other men; he had been singled out to possess it either by Divine Grace or freakish chance. What he must do, simply, was meet someone else who shared with him this wonderful peculiarity (who would have also, no doubt, apt responses on the very tip of the soul's tongue) and by means of so auspicious an encounter—such a pairing of paragons—the words he had so often wished to speak would at last enlarge themselves from his throat and go forth, spoken aloud and audible to human ears. Then— ah, then! and *mirabile dictu*, he would say to himself, with some precision—they would be two souls fixed on earth but exchanging comprehensions as magnificent, and insights as limpid, as the vistas and atmosphere of Heaven.

Caesar, requiring therefore a fellow-interpreter of the spiritual voice, had not far to seek. Given the isolation of his dwelling, how seldom they saw visitors up there, how thin on the ground were the inhabitants of that remote fastness and how ramshackle their moral and intellectual attainments, it is no wonder that he looked, to liberate the baffled eloquence of his inner being, to his wife Bonne.

What Bonne knew of this was only that an additional strangeness had been imported to the life she lived with Caesar. It was plain to Caesar that for his desired colloquy of the spirit to take place, the souls must call spontaneously to one another and not be introduced by some third party; not even by so close a relation as heart or mind. Accordingly, he had not told Bonne that his soul would, from time to time, at what it held to be promising moments, turn its alert and sudden ear towards her very own soul. Nor had he explained that this questing soul of his would insist, now and again and for hours at a stretch, on keeping Caesar's body, where it lodged, neighbourly to hers; so that the two souls might remain within spiritual earshot in case hers, as his thought possible, spoke unexpectedly, on a whim, out of the blue.

At first (it was two years since Caesar had been visited with this hope of enlightenment and had embarked on these exercises) Bonne had blushed, for in the decade since they married their sexual friendship had faded. She now supposed, therefore, that it was to be reanimated, when if she sat on the grass here, or a wall there, Caesar came and sat close beside her; or if she chopped vegetables on the kitchen table, Caesar stood across from her, leaning close and with his eyes weeping in the onion mist. Still at first she thought so, and therefore did not mind it, when Caesar followed her on a walk up to the meadow, or down over the bridge to the serfs' village, keeping always within a pace, impossibly close, either behind her as if urging her on, or walking backwards before her, turning the side of his face to her face, and sometimes bending double, walking backwards, and turning the side of his face, his ear indeed, to her stomach, as if to hear it rumbling.

That she had misconstrued these courtesies, however, became clear to her at last, when on something like three well-spaced occasions a fitful flame of joy woke in their bed and each time, or ever they had climbed into the apotheosis of their lust, Caesar stayed, stark, rapt and listening, intent only upon her but as if she came between him and herself; as if she were an impostor, a changeling who had stepped full-grown to their bed, a thing of witch's blood masked in Bonne's own human form; as if she had become a fraud, a cheat and not what she had promised.

She grew weary, too, of looking into his ears, for always in these fits one ear or the other turned towards her. Whatever impulse had been left her, as Caesar's associate in this repertoire of odd behaviours, to speak in any of the carnal, spiritual or usual languages, was quite abashed by these pink and predatory ears. She did not know what they were doing, flourishing themselves in front of her, except that they were to her as bottomless pits impatient to be filled. Who can feed a famine? Who, save a bird on the nest or a mother her milk, will give freely what is to be snatched away as soon as it is presented? Bonne's voice was hushed.

In the end she, who had begun by hoping that these antics of Caesar's were in fact the first signs of his return from an inclination towards self-despair and the attractions of madness, came to see that this inclination had, on the contrary, steepened, and he himself accelerated. She saw this in the deranged appearance with which he would confront her, at the end of one of those passages of his no-longer understandable attachment to her person, and stare at her for minutes, or if she could not escape for hours, with his hair on end and the expression on his face of that ancient king Whatwasisname of Corinth whose destiny, in Tartarus, had been to roll uphill a rock which always rolled down again from the summit.

Caesar, for his part, nowadays found Bonne more elusive than she had once been. It had occurred to him recently how ironic it was that his soul's attempts to draw forth the voice of her soul, and so in turn find its own tongue, had all but extinguished ordinary talk between them; and that his attempt to join their two souls in Divine argument had forced their two human selves apart; and that the voice with which Bonne used to sing her way about the house was now as mute as a swan's; and that the silence of the heart that spread about their lives would fill eternity.

When he scanned the catalogue of mysterious sorrows that had accompanied his soul's wooing of the soul of Bonne, Caesar's determination faltered. That Bonne no longer sang! This alone hinted that he should look in some other carcase than his wife for the soul that was to make his own soul speak. Sooner or later, this he must do, for wherever Bonne's singing voice was gone, the rest of her was dwindling after. Reclusive and hysterical she had become, and there was not much time left for him and her to achieve anything together. Would he, then, waste what little time was left? Or run defeated from what might, the next moment, yield to his desires!

Clenching yet again his indomitable will, Caesar subdued the fears and griefs that opposed him until they were no more than an ache at the centre of his being. He tightened his belt over the pain and took it as a goad to his singleness of purpose: he would attempt once more, for a month say, or a season, the task of bringing home that message from Bonne's soul.

What choice had he? During this past hour spent with the young newcomer—was it only an hour?—he had been reminded how rare visitors were and how uncertain, for his purpose, their credentials. It was plain to him that Bonne, for all that she had failed him so far and dilapidated as she had now become, was in the present state of the balance a likelier hope than the infant wiseacre, the pompous urchin blown about between self-esteem and self-pity—and evil, it now seemed, into the bargain—that Amanieu had so far shown himself to be.

## Chapter 5

# THE VOICE OF THE CORNCRAKE

"**B**ECAUSE of the peace," the urchin was saying, "my career is ended before it began. I'm not rich. I'm the seventh son. My father kitted me for soldiering and wished me good-bye. The silk I got from a woman. The boots I came by." His head turned coyly on its stalk. "Loot," he said. "Booty of war."

His host had merged with the shadows, diluted himself with the dimness; gone off into a brown study. The young man's voice went up the scale, keening to be heard.

"There are six daughters," he said, "and I am the thirteenth child. I am a seventh son and a thirteenth child: as also the first-born of my mother, for my father's married three times."

This very curious speech half roused the other man from his abstraction. There had been a whiff of weirdness in the tone of it, a musk of half-madness, that along with the gloomth and the garlic, the ripe fish and the raw wine, made dizzy his reawakened mind.

He stood up.

"Come into the sun," he said. "Let's go outside. Come and sit in the sun."

They sat on the ground, leaning against the house, not in the sun but in shade thrown by a tree filled with plums. They still had the wine.

There was a clatter of crockery in the room they had left and a sharp tongue spoke at them invisibly from the doorway. "You'll get drunk," it said. "Where's my lady?"

"She'll eat tonight. She's watching the bees. When I've got drunk, Gully, I'll thrash your old hide."

"Stinking fish!" the doorway said.

"The house was here, you see, is here; the old manor. I'll keep it under the east wall, build it into the wall. I put the gatehouse there, the keep up there, and that's as far as I've got. Eighty-three courses of stone, of excellent draught, the keep. In height over a hundred palms. My men live there, my hired captain."

"Hired? Hired men only? Do you have no knights? Are you not a lord?"

It had become for Caesar one of those afternoons that is half a dream. There was a haze in his mind, and it was stiff work answering the mundane little questions.

He was a lord still. "Yes, I am a lord." He looked across the ground before him to the pile of stones and scaffolds that might make a wall. "I am a lord in Gascony. I am not, though"—he made a gesture of apology, but as if to himself rather than to the boy—"I am not *in* Gascony. Do you know what a captal is?"

"Captal is a Gascon word—a Gascon lord." The young man's voice sounded as if it were listening, rather than speaking.

"That's right. I am the Captal of Yon, in Gascony. I had a misfortune, I had to leave. I gave over Yon to my brother. I am a lord who cannot live in his lordship. Bonne and I came here to the Minervois, to this bare holding of hers."

The urchin's face now swam into Caesar's vision. It came up before his own face and filled his sight. It was all jerks and spasms; the eyes blinked and the nose sniffed, and the long, long mouth writhed and twitched in a frantic and nightmarish independence of its own. The creature was over-excited and at the sight of him Caesar felt that he was about to be sick.

The child said, "You are the Captal of Yon."

There was an emphasis in this from which Caesar flinched. He yawned protectively and began to babble. "This place is not quite a lordship, you'll gather. Maybe another man could work it up into a lordship. There's plenty land, not enough people."

He ran out of talk and there was silence. Foolishly he said, "I lost a wit in Gascony. I lost one of my wits."

"I know," the youth said—the terrible youth. "I know you did. They called you the Madman of Yon."

The Captal's face with its ceaseless smile looked back at the boy like a shade looking out of Hades. "The Madman of Yon," he said, and all the moisture had gone from his mouth so that his tongue creaked. "The Madman of Yon? Not of me, no, no."

He put himself into a stupor, fell into a sleep, compelled the heat and the wine and the exhaustion of his mind and senses, heart and flesh, and indeed his soul, to remove him from the day; but not soon enough to escape the voice of the corncrake.

"You are the Madman of Yon," it said, "who killed your little boy."

## Chapter 6

# STUNG

IN the last of his dreams he heard dogs bark and he woke to a commotion of men and horses. It was late in the day and everything was low sunlight and long shadow. Vigorce held a horse by the bridle while its rider leaned down from the saddle, pointing behind him to the gatehouse. Two more riders came under the archway. The first jumped to the ground and slapped his horse out of the way, the second carried a burden in his arms and made ready to hand it down to the man on foot. Here came Vigorce, however, suddenly on the spot, and took the burden instead and began to walk to the house.

They met at the door.

"Give her to me," Caesar said.

In his arms Vigorce held Bonne, stark naked and with all her beauty but her eyes open to the evening air. She was bright red. He turned Vigorce by the shoulders so that Bonne was out of shadow. She flamed all over, all her skin flushed and glowed a bright carmine as if she had bathed in cochineal. Under the skin her flesh was swollen, her eyes and lips were puffed up. Caesar found, to his dismay, that the strange sight of Bonne, possibly *in extremis* but painted with this lustrous and living glaze, drew his hands to touch and his eyes to wonder more than it woke him to compassion.

"Give my wife to me," he said again. "What happened to her?" When he had asked this a deep fear opened in him.

Vigorce looked up. His face was clear and vivid. There was no set to it, the marks of his life had vanished leaving it as wet clay, fresh made, still making—each moment saw a new emotion light on it and go: and it was not as if the flow of feelings came out from the man, but as if they reached him now and entered him, as if you saw him accept visibly his share of passions.

Caesar saw there hate, jealousy, grief and a thirst for vengeance; then he counted love, pity and—all these signs were strange, but this was strangest—a fear that reminded him of his own. The face of Vigorce went on changing as a dying mullet goes from colour to colour. Caesar was puzzled by what he had read in it and startled by

the display of a self turfed suddenly out of hiding into the daylight: he
turned away his eyes.

He thought, if his hand touched Bonne's skin it would burn. His
fear of what had happened to her, the fear he had been surprised to see
mirrored on the other man's face, came to his tongue.

"What happened to her?" he said again, and now he added, "What
did she do?"

At this question, "What did she do?", the spate of facial meta-
morphosis ended and Vigorce nodded deeply as if Caesar had hit the
nail on the head. When he spoke he did not look up. The voice came,
as it were, out of that vigorous crop of black hair etched with grey, but
now the hair straggled all over the place and was hardly black at all
and a patch of bald crown showed. The pathos of this matched oddly
with the young-eyed passion of moments ago, as if the man were
living both ends of his life at once.

"She was naked on the hillside," Vigorce said, "and stung senseless by the bees." With his face turned down to Bonne's bright
radiance the voice was hard to catch, and it came in a mixture of
mumbles, sighs and gruff barks. Caesar bent his knees and hips to get
his ear to the story. "I think she went in among the bees. She stripped
naked and went in among the bees," Vigorce told Bonne rather than
Caesar; and indeed shook her a little so that her swollen flesh jiggled;
and it was altogether as if he were reciting her sins to a recalcitrant
child—Who went in among the bees, then?

The sorrowful head hung close over her bosom but Caesar
glimpsed her face pouting, and the fall of russet hair that the evening
wind of the mountains had laid, like pale, flickering sunlight, upon
one fire-red breast.

Vigorce lifted his eyes off Bonne and spoke at Caesar's face. "They
found her!" His speech was suddenly clear and spiteful. He had come
to his point and Caesar would learn now what had provoked these
amazing intensities of fury and desolation. "Your common soldiers,"
Vigorce said, "lay round her on the grass and picked over her bare
body." So there it was. Caesar stared at him, enlightened: his hired
captain worshipped Bonne, and the touch of the soldiers had pro-
faned her.

Caesar saw in his mind's eye the three soldiers on the green hillside.
One knelt with his hands clasped and seemed to pray, like a saint in a
painting; he was at Bonne's head. Her hair, more yellow than in life,
spread in a fan about her on the grass, and from this her scarlet body

stretched, portraying less the stupefaction of a thousand bee-stings than the languor of an opium-eater. She half-lay, half-sat, still able to lean on one elbow and to bend one knee, and regarded an azure sky across which three magpies flew one way and a stork, the other. Grasping her left (or in the painting, topmost) breast, were the five fingers of a soldier who had sensibly sat himself behind her, and whose other hand was plucking out bee-stings. He had an expression of cheerful, if self-indulgent, goodwill. On the face of the third soldier, however, lechery was painted. He lay on his belly on the grass, and across the foot of Bonne's raised leg, and was drawn on a downhill line so that Caesar could watch him where he peered up between the molten thighs and along the hectic joys of Bonne's inflamed trunk.

Caesar liked this picture for its colour, its composition and its moral simplicity of showing one who prayed, one who helped, and one who leered. He came away from it, however, to find desire lifting in him, stronger and more heated each moment, while to this end his eyes traversed the glistening ardour with which Bonne's skin now held fast to her over-sumptuous flesh.

The thought darted into him from nowhere like a bird out of the sun. "She may die," he said, and took her out of the captain's ungiving arms.

Her skin was hot on his hands. Lust went. The sight of her sheen was no more than if it had been on a boiled lobster. As she lay there swollen with poison, the love of her flicked like a whiplash round his heart, more seemly than the physical pang of a moment ago, but more feared.

He carried her into the house and through the dark hall, and laid her on the bed.

## Chapter 7

# FLORE AT DAYBREAK

A N hour or so before dawn the night went to rest. It left behind it a limbo between sleep and waking, between the dark's repentance and the evil of the new day. Amanieu descended from his nightmares (in which he had everywhere triumphed) into this ambiguous lull. His black eyes stared at the impenetrable void, itself as black as pitch; not yet paled by hints of sunrise and long unlightened by the vanished moon.

This was his favourite hour.

He found himself on a soft bed, and he stretched along this comfort until his nine toes would have cramped, and hung there for a moment chewing his tongue while the sinews safely ceased to creak, then fell at ease and with his hands under his head exchanged black looks with life. It had been some days since he cursed his father, and he did so now; a good curse, he felt his skin turn white with hatred. He cursed his six brothers with venom, and his six sisters with spite. Then, for the very first time—inventiveness refreshed perhaps by altitude, and by rest, and by the sense of holiday that had sprung in him at having found a refuge far above the anarchy, famine and disease that ravaged the land below—he cursed any child that might have passed from his father through his mother since he had left home. At this masterstroke he felt the colour return to his cheeks. His mother herself he remembered jealously and wished her well; but doing so he looked askance into the blind space about him, as if he feared spies.

A cold air crossed his face. It was fresh with dew and carried an essence of the wild scents of fruit, herb and flower that rose from the steep hillsides. Somewhere among these perfumes, eluding all the cunning of his senses, either a forgotten memory or an unseen promise lurked, like a wild beast debating whether to emerge from its forest. He glimpsed its presence among the trees; he felt something shift inside him as a sleeping man is aware of his body turning; then it was gone.

Above him began a weakness in the dark, the first tincture of dawn, and there was a footfall on the stair.

Thereupon Amanieu experienced a great shock—he could not make himself move, he was like a spellbound man. He lay stock-still and listened, as if he had a hundred ears, for the footstep he had heard outside his door to be followed by another within the room. What room? He had forgotten where he was: he called in his wits like scattered outposts and was reminded—he had slept the night in the madman's new gatetower. Indeed it stank of mortar: where now was the smell of flowers?

Out of the thinning dark the doorway grew, black and inscrutable to his gaping eyes. A face glimmered at him and whisked away. Feet passed down steps on tiptoe. His chains fell from him and he jumped to the door which opened on a spiral staircase. He saw someone below him, a child's hand on the pillar beside his foot, and a child's face turned up to him. Her mouth opened as if she was going to speak, or laugh, but she smiled and went down out of sight.

He was not quite woken from the spell that had tied him to the bed—although here he was, up on his feet—and not completely woken from the night, nor from his hour of familial evocation. For these reasons, no doubt, he stayed there some time after she had gone, with his hands grasping the lintel and his head out in the stairwell. At length he raised his eyebrows, stood up, stamped his feet on the stone floor, for he had slept with his boots on, and went out to see the day break over the hills.

No dog barked, and no cock had yet crowed, when he stepped from the gateway of the future castle. The sky was white, a canvas waiting for the sun. The ground was still in twilight and black with shadows, but he could see far—the air about him was luminous as if the ground had a light of its own. The top of the sky became lit with blue and over the hill across the valley daylight began to flow. The air shone, yet still the sun had not appeared.

The edge of the sky glowed with fires of red and purple which descended onto the hillsides (that had been grey) and proved to be their true colours. The bottom of the valley, and other valleys that opened from it, filled with mist white as wool, as if there had been a great shearing of sheep overnight. The sky was suddenly all blue, the mists wisped away into nothing, and the sun lifted like gold into the air. Where there was rock it gleamed pink and glinted yellow in the slanted light, and where there was meadow a million flowers filled the glance of his eye. Below him in that dawn the girl's voice sang.

For this moment he knew that life was a dance. The sun warmed his face and breast and the fresh, moist air still lingering here brushed his neck, sending a shiver down his body. He was about to set off running down the hill—all childishness—when such a pain began in his head that he shut his eyes. He remembered that he had gone to bed drunk. He turned away from the sun and gathered himself back from his infancy, from the cradle, so it seemed: an emotion with no name to it washed through him, and he felt a furious scowl compress his face. After a while he found himself stooped over, standing there staring at the ground, at his feet, with nothing in his mind. When he straightened up he creaked all over like an old house in a gale. He passed a hand round his meagre waist and made a wry mouth, looking about him. This place was doing him no good. Drunk yesterday, awake this morning to a fit of the horrors because an early-rising child ran past his room, and now wandering out in the morning mist without a weapon to his name. He went inside again, up to his room. There he got his long dagger and belted it over his shoulder and set off down the hill.

A dog pelted growling and snarling out of the arch behind him and he smiled—for the first time, indeed, that day. He came round kicking and caught the beast on the side of the head with a full swing of his boot. He watched its eyes blink and close. It fell down on the grassy track and blood came from its ear; a big dog with jaws like a wolf. He kneeled down and put a hand into its thick ruff and pulled gently, as if he liked the dog. The eye opposite to the bleeding ear came half open, and he spoke to it. "Amanieu's here to stay," he said. "We must become friends."

The dog withdrew its interest and began to snore, and Amanieu went downhill swaggering and mocking himself, for it was not his habit to conciliate a fallen foe: was he growing tame in this mountain air?

He made his descent on long, steep strides, landing with poise on sprung heels to take care for his headache. His feet whished through long grass, white lilies and yellow gentian, the last of the pale high buttercups and the first of the wolfsbane, through cornflower and asphodel, bellflower and vetch, columbine and snapdragon, and innumerable worts. Every step crushed their scent from them and brought paradise to his nose. Poppies flourished in patches of red and yellow. The ground flattened. He stood in a damp meadow among rampion and yellow-rattle and he saw, across the stream before him, the object of his journey. She waved to him and he waved back. She beckoned with a lordly whip of the forearm and he sat down on the river bank to take off his beautiful riding boots, and stayed there cooling his feet in the rippling water, while his headache diminished as if it were trickling out through his toes.

The girl came to the other bank and called over to him. "Come on. We've to pick every one of those we can find!" She held up a bunch of blue flowers.

He was struck by the sight she made, the pale figure against the green field, the pale-haired child in the pale frock. The sun's brightness splashed off the water at her, and against the dusky green she hung before his mind as a vision of light and spirit instead of life and flesh.

"What are you staring at?" she cried.

"I don't know," he said.

"Well, come on across!"

He paddled across the shallow river. "I was day-dreaming," he said. "What are the flowers?"

Her hair was cream-coloured and hung to her waist, a child of twelve or thirteen. Her lips were pink, pouting full and plummy, her complexion gilded by the summer and her cheeks rosy, brushed a little by this meeting. The face was oval and escaped being long, and with that colouring it was fortunate in the eyes, which were chestnut, dark and seeking eyes.

"I am staring again," he said, making a compliment to a child.

She met this with an ironic smile, as if she had been eavesdropping and heard herself insulted. "The flowers," she said, "are blue pimpernels. Gully wants them for Bonne, my mother."

The ache was back in his head. "I've heard of blue pimpernels," he said. "They're not common."

"Here," she said. "Take one, then you'll know what to look for. It's to cure my mother." She cleared her throat. "My mother has been stung all over by bees. She's nearly dead." She saw that this news perplexed him. "Yesterday, when you were drinking with my father." She laughed curtly. "You were as drunk as a lord," she said. "You missed all the excitement." He saw that her breasts were already full. She flushed and grew serious. "You go to that end of the field. I've got this far from my end. We'll pick till we meet."

He walked away across the rye-grass and then stopped. "What is your name?" he asked her.

"Flore," she said. "What's your name?"

"Amanieu," he said.

She smiled. "That's a pretty name;" she said, "Amanieu. I'm not laughing at it—I like it."

He smiled back at her. He did not mind that this girl thought his name pretty. Men were bones who had laughed at it. He walked to his end of the field and started to pick flowers.

*     *     *

He did not find many pimpernels. The grass on that pasture came hardly to his knee, but for the most part it grew higher than the flower he hunted. He found a comfortable crouch and took a patch at a time. His eyesight was sharp but its usefulness was diluted by fits of abstraction. The pose and the occupation were restful. He could hear the soothing carol of the river, and the earth, wakened again by the sun, had begun to give out the heat that had been storing in it nearly half a year. Insects buzzed and droned and birds sang, and were silent, and sang again. The girl too sang and stopped, and then sang again. Amanieu was adrift on sounds and sensations, among such pleasures as rolling the tufted grain under his toes; drinking in the charms he had discovered—since it was the present object of his day—in the blue of the pimpernel, esteeming its petals for being rounded which he would equally have admired for being pointed, or straight across; reflecting on the strangeness of being in this mountain morning, and this river meadow; and keeping always at the far edge of his mind's eye the child who was working her way towards him faster than he to her, finding and gathering the flowers she wanted with a quickness that was, apparently, quite beyond him.

"I settled the dog, though," he said to himself.

He hunched down in the heat, into it, sitting on his heels with his wrists on his knees and the hands loose and dangling. He let his eyes half shut and slipped into a daze. Colours came to him shapeless through his eyelids, green below and blue above, and across them darts and flashes of iridescence, birds, dragonflies—perhaps tricks of light. The heat and freshness of the air met on his skin. He was in the pure scent of the grass. Something in him suggested this was in the past, not of now; but he knew this was now, certainly it was now, and he was here in this day. He had arrived at the eccentric house up the hill yesterday morning, got drunk in the afternoon, and slept the night through, among the usual nightmares. Now he was here in the mountain valley, and he marvelled at the distance he had come from the burnt and harried plain below. He had travelled lifetimes in a week's journey.

"Hey!" she said. "Wake up! Is this all you've got?" She was down beside him, her face a foot away, leaning towards his own. The mouth was a little open, smiling but earnest. There were faint freckles on her ruddy cheek, and a sweep of hair fell artlessly across one eye which peered darkly through at him. Despite the urgency of her questions she had a look of being settled there for the day. Her breath on his face was the sweetest pleasure he had known this age, and he saw her notice this, the satisfaction in her eyes and the excitement that drew inwards her plump and eloquent lips. He pushed the hair off her face, and back over her shoulder. She tilted her head to help him.

"So! There you are," he said. "I seem to spend all my time here dreaming." He picked his small offering from the ground and added it to her bunch of the blue flowers.

He sat up to put on his boots.

"Carry them," she said.

"Since I have brought them," he said. "I'll wear them."

They set off along the bank of the river.

"What's the knife for?" she asked.

"Fighting," he said.

"There's no fighting here."

"I've not been in a place where there was no fighting for three years," he said. "I'll believe it when I see it."

"Don't you believe me?"

"I believe you," he said, "but it may follow me. I'm not lucky."

"If you've been fighting for three years, not dead and not maimed, you are a bit lucky."

"So I am," he said, "so I am! Though I have lost a toe."

Their way left the river and began to climb. The girl started uphill in a lazy walk, for though it was less of a slope than the one opposite, where he had come bounding down among the flowers, the morning was well on and the heat strong. They did not speak while they climbed the narrow, trodden path made by goats or sheep. They left behind the sound of the river, and the birds and insects that abounded on the meadow, and crossed a green hillside from one group of oak trees to the next, now in sunlight and now in the trees' shade.

The child led and he followed. The character of her slow progress up the hill was one of sympathetic concession to the heat. She did not surrender to the sun's force, but took her part with it in the business of the day: the legs found a rhythm and kept it. They accepted the heat—as it might have been the sea—for the medium in which the slow climb up the hill was taking place. The thigh bore up its weight of sun-filled sky as a thigh, wading, must push through the resisting water; the calf rose and dimpled (pausing, say, for some breaking wavelet to get by) with irresolute musculature: until the foot that had been pensive while in the dust, as if wary of crabs and spiny shells, carried through its sensitive but definite step.

All the length of the climb it was this motion of thigh, calf and foot, of this leg and that leg turn about, endlessly on and up in front of him across the green hillside under the hot, bright sun and through the dappled shade of oak trees, that spoke to Amanieu. The two legs rose in their turns as if thinking about something else, rose with an indolent air half-mindful, and half-removed to a hidden place where they lived together with Flore: but rose purposeful and sure on their poised, slow, perpetual, solemn pull of sinew.

In every part of Amanieu resonances thrummed. Some sounded on a note he did not yet hear, and echoed emptily in far, incorporeal reaches of his being: but closer to home, where the Amanieu of flesh and blood lived, the reverberations that stirred in him were friendly and familiar. One moment he was stepping along in a state all but asleep, what with the heat, his hangover, and the child's lulling, unaltering lope, and the next thing he was wide awake—his head swept—himself rested and intelligent—while his desire for the girl leaped in his body.

His step slowed until he stopped, to let body and mind adapt themselves to this latest (the third, it was) of the day's rude awakenings. He looked at the ground. A smile came onto one end of his mouth and ran along it like a rippling wave, and off again. He frowned. The girl's bare, brown feet had entered the circle of his downward look. With an effort of will he brought his look upwards and soon found himself regarding the top of her head (which in its turn was bending a little, though not that much, downwards): the creature was staring at his poignantly aware loins. He lifted his head and saw the sky.

His mind was like a pudding stirred by twenty spoons. Taken by a mere child! Inside him an entire geography of cataclysms took place, the ice on many rivers broke and was carried into a rare accumulation of volcanoes. Steam, smoke, cracking and heaving sounds and sensations ravaged him from within. It could not be the child—but it was!

It was humiliating—surely?—to be so exercised by an infant, and it was then absurd to be struck dumb, petrified, to be made a statue of by indecision.

The infant expelled a long breath. He felt himself shake; he felt himself a giant about to burst open. She came into his view again, walking on. She *was* an infant. The long hair was the colour of cow's cream; it moved and spread upon her back like insubstantial cloth. It partook of her colourless linen dress and together they shaped her languorously climbing form, and fell from it and moved with it and against it.

Which end of childhood did she inhabit?

She stopped and turned her head. She watched him for a long time, while the tongue curled from the side of her mouth in a sign that meant one thing from a child, but another from a woman. She was not far away, a dozen paces. Her eyes upon him were serious with questions, and they were dark and warm. She set off up the hill again, as before.

*Chapter 8*

# QUARRELS

THE roan stallion stood higher than its companions. It was taller than Caesar's Andalusian horse; not so fat, but taller.

"He's a German," said Jesus the Spaniard. Jesus was a tall creature himself. He stood straight and lordly but his eyes shifted as if they looked for exits from tight corners, or wealth left unminded. It was he that yesterday brought home the bee-envenomed Bonne, naked across the withers of his horse.

"That's right," Vigorce said.

"D'you not see Norman blood there? Look at the size of him!" This speaker was a miniature man and for that was called Mosquito. He had a broad and happy face, and a contented air unusual in such a little man. It was to him that Jesus had handed down the stung and scarlet Bonne—and from him that Vigorce had at once removed her.

"No," Vigorce said definitely. "There's no cross-breeding to that horse. He's German right enough, a Mecklenburger, and I saw them in Burgundy. As strong a warhorse as there is. He'll work through a whole summer's day of fighting." He stood in the arch of the stallion's neck with the animal's chin on his breast. "As fiery as Hell in his rage," Vigorce said, "or twice as patient. See!" He put up his long arms and pulled the dark and silky ears. The horse pushed its head sideways to glance for a moment into the eyes of Vigorce, then settled again and stood still and comfortable in the shade of noon.

To south and west of the manor house the ground fell away, and in that immediate space a capacious lean-to shelter had been made. From the corner of the house a heavy beam ran to a stone pillar; this was the main strength of the roof. Lesser pillars of timber and lighter beams carried it to the sides, and the space was bounded by the walls of the house, by a stretch of rock face, and by a stone wall at the far end on which, in wintertime, the north wind struck bitterly.

Here Caesar's garrison took their siesta. Solomon, indeed, slept under that north wall, a respected casualty—once the first hilarity was over—of the war with the bees. His comrades and his captain felt too much that a new pitch of animation had entered the life of the household for them to be able to sleep. For long enough it had been a place wanting nothing but energy to move its fate towards the crisis: now events had brought their own activity to bear. Here was this mysterious stranger within the gates, and there was the lady at death's door.

The habit of life in this remote fastness was a dull one. Events of moment occurred seldom, and when they did occur they showed no sense of their own importance, they brought no mood with them to change the state of the air. Indeed, all the mood of life, all the temper of the air depended on how things stood between Caesar and Bonne. Their long and unfought war, of hidden battles and invisible manoeuvres, had the mysterious character of a charcoal-burner's slow, smouldering fire of embers covered-in with earth that would let no fumes, other than its own, live in the air about it.

The last true event had been the departure of the masons in the spring. The day of their going was a symbol of catastrophe, since it proclaimed the poverty of the house and suggested that the ramshackle world up here had begun to end. Yet Caesar and Bonne, who had been as affable as dignity allowed for the week after the master mason said he was taking his men off the job—having bondsmen up from the village to help dismantle the scaffolding, and so forth—had on the actual day that the masons left wrought up their impalpable conflict to such a height that the air hummed as if thunder walked the hills. Men had headaches, could not hear plain speech, and shunned all work or talk that needed them to think. When the small convoy of two wagons and a few pack animals set off down the hill, it was the masons that looked uneasily towards the house, not the house that cast foreboding looks on their departure.

Now, however, Bonne had descended at a stroke from that haughty warfare where lightnings flew unseen among the clouds and had thrown herself, or been thrown, to the brink of death. Her dying, if it took place, would be not phantasmagorical, but fact. Something had been allowed to happen, at last.

The man at the end of the horse-shed turned onto his back and snorted as if he was waking up; but he slept on, snoring from time to time.

"He's breathing well," Mosquito said. "He's better."

"The Jew is drunk," Jesus said. "He drank a bucket of wine."

Vigorce came from under the German horse's throat. "It was wine boiled with fennel, medicine for his bee-stings, and it was by no means a bucket." He stood beside the Spaniard and looked down over the plain that ran south to Aragon, to the Pyrenees. "You've disliked him since he came. That was at Easter. Now you're speaking of it."

Jesus's lips, pale, bone-like parallels on a thin face that looked as if it had been narrowed in a vice, were turned up with relish into a sneer. "Now is the time to speak plain," he said, looking at the view.

"Speak plain, then," Vigorce said, continuing also to regard the distance.

"This family and this house are going to pieces," Jesus began at once. "Say the lady dies—" here Vigorce stopped breathing for a while, and his eyes fell sideways "—although of course it will be a splendid thing, to have been stung to death by bees." To this splendour he gave a formal sign of appreciation, bowing his head stiffly as if his neck hinged on rusty metal. "The lord is mad already, the castle will never be built, and there is no money. Now we have this adventurer in a silk shirt, a thief and back-killer if I ever saw one!"

Little Mosquito said, "Why do you think so? He says he's come from the wars. Why not?"

"I daresay he has," Jesus said, and dropped a mere speck of a glance, a fidget of the eye, on Mosquito so far below. "There are pickings in the wars, so I daresay he has. I still say he's a robber. Consider this horse. It is fat. It has no mark of wounds on it. It is two years old, barely—hardly got its growth. This is a cheerful, innocent, untried horse that has never been to war." He turned to Vigorce. "Am I wrong?"

"No, I think you're right," Vigorce said. "Go on."

"A German horse," Jesus said, and nodded several times, and some way into his next words as well. "German armour he has, too; brand new chainmail. His sword is German, very new, unblooded most likely; and the grip's unworn, unsweated, virgin."

"What do you mean?" Vigorce asked. "I understand that all his gear is German and all of it new, and the horse German, still very young. So, what are you saying?"

"Everything is of the best," Jesus said, "weapons, armour and this Mecklenburg horse. It is a rich man's gear." He smiled. "I see a young German noble, a knight—no, a would-be knight—on his travels." He put his smile away. "Met his match," he said flatly.

"Oh-ho!" Vigorce said. "I see." He thought about it. "Why not in the wars? He could have killed the German in fair fight."

"A German lordling in these wars? I doubt it. On one side, the Count of Barcelona, supported by the King of England and renegades like the Count of Foix and *their* cousin—" here he nodded his head up at the house, pleased with the passing insult"—Roger the Viscount, of Béziers and Narbonne, and so forth: and on the other side, Count Raymond of Toulouse and anyone who's stayed loyal to him. No Germans in that. Some mercenaries, perhaps, but no baby barons on their first outing. In any case the wars have been over six months now; a good six months." Jesus sniffed the air like a dog questing with its nose. "It all smells more recent to me, this little lark."

"All the same," Vigorce said, "what's going on down there? Disbanded armies, troops of mercenaries, gangs of brigands—all living by the strong hand. You could not blame the man for being there, and killing this German of yours in a brawl."

Jesus shut his eyes tight and put up his chin till his beard pointed to the roof of the shed. "That is not how it happened," he said. "I feel it in my bones. This German of mine, as you call him—" and he smiled again "—was murdered by our new friend."

"That's likely enough," Mosquito said agreeably. "Why should we care?"

Jesus descended towards Mosquito by bending at the knees, and remained there, sitting on his ankles. "I care, because I have taken a dislike to him," he said. "I care also, because he has wormed his way into the house where he has no more right than I have; this family of his, of Noé, who has heard of that? Whereas my family—"

"Yes, yes!" Vigorce said. "We have heard, certainly, of your family, and often enough too. The fact remains, you're hiding from the rope yourself up here; from several ropes. Sit still, you idiot!" Vigorce put both hands on Jesus's head and pushed down. "Don't be such a goddam play-actor. You told me yourself, when you came here, you were a thief on the run. It shows in your face still, for all your airs and graces."

"I know it shows," Jesus said. "You can take your hands off me." He jerked his head impatiently. "Sure, I know it shows. As soon as I started thieving, it showed in my face. It was hopeless. I could make nothing of it at all."

Mosquito said. "It goes against the grain with you to be a thief, so your face gives you away. Now I was born to cut purses. That's why I'm this height; it runs in the family."

Vigorce came back to the point. "You had more to say about the visitor, Jesus. You've been spying on him, since you've had a sight of his armour. You think he means us harm? What harm can he do us? Why should he?''

Jesus rolled his head about and lifted his eyes to Heaven, so that they showed white. "Maybe I'm tired of this," he said. "Listen, I'll tell it all at once, what I think." He looked across at Mosquito and up at Vigorce, to see if they were attending closely. "Very well. I say this place is going to pieces. Well, let it. If the lady dies or not, the lord will go more mad than he is; he will go all mad and die, or kill himself. The girl will go away. We can live here as long as we want, once they've gone. No one will want the place. No lord will come and take it. Well?''

Vigorce was glaring at him, darkly. Mosquito said, "Perhaps. Say the rest of it.''

"This . . . this newcomer," Jesus said. "He is out for what he can get. He'll spoil it for the rest of us. He wants to make something for himself. There will be nothing for us, and even if by many miracles the family live through all this—'' he revolved a hand by which the others understood, easily enough, that he meant the general atmosphere of failure and decline in which they spent their days''—even so, he will do us down.''

"I don't get the hang of this," Mosquito said. "You don't say, he is our enemy?''

Vigorce cut in. "That's what he *is* saying!''

"No, I'm not," Jesus said. "I don't say he's our enemy. I say he has come across this place, and now he has chosen it. He has things to do with himself and he'll do them here. Can't you tell that, by looking at him?''

"No," Mosquito said. "Not me. Even if he has things to do here, and he has chosen this place, what's wrong with that?''

"Oh, nothing," Jesus said sarcastically. "Nothing at all. Except that he seems to me to have killed a stranger simply to get his horse and armour. What will he do here, to have his way?'' He threw his hands in the air and sat dejected, looking into some middle distance between himself and the horizon.

There was a short silence, then Vigorce spoke. "The lady will not die. That woman in the house knows medicine.'' There was more silence, and Vigorce spoke again. "What do you say to all this, Mosquito?''

"I say nothing," Mosquito answered. "I don't know how to think like that, the way Jesus thinks. I'm not against it, I just can't get a grip on it."

At this, Vigorce grew ill-tempered. "That will hardly do," he said. "Jesus makes sense in some things." Jesus threw his eyes into a fit of rolling. Vigorce knitted his brows in the effort to experience (as Mosquito could not) the Spaniard's ways of thought. "This stranger is to be reckoned with. He may be just a lad, but he's been to the wars. He looks clever and wicked and not to be trusted. A crafty boy is dangerous. Now: what do you say, Mosquito?"

Mosquito shook his head, smiling ruefully. "It may be true. You describe me as a boy. Dangerous? If I told either of you, you were not dangerous, you'd stick a knife up my nose." He scratched inside this organ. "I tell you what—he's got an air, something about him. I like his style."

"He has a way with him, you think?" Vigorce pounced on this. "I feared that, I feared that too. Style, you say—style. He could make his way with my lady; put his thoughts in her head." Vigorce shoogled his fingers in front of him. "He could have her in the hollow of his hand."

Jesus jumped to his feet with a howl of frustration. "You do not hear a word I say! You can't listen, can you? My lady this, my lady that! My lady in the hollow of his hand!" He held out his own hands to Vigorce as if there were something to be read in them. "See this! See!" He spat into the palms of his hands and waved them at Vigorce again. "Was my lady not in the hollows of these hands last night? In all our hands—and what of it? I spit there, I spit! I'm talking about realities, not about your dreams. You and my lady—oh, yes! Huh! I spit in these hands, and I wash her off my hands with spit—see, see!"

Vigorce saw, and Jesus came to his senses, simultaneously. At the very moment that the Spaniard threw himself towards safety, Vigorce threw himself at the Spaniard. Jesus had put all his effort into a bound of which everything took place but the separation of his foot from the earth; for Vigorce had grasped the ankle. The effect on Jesus was as if he had been a man who, not realising that he has been fettered to a wall, sets off to win a race.

He cried out, "Ay-ay!" so that Solomon woke at last and Mosquito laughed aloud, and then he fell for a long moment to the sound of crackling gristle from disconcerted joints, and hit his nose on the ground with a thud, but his head with a hollow noise upon a stone.

When Vigorce turned the fallen man over, it seemed as if he would be cheated of his vengeance; Jesus lay there stunned. The captain sat beside him on the ground and whistled soundlessly. He fingered the bump on the head and then patted the cranium as if to say, nothing much wrong there. He looked about him and had an inspiration. He took the worn leather gauntlets from his victim's belt.

When Jesus came to himself he groaned and put a hand to his head. He let the hand fall. Later he sat slowly up. He looked at his old gloves there on his hands, and wondered. He leaned forward to peer at the gloved hands. He lifted them to his nose and sniffed, but the nose was full of dried blood and told him nothing. He put his face towards the sky and began to pull with one glove at the other. He could not get the glove off, and tried the other hand. The leather started to draw off and then came suddenly. Horse dung fell to the ground, and the glove was filled with it, the hand covered. He tore off the other glove and got himself to his feet. He steadied himself, and had a thought, and bent carefully for the gloves and stood up again. He had not once looked into the horse-shed, and now he took one step away, downhill.

When Vigorce spoke, however, Jesus stopped. "Now," the captain said. "When you look at your hands you will not think that they held the lady there, and naked, unless you think also whatever it is you are thinking now."

Jesus turned to look at him. His face had no expression from within. It had dirt and blood on it. The eyes were the same as ever, dark and unlit depths, like the naves of long churches in midwinter. He turned away and limped off slowly.

"That was hard on his pride," said Mosquito, who had begun to whet a long and narrow dagger on the soft leather sole of his boot.

Vigorce made an unsuccessful laugh and rubbed his hands over his outsized face, over his black, greying scalp. "You can put that away," he said, "I'm not quarrelling with you."

"Your temper's cool now," Mosquito agreed, "but I'll put him away in my own time." He went on whetting the knife. "What about Jesus and his pride? What do you think he'll do?"

Vigorce said, "He won't do anything. It is a part of his pride to have it injured now and then: the greater the hurt the greater the solace. I have comforted his pride."

On the long side of the shed five horses were stalled, and Solomon came down to his fellows leaning on the stalls as he passed them.

Mosquito jumped up. "Sit on this log, man. How do you feel?"

"I feel well," Solomon said, "but I stagger." He had a bald round brown head, wrinkled like an old apple. When he had sat down, Vigorce touched the top of the head lightly.

"How does that feel?" Vigorce asked him earnestly; he had a great kindness for Solomon. "It looks all right," he went on. "It's not red now. The welts have gone down, almost all."

"I think it feels fine. It doesn't hurt."

"They were bad stings," Vigorce said. "They were African bees."

"How's the lady?" Solomon asked.

The captain's face twisted. Lines pulled from the jaw to the inner corners of the eyes, chasms opened on the brow, and a pitiful expression enfeebled the full mouth. Where Mosquito had been about to resume his seat on the log, beside Solomon, the captain plumped himself down. "I was so busy about her—her pride," he said, "that I forgot. She is at death's door, Solomon. You have been lucky."

Solomon made a dry sound, disagreeing. "Lucky? Did I ask to play with the bees?" He shook his head. "She made a fool of herself, yesterday."

He went on shaking his head in an elegiac rhythm.

Onto Vigorce's much worked countenance, roused even by this temperate complaint, ran the scarlet of his ready anger. He leapt to his feet and hit the flat of his hand three times on the stone pillar. "Ah!" he cried in despair. "We must do something!" When he turned to them, his face was enlightened, wild with an idea. "I shall fetch the priest," he said, "and we shall have prayers out of him. We shall have prayers out of the whole village!"

Mosquito had grown wary. "The priest! Do you think he'll come?"

The change of spirit in Vigorce was so great that it put him beyond taking offence. With that powerful body, the large head, his face alive with resolution and blood in his eye, he was the very picture of a captain in the field about to hurl himself on his enemies. In no time he was urging an indignant bay horse across the slope to the bridge, at a pace between a canter and a scamper.

Mosquito was irritated, and sat cracking his knuckles until Solomon made a face at him.

"He's besotted," Mosquito said. "He's crazy. He wants the lord's wife for his woman."

Solomon's sixty-year old eye became lively. "She's a likely woman," he said. "She's still a beauty. She's got a fire in her."

Mosquito cracked his knuckles to this. "She's the lord's wife," he said.

Solomon shrugged. "It's the heat," he said peaceably. "Lack of occupation. Craziness grows."

Mosquito remained gloomy. "He'll foam at the mouth soon." He seemed about to fall asleep, then said suddenly. "Hey! Did you see what he did to Jesus?"

"Not clearly. I was half asleep. I saw Jesus go off in a huff."

Mosquito described the insult and the reciprocal outrage. When he had finished he laughed, but shook his head as well.

There was no laugh from Solomon. When he spoke, it was about something else. "He's gone to fetch the priest. Why do you think the priest won't come?"

Mosquito became uncomfortable, but he got it out. "The priest calls the lady Bonne a heretic."

"I don't mind being called a heretic," Solomon said. "There's no need to be delicate; but I must say, Mosquito, you're an easy man to get on with."

"I like a quiet life," Mosquito said. "Isn't it marvellous how unquiet this place can be. Even today's siesta!" He waved a hand at the place where Jesus had been laid low. "And yesterday, with the bees!" After a while he said, "Last year the priest was crazy; about the lady, I mean. As Vigorce is, now. He'd just arrived then, a new priest. He really went for her. The lord had not gone so peculiar last year, but he was hanging on by a thread. The lady was a lot left to herself. She didn't have the child with her much—the child began to play with the serf children about then. That's bad, you know?" He looked gravely at Solomon, who gave a little bow to show that he understood this to be a solecism, letting the child play among the serfs: a pulled thread in the fabric of life. "The priest," Mosquito said, "Talked religion to her, and she talked it back to him. Sometimes you could hear them right across the yard, wild and excited, shouting and stamping the feet—sometimes you heard crying, and that was the priest. Isn't that curious?

"One day it came to a head. It came to a fight." Telling his story had cheered up Mosquito, and he grinned. "I think the priest jumped her, there in the house. She fought him off. She's a strong woman. She fought him. Vigorce and I ran over to the noise. As we got there she knocked the priest down with her fist, and he gave up. He was half out the door with his head hanging down the step. Then the lord came home from one of those long walks he goes.

"'What's this?' he says. 'He tried to rape me,' the lady says, and at the same time the priest says, lying there on the step, 'I was struggling with the Devil in her. She's a heretic.' The priest looked like nothing, like a strangled chicken, but the lady was in her pride, her dander up, not upset at all. Now," and here Mosquito leaned forward and tapped Solomon's knee, "Vigorce was gazing at her like a man star-struck—and she looked fine, shining with fury, all her dignity on—oh, yes! But Vigorce wasn't like a man looking at a woman he wanted. It was as if he'd seen the Blessed Virgin."

He crossed himself and then ducked his head apologetically at the Jew.

Solomon twitched his neck impatiently as if a fly had tried to land on it. "Come on, come on," he said. "What did the lord do?"

Mosquito resumed his tale. "The lord Caesar looked at the priest down on the floor, and he said, 'Rape!' and took the word in: he took it onto the tip of his tongue and drew it in slowly, for the taste. I saw him do it. Then he looked at the lady, hot and raging but smiling as well; very mixed to see, she was. The lord looked at her and he said, 'Heresy!' and he tasted the sound of that too. Then the lord saw Vigorce staring at the lady and he snapped his fingers under his nose and brought him down to earth. 'Now, now, captain!' he said."

Mosquito rubbed his stumpy nose and his eyes were bright with the remembered moment. "Then he looked at me," he said, "and he cried out, 'Well, Mosquito, we can't hang them all!' and went into the house!"

This appealed to Solomon who laughed deeply until he fell into a cough that shook the phlegm from his chest. He thumped the log he sat on with his fist. Mosquito watched him, and himself laughed in sympathy. As the laughter died down, Mosquito stood and stretched. "I'll get the water," he said. "You take it easy, but you might see their halters are tied fast, or they'll come for it before the chill's out of it."

Solomon passed his hands lightly over his shining head. Another chuckle came out of him. "Heresy," he said, "to refuse a priest!"

Jesus came into the shed, carrying two leather bags and his big cloak, and with his long sword at his hip. He brought his small, cream-coloured horse, part Arab, out into the sun with its saddle on it, and threw the bags across its back. Over the top of the horse he nodded, with great solemnity, at Solomon, and Solomon returned this greeting. Jesus made a roll of his cloak and tied it behind the saddle. He came round the horse and spoke to Solomon. "Are you well?" he asked.

"Well enough," Solomon said. "I'm well."

"Good," Jesus said. "Will you tell them, I am hunting carrion?"

"You're going to look for the body?" Solomon asked him.

"Ah! You heard then!" Mortification, despite his best efforts, turned away the Spaniard's face.

"I heard some, not all. I was coming and going in my sleep."

"Ah!"

"Jesus!" Solomon said, and the man's face came round again. "If you will set out in the heat of the day, take this," and Solomon threw his wide straw hat spinning at the man on the horse. Jesus actually hesitated, to make up his mind about this offer, and then caught the hat after it had passed.

Solomon blinked at such dexterity.

Wondrously, Jesus smiled, and it was like a moonflower opening in the night. He said, "When I come back . . . ." He shrugged. "Ach!" he said. He put the hat on his head, and hit the air between them with his fist, by way of farewell.

Solomon lifted a hand, and the little cream-coloured horse ran down the slope with the Spaniard's long legs dangling down its pretty sides.

## Chapter 9

# PIMPERNEL PASTE

**B**ONNE swallowed a little of the wine that had been boiled with fennel in it, but for most of the time after her battle with the bees she lay in a stupor. It was Gully the kitchen woman who coaxed those few drops of liquid down her, splashing the rest on her fervered skin: and here now was Gully once more, with her paste of blue pimpernels—the sovereign remedy, she said, but late, late in the day!

"You can't find wild flowers in the dark, Gully!" Flore protested. "You spent enough time yourself stewing them up in the pot!"

This was the right answer. "Flirting is no help either," Gully said with pleasure. "And what I do in the stew-pot is my business! Here!" She handed the basin that held the hopeful medicine to the girl, and threw back the linen sheet that covered the patient.

Bonne lay on a wide bed, wood-framed and corded across with leather. Its curtains had been turned back when the day warmed to let the air pass freely. The wooden shutters of the window were open as well and Caesar sat there on the stone seat, the whole of him canted to one side as if he had been sitting very upright, and so fallen asleep. His eyes were closed, not tight shut, but with the eyebrows up in an effect of surprise, and the lids descended. He had passed the night here with Bonne. Some of the night he had lain beside her, smiling his perpetual smile into the dark hours, but he had not slept until now; and this was hardly sleep, since he could hear what Flore and the woman were saying to each other.

He did not open his eyes. "What do you bring?" he asked.

"Blue pimpernel paste," Gully said. "It is famous for stings, and other things too."

"When you can find the flowers," Flore said.

"I told you where to look," Gully said smartly. "They call me a wise woman. Here we go!"

She began to slap the pulpy ointment she had made onto Bonne's body. "The poison's all everywhere," she said. "We must send the cure in after it." She was not so fierce with the face, which she smote firmly with fingertips, but from neck to toes she slapped the stuff onto the skin as if she would force it through.

This morning Bonne's skin was no longer scarlet, but pink and puce, white and yellow. To Amanieu, who leaned watching in the doorway, it was as if she had been made from a vein of ill-blent marble—except that she was in a state of continuous bounce under the strange treatment. Gully slapped her lady madly upon belly and sides as if she thought one kind of sting might eliminate the effects of the other; as indeed she did. She beat even upon the proud breasts, strained and streaky though they were.

"Oh, be careful!" Flore cried, welling with sympathy and envy together for her own immature bosom. "You will damage her!"

"Is she not damaged now?" Gully cackled, quite carried away, you might have thought; but she moved almost at once to the arms, where she administered the ointment by holding an arm in the air with one hand, and slapping it hardily up and down, backhand and forehand, with the other.

After a time something occurred to Caesar, and he opened bloodshot eyes. "You said that stuff was good for something else beside bee-stings," he said. "What?"

Gully, who had just finished the legs, paused for a while to catch her breath. "It cures madness that *I've* heard of," she said. "Mary Mother!" she said. "I'm old. This is too much for me." Flore dipped her hand in the basin diffidently and began to pat her mother's carcase. "You'll never do it like that," Gully said, but flopped onto the bed, panting. "The lord will have to finish it."

"Nonsense," Caesar said. "I couldn't smite Bonne like that, as if I was salting so much meat."

Amanieu, looking down upon the stung, marbled and now again provoked flesh, and upon the fair, forlorn face that lay visible (at least to him) beneath the disease or death that blotched it, felt a very curious pang. It was a sensation not precisely humane, a weird feeling of the kind he had known once standing under a willow tree at full moon: he had been told this was a perilous thing to do, for some people.

"Get up a moment," he said to the old woman who sat on the edge of the bed, "so that I can turn her over. I'll finish it."

He gave Flore an encouraging wink and started to beat the last of the blue pimpernels into her mother's back. He wondered if they would need some more, if they would grow up overnight, replacing themselves as fast as dandelions: if they would go picking them again tomorrow.

When Amanieu had slapped the final dollop of paste onto Bonne's bottom, Gully said, "Now, rub it in. Rub!" She had moved to the other side of the bed, near Caesar's window-seat. "There's something else the blue pimpernel does," she confided to him, "or so they say. It's not a thing I'd do, you see: but I've been told!"

Caesar, now that Amanieu was rubbing his hands over Bonne's body, felt that something was wrong. He craned his neck first to one side of Gully then the other, to make sure that nothing luxurious entered the action which Amanieu brought to those smooth, rhythmic strokes of palms and fingers upon Bonne's thighs, the backs of her thighs, behind her knees. "What did you say?" he asked Gully, much distracted, however, by the scene on the bed.

"The blue pimpernels," Gully said, "can create the force to speak with spirits."

Caesar's wild blue eyes, which had been gliding left and right to pass his rapid glances either side of Gully's wagging old head, slid to a more central station and fixed themselves on hers. He sent his mind and hearing back a few moments to pick up what she had said. "Speak with spirits!" he said. "These blue pimpernels?" He looked. "In that basin!"

Amanieu moved Gully with a shove and turned Bonne belly-up on the bed again. Now it was Flore who watched him like a hawk. If only she were a year older! She had roused him coming up the hill, but she was too young—he was sure to go crazy for Bonne, they all did. Through the door she saw Mosquito drawing water from the well, which was in the hall, just above the kitchen steps. She gave him a nod and managed a tight little smile: she'd throw herself at him one day, if she had to—she had seen him refusing to react to Bonne. He pulled a bucket from the well and came to watch.

Just as Flore wondered if Amanieu was about to start stroking her mother's bosom, and laying his long fingers down the insides of her thighs; and as it came to Amanieu that he was, suddenly, irresolute to continue on the foreparts what he had begun so masterfully on the hind; and as Caesar in one movement got up and snatched the magic bowl from Flore: Bonne woke from her poisoned sleep.

Her golden, catlike eyes looked into Amanieu's black, basaltic orbs and understood his weaselly face. She closed them and laid a fragile smile on her lips.

Caesar pushed forward. He smeared hastily onto his own forehead a tiny scrape from the basin, held his long, wolfhound's face over Bonne's and fixed on it, in anticipation of a second awakening, one of his most concentrated regards. If the paste of blue pimpernels could evoke the inmost voice of the spirit, then now, if ever, he would hear Bonne's soul answer to his!

Her eyes opened again. The gold look blundered into the startling blue. Her voice was clear, but diminished to a fortieth of its true size. "Christ!" she said. "Do I still live?"

The eyes rolled in their sockets to search out Amanieu, at the other side of the bed. She reached for him, but failing and letting her arm drop, and then pointing at him instead of clutching, she made plain her disappointment. "I thought I was dead, and in Hell!"

After that, the people round the bed remained for some moments stuck fast where they were, as if they were in the first stage of being transformed into pillars of salt, or red sandstone, or anything doomed to stand for centuries in the same place. Mosquito, however, seeing the flickering tongue that raked the cracked lips, brought his bucket up to the bed and gave Bonne water from an iron ladle, and she slept.

## Chapter 10

# LIGHT AND DARK

WHEN a whole day had passed Bonne still slept. Her skin was near its usual colours, the flesh within more placid; she breathed deep. Even her beauty was on the mend, but still she slept.

On the day following, therefore, the blue pimpernel cure, and at the same time in the afternoon as it had yesterday been administered; and Gully and Caesar being this once of the same mind—namely, that Bonne was now set into her sleep the way you can get stuck in a bad habit, like drinking—they took her out of bed and restored her as far as possible to the daily run of the establishment.

Their thought was this, that Bonne had an imperious nature, and whereas you can dominate a bed or bedroom, provided they are of a certain history, by lying asleep; yet you cannot sit forever among a household's affairs with your eyes shut and yourself elsewhere, and experience a sense of rule.

Accordingly Caesar summoned Vigorce, and Vigorce summoned Solomon and Mosquito (Jesus being absent on his errand), and besides these there was Amanieu, not to mention the old woman and the child, and the seven of them pulled the long table from its shadows—the wide elm-board as thick through as a man's hand is broad—to a place near the front door, so that the sun spread over one end of it while the other end rested in that cool corner of the hall where the well was sunk. By the well-head then, between the outer doorway and the steps down to the kitchen—you might say at the very hinge of the house—Bonne was served up, dormant, upon the table.

Suddenly when that was done—when Bonne was leaned, half-sitting, on a pile of pillows and cushions, and Gully had washed her lady's face and hands with warm water and a little vinegar, and gone off to the kitchen; and the yellow silk dress which was (excepting perhaps her enamelled Persian birds) Bonne's dearest possession, lay along her sleeping form; and Flore had kneeled beside her on the table and combed her hair, from which fell some stings and a dead bee, and thereafter, stricken by aimlessness and having no kitchen of her own, vanished into one of the black patches that lay about the house—after everything was done, a bad humour settled upon those remaining.

The talk natural to such shared and anxious activity ended, and nothing followed; Solomon and Mosquito went out. The men left in the room had separated into their single selves, each of them cast in a pose that said a good deal about his character and its relationship to Caesar's wife.

Vigorce sat on the top step with his back to the doorpost and his legs along the threshold. Most of the flies passing in and out of the house paused to address him, and the petulance that sprang from this made his unhappiness strong in him again. The muscles behind his shoulders creaked with anger. From where he sat, he looked up at everyone.

Amanieu sat on the edge of the well, collecting an unhealthy chill into his kidneys, planted by Bonne's side like a usurping consort on a coeval throne, and facing like her down the table but with his eyes open, squinting out of darkness into light. In his mind, Flore walked.

Caesar stood at the foot of the table, very straight for him—bending a little back in the middle and down from the top. His figure shone, gilded freakishly by the afternoon sun, even to the rope-coloured, grey-streaked hair. He stared from the shower of light that sprinkled him to the shadows, where Bonne's true, golden beauty gleamed forth out of her darkness and dreams. As self-absorbed as a god of old mythology, or a buffoon of any time, Caesar shared also their gift for the histrionic. In his case, however, it was an inconstant gift, which came and went, so that sometimes he would mistake the fancy for the fact: attempting the theatrical when Apollo was not in him, he would take his stance and wait for eloquence to flow—and hear (amazed) silence trickle by. This had happened now, and it was the force of his astounded dumbness that exerted the general silence, like a heavy but inescapable article of faith, on everyone in earshot.

There he was upon his chosen ground, caged in brilliance, marooned in a dazzling pool of sun, dumbfounded and meaningless. Sunlight pressed on him from without and silence pushed outwards from within. He reacted like an olive stone squeezed between finger and thumb. For one transported instant, and as if his soul had vaulted into the sky, he looked down on himself and saw a man who gazed from brightness at a woman that hid in the dark. He saw a man always about to dance in light but kept, by a medusan eye, stone-still and blind.

Mosquito came back to draw water for the horses. Across the

doorway sprawled his captain's legs, forgotten by their owner who sat in a trance. That officer's men were used to his falling into catalepsies before the lady, yet it seemed to Mosquito that with Bonne already entranced on her own account Vigorce had, this time, run past himself. A second look, however, discovered that the captain's eyes were fastened not on the lady, but the lord. They gazed up at that illuminated person with a dull stare that looked as if it saw a ghost: their aim, also, was inexact, as if they thought some of Caesar might be found up among the rafters. Flies crawled and buzzed unheeded now about the captain's massive head.

Mosquito was not a dwarf, but he was no taller than a boy and had a boy's proportions. Phlegmatic and down-to-earth (due, Solomon said, to his brains being near the ground) he let people excite themselves, and cataclysms shock the earth, without troubling his own emotions to respond. He had one obsession—to keep as much space around himself as was accorded to a full-sized man. The raptures and morbid passions that steamed in the air of this place touched him to no more than irritation or amusement. He was neither their friend nor their opponent, and by them he was uninfected.

He now allowed his head to precede the rest of him across the threshold, and perceived that Caesar was in an ecstasy. It came to him that the whole room might be under miracle or magic, and he peered round the corner at the well. His eyes were small from the daylight and at first he could hardly discern the lady; but there she was, sleeping on. He kept his head still and rolled his eyes along to the visitor. A look as fast and cold as a fish struck into him. If there was a miracle, it had not reached that end of the table. Mosquito blinked his eyes up at the roof, where he saw nothing to explain his captain's unfocussed way of watching Caesar. There was, to be sure, a definite sight to see up there, a thing easy to describe—a fluttering glow in the rafters, he could call it: but the earthly chill he had received from Amanieu's eyes, the assurance they bespoke that unspeakable mysteries lay unfathomably deep in mere, ordinary men, had disposed Mosquito against the miraculous and magic. The glow in the rafters, therefore, he reckoned to be simply a piece of light tossed up there like a leaf by a passing wind. Yet he stepped over the stretched legs of Vigorce almost as if the captain were a log in an enchanted forest; he contrived to work his way between the doorpost and Caesar without touching him—very much as he would have done had his lord been spellbound into a tree; and he walked discreetly to the well where he let down the bucket from a station as far as possible from Amanieu, as if the latter had been an actual and natural specimen of poison ivy, or the giant and itchy hogweed.

The well was low, so far into the summer, and the bucket took some time to reach the water. During its descent, Mosquito began to shiver, and knew himself to be under the stranger's chilly eyes. When the bucket was on the way up, Amanieu spoke.

"You are used to this," he said.

Mosquito hoisted the bucket to the top. "I do it each day," he said.

"I don't mean that," Amanieu said.

Mosquito pulled the bucket onto the edge of the well. "Ah!" he said.

The shivering ended, so he flew a glance at the questioner. That mysterious youth had a friendly smile on him. Despite the sense Mosquito had of this visitor, that he was not a man like other men but a creature made of earth dug from deep and dreadful pits (through whose floors the sulphur smoked); despite the weaselly face and reptile's eyes, Mosquito felt at this moment his own honest, human spirit respond to the hint of warmth.

Therefore he asked, "What *do* you mean?"

Amanieu indicated Bonne behind him on the table-top, and the two stunned figures near the door.

"I mean that being here is like watching someone else's dreams, and that you are used to this by now."

Mosquito stepped inside the kitchen and emptied the bucket into a wooden chute that was fixed to the kitchen wall, and which ran out through the horse-shed to the water-trough. Far away, as if from the farther end of the chute, there was a sound like a faint cry. He listened, but did not hear it again.

A thought came to him, and he put it to the stronger. "If watching these three—" he jerked his head at Bonne and the two men "—is like watching someone's dream, whose dream would it be? They can't share the same dream. They can't have the same dreams as each other."

"Is that true?" asked Amanieu, much struck. "Perhaps it is true. All the same, do you not have the sense that they dream one dream, and that you live in it along with them?"

Mosquito did not like this idea. "I don't dream much," he said, "but my dreams are my own."

Amanieu was annoyed. "Who cares about your dreams?" he de-

manded. "The question is your lord's and lady's dreams. Perhaps he
has a dream with her in it, and perhaps she has a dream with him in it,
and perhaps sometimes she in his dream and he in her dream, meet.
What do you think of that?"

Mosquito gave time to this, while he studied the two figures in the
stranger's conundrum. He said at last, "I think dreams or madness, if
you live them, will be the same. Can you dream enough to share
another's madness?"

"What?" exclaimed Amanieu. "What an idea!"

"What did I say?"

"Say it again!"

Mosquito found that he had forgotten what he said. "Tell me what
it was," he asked.

"You are better off without it," Amanieu said. "I shan't tell you.
Fill your bucket."

Amanieu had his answer and he paced about the room, through the
dark places and the bright, appearing and disappearing. He planted
himself opposite the table, equidistant from Bonne and Caesar, and
on the border between sunlight and darkness. He studied their inani-
mate forms. Bonne slept on, resting well, it seemed, golden and
beautiful in the murk. Caesar, on the other hand, looked rather fallen
in on himself, as if his present fit of mystical dementia had run its
course and the fatigue of relaxation was about to strike. Amanieu took
another turn about the room (and he noticed, in passing, that Vigorce
still sat in the doorway looking with stupefaction at his master) which
he brought to an end by sitting, once more, upon the parapet of the
well. Mosquito poured another bucketful of water into the chute, and
again after a few moments, heard that sound of a faint cry. He decided
that it must be made by some trick of the falling water and returned
the bucket to the well.

At this moment a commotion from outside the house began to be
heard, but it was not yet so loud that a vast sigh from Caesar was
rendered inaudible, and descending from his elevated state to the
hard floor of physical fact, he staggered about as if he had been a long
time at sea, and then sat down floppily on the end of the table.

Vigorce, who had been spellbound by Caesar's visionary exaltation, was by its ending released from thrall. He did not rush to resume
his duties as captain of the garrison, but sat for a while lost inside his
mind, wearing an expression of amazement and shaking his head to
clear it, like a dog with canker in its ears. The noise of many voices

was growing insistently louder, and pausing only to throw a last bucketful into the chute, Mosquito followed Amanieu to the door.

The captain still had his legs stretched across the threshold, and onto them—just as Vigorce looked up and seemed about to get to his feet—pitched Solomon the Jew, his life's blood pouring from a dozen great hacks and wounds.

"They want their priest," Solomon said, and died.

## Chapter 11

# THE PEASANTS' REVOLT

"THE priest!" Vigorce hit himself on the head with the base of his hand. "The priest! I left him in the horse-trough!" He looked up at Mosquito. "Did you not see him? Have you not watered the horses?"

"What the hell are you talking about!" Mosquito shouted. "Look out there!"

A mob of peasants, with scythes and billhooks waving above their heads, and knives and sickles in their hands, was coming at them. The mob was slowing down as it approached.

"Anyway," Mosquito felt impelled urgently to explain to Vigorce, "in the morning I water the horses from the tub."

"Of course," Vigorce said. "Of course, so you do. Then the priest has spent the night in the horse-trough." Slowly he started to laugh. "He *slept* in the horse-trough," he shouted, and at the thought of such a joke his laughing grew into a fit and he thumped his knee with his fist: but it was not his knee, it was Solomon's body, and the fist fell into a mess of blood and liver with a terrible sound. When this gruesome thing happened the captain's laughter was still ascending, and it was one of those runaway bouts of exuberance which, like a stone tossed in the air, will not come down to earth until it has first climbed to its apogee. Vigorce was driven to laugh more and more throughout the very minute in which the shock came to him—that Solomon's butchered corpse was lying fallen on his lap: and of realising that all the time he sat there, by some strange dispensation of his mind making jokes and laughing, he was weltering in another man's gore. The warm blood soaked through his clothes, it steamed on his hand, and when he contrived at last—shuffling Solomon's corpse off his knees, letting it roll from him as he came gradually upright—to come to his feet, his whole front was painted with blood. The laughing reached its peak, and began to loose its hold.

Vigorce splashed his hands on himself. "Oh," he cried, "he is as full of blood as a pig." It was all his disordered elements could muster by way of lament. You could tell from the tones of his voice that it was meant for mourning, but he knew as well that it was a wrong thing to say of a Jew, and that whatever insult had been spared Solomon in his killing had now been administered by his friend. He laughed again, but there was not much to it; it had become a light, silly laugh. He stepped down from the doorway and the corpse, and a little way towards the mob, and stopped there.

"Good!" Amanieu said, as if it were an oath. "Is there a weapon in this house?"

The number of peasants was about forty. Some were women, and the weapons with Solomon's blood on them were distributed without distinction of sex. Nasty blades they were, Amanieu thought—the hooks and cleavers, some of them fixed to poles, that were the inevitable armoury of mutinous serfs.

Amanieu's long knife was in his hand. "Give me that cutlass," Mosquito said. "Here's the lord's own sword. I don't think he'll be using it."

The sword was long, but Amanieu knew it would work for him as if he were St Michael. "Good," he said again.

"These are father's too," and here was Flore with two short spears, weapons much favoured in Gascony. Her eyes flared at him with such a light that his mind stopped for a moment. "Mosquito's right," she said, "Father won't be ready—he'll be mysterious for a bit yet."

"Find a safe hole," he said. "Get out of the way!"

"No," she said. "I'll see what happens."

Caesar, in a manner of speaking, now intervened. He stood to his full height and stretched out his arms—a man waking from sleep—and looked out of the door. He said, "My people!" with a pleased smile, caught up his astounded daughter by the waist, and passed over the shambles at the door avoiding, apparently by a fortunate accident, everything that had issued from Solomon's body and might have dirtied his feet. He stood Flore on the ground and with a hand on her shoulder urged her forward with him, until they stood beside Vigorce (reeking of blood and laughing, occasionally, a decrepit laugh) and regarded the peasants from a closeness at which it was possible to make out the colours of their eyes.

To Flore Caesar said, "Move sideways a step or two. Vigorce stinks, and besides, he's gibbering." When they had made some distance from the wretched captain, Caesar spoke again. "There's the old goat-woman. How did she come by my Spanish hat? I asked her to her face, but got nothing out of her. She's an inflexible old bitch."

"She's got a scythe, a scythe! She'll reap my poor legs." Flore trembled, from the soles of her feet up to her shoulders. "What did you bring us out here for?"

Caesar laughed, a thing he could do at will; to his mind it was a fool's gift, and he was confirmed in this view by the deranged cackle that broke out in sympathy from the left, so exact did that echo seem to him. "Sounds like a raven's croak," he said, gabbling to keep their courage up. "What do you make of that, my girl—demented ravens on the left? What sort of omen is that?" His fingers on her shoulder pressed hard; the intention was companionable and contrite, but the pain was annoying. "I've done it now," he said. "I've let us in for it."

Flore was now trembling throughout her whole self, and her right foot had begun to kick at the ground all of its own will. "Omens!" she said. "O-O-Omens! What do I know about th-that? I'm not educated, am I?" Caesar twisted his face at this: it was a sore point. "My mother was educated, not me though. Oh no! Look at this!" Suddenly she shouted loud. "Look at us here, a madman, a f-f-fool and a sacrifice!" Such cogency of phrase won a glance of admiration from her father. "Not me, though, I'm going back to the house!" But she did not move. Alas! She could not move. "This is just what you'd expect from living here! Just what you'd expect! Life here is vile, you and her, vile! I'm going away! I'll go tomorrow, or the day after!"

"Where will you go? Don't be silly. Girls your age always start saying that." Caesar remembered something. "And you must not speak like that about your mother."

"Of course I'm going," Flore shrieked. "That old woman will cut me in *two* otherwise!" How she was still standing she did not know. "Why don't they come and cut us up?"

Caesar smiled cheerily at the bloodthirsty faces in front of him. He was impressed by the fact that Flore, in her hysteria, had combined the solution to her two woes—the misfortunes of their home, and the fear of being sliced in two by the scythe-bearing crone—into one: she would leave tomorrow, or the day after. That her plan did not make sense, when you faced the imminence of the inflexible old bitch—"I'll have that hat off her if it's the last thing I do"—was beside the point. If Flore was able to throw all her difficulties into one pot like this, and make a digestible soup of them, she was a better man than he was. Her last question, too, was a good one—why didn't the peasants start chopping them up?

"Stop shivering!" he said to Flore, and sought for a compliment to remark the new esteem with which he viewed her. "You *are* educated," he said.

"God dammit!" Flore exclaimed, and kicked him on the shin. "Speak to them!"

"I am truly sorry about this," her father answered. "When I saw the serfs and came out to meet them, I had no idea they were on the rampage. I must have been in a daydream. I did not see poor Solomon until I was going through the doorway. Poor fellow! They always kill Jews when they're in a state, if there are some handy. Perhaps they don't want to cut us up at all."

"Ask them, then!" Flore said, and after this sarcastic jibe found herself sitting on the ground. Her father had let go of her shoulder and walked even closer to the peasants.

Caesar missed the sarcasm and took the sneer for an example of that talent he had newly perceived in Flore, for responding to life with neat and irrelevant answers. The fact that her solutions made no sense, need not mean that they must fail: he had lived long enough to understand that! Accordingly, he stepped forward to ask these men and women, wielding their bloody hooks and blades, what was holding them back. A natural delicacy, however, prevented him from putting the question in its starkest form, so he merely asked them, "What's the matter?"

"We want our priest!" Surprisingly, these words came from the inflexible old bitch.

"That's my Spanish hat," Caesar said, and grabbed it, quick as lightning.

"Keep your hat!" she said. "We want our priest!"

Caesar took the hat and turned to Flore. "I've got my hat back," he said, to show that something had been won.

Flore bit her knee and looked at him as if he were a figure in the far distance.

"We want our priest," the old woman said again, and waved her scythe up and down so that the man beside her took a nick from the fearful blade that cut his ear half off.

"We want our priest!" the peasants shouted. "Give us our priest!"

Sitting there on the ground and looking at the knees of the mutinous peasantry, Flore had by this time spied in the lower reaches of the crowd a few of the dirty little children she had been accustomed—never again!—to play with in the village.

"Rosine!" she yelled under the mindless grumbling of the serfs, who would plainly go on asking for their priest back until their blood was up again, and they felt ready to chop her and her family into sausagemeat. "Rosine! Rosine!"

Rosine caught on. "Yeah!" she yelled back.

"Rosine, the priest is in the horse-trough!"

"Where?"

"In the horse-trough!"

Rosine giggled at this news and Flore covered her eyes. Often she had hanged Rosine in play, or had her disembowelled and then quartered by horses, and even then she had to be quite bullied to prevent her from giggling and making a mockery of the proceedings. How Flore wished, now, that she had played these games more realistically! At this juncture, fortunately, Rosine's mother, a fat woman composed entirely of pumpkins, shook her daughter furiously just as Flore used to shake her, and asked her why she giggled. The answer passed upward.

"The priest is in the horse-trough!" the woman made of pumpkins bellowed, and her voice was as the voice of Dido lamenting Aeneas. "They have put the priest in the horse-trough!"

For a moment or two everyone shouted that the priest was in the horse-trough, but the general note was of suspicion and incredulity, and no move to rescue the priest took place. Caesar, looking down upon these cantankerous people, was reminded of the lowered head and up-from-under look with which an ox tells you it will not be tricked into accepting the yoke. Caesar thought the image was quite apt.

"There you are!" he said. "The priest is in the horse-trough. Don't stand staring—go and get him out!" Finding the Spanish hat in his hand, he clapped it on his head as if everything was now arranged, folded his arms and frowned towards his feet, and tapped the fingers of one hand upon the other arm. He looked autocratic and impatient: in fact, he had forgotten what it was he wanted to do, and was trying to remember where his life had been before the turbulence broke out.

"Flore," Rosine shouted from among the mob's restless feet, which had started to shuffle with the uncertainties of the situation. "Flore! Where does he mean? Which horse-trough?"

"Round the back," Flore shouted into the rising dust. "The meadow below the stables."

"Round the back! Round the back!" the woman made of pumpkins almost instantly bellowed, and led the main element of the church party round the corner of the house. "Save the priest!" they were shouting as they went from sight. Among the few who stayed was the old woman with the scythe. She stared at Flore where she sat on the ground.

Flore had now entered a vacuum of the perceptions in which she was unaware of fright. She returned the goat-woman's look and stood up and brushed off her frock.

"Well, my dear," Amanieu's voice said, "you will know the child again." He was talking to the old woman.

"No," she said. "I'm blind. But I'll know you."

"I believe you," he said. "You have the gift. Your toes will curl up when I am near." He studied her face. "You don't look blind."

"They say I'm hard to look at," she said proudly. Her blind eyes moved from Amanieu to Flore, who stood now beside him, listening intently to this quick intimacy of converse between two who were, in all apparent ways, opposites.

A small silence ran between them. Flore saw that they both contemplated her, and she blushed, looking askance into the old woman's harsh, blind gaze.

Amanieu spoke again to the old woman. "Can you still mow, blind as you are?" he asked her. "Is that why you keep the scythe?"

"Yes," she said, "because I can mow a meadow, and because the scythe is mine." She hefted it. Flore saw that the blood from the man's ear had dried on the blade. "I must go back to my goats," the woman said. "I could have found you," she said to Flore. "I smelled fear on you."

"Go to your goats," Flore said, and turned away. She found herself, at once, spectator to a communion very different from that between the old woman and Amanieu. Vigorce, fouled and stinking obscenely with Solomon's staled blood all over him, sat upon the ground and chattered. Opposite, his head not much higher than the captain's, Mosquito stood. Flore saw the little man step forward and then at once step back, and shake his fists despairing at his sides.

"What's wrong, Mosquito?" she asked.

"I can't touch him," Mosquito said. "If he stays like that he'll go mad. He must be cleaned, but I can't do it."

Flore said, "He seems mad already. Still, he must be cleaned."

"He may not stay mad," Mosquito said.

The few peasants remaining had tucked their weapons politely out of sight. There was no temper left in them. She could see a few walking back to their village, and there was Amanieu—God rot him!—making his farewells to the old woman down at the gate-house. Where was her father? Never mind. "You two," she said, "come here!" She commanded two young women to come to her as if she had been her own mother, and they came. "Take the captain to the river and give him a bath. Get something for him to wear, Mosquito, when he's clean. He's bound to have spare odds and ends, and if Solomon's left any, they'll fit well enough. Make them bring back the clothes he's wearing: we'll bury them with Solomon." Mosquito ran up towards the new keep where he and his comrades lived.

The two women had Vigorce on his feet.

"All this blood!" one of them said, chiding him sweetly, coaxing a child.

"Hush!" the other one said to him from her side. "Hear yourself go on, man! Chatter-chatter, and saying nothing!"

"My friend's blood," Vigorce said, suddenly coherent.

"Still, it's doing no good on you, is it?"

"No," he said shouting, and wept, "it's no good!"

"There," the second woman said. "You must think more easily on yourself. After all, he was a Jew."

"That's right," her companion said. "You think that: after all, he was a Jew."

Far inside Vigorce, and as if trapped in the ruins of a tall building; as if caught under the beams and the blocks of masonry whose collapse had united whole floors of rooms, and squeezed corridors that ran across, or above and below each other, into one mass of rubble: as if buried alive under the tangled wreckage of what had been only an hour ago the familiar tenement in which he lived, the sanity of Vigorce found a voice and sought for it an outlet.

"A Jew," he said. "Yes, he was, wasn't he? After all, he was a Jew!"

Flore watched them go down the track towards the bridge, whispering their kindness into the captain's ears.

# Chapter 12

## TASTE OF SALT

BONNE'S voice—Bonne's voice!—came sounding out of the house. "Gully!" it said. "Clean my doorstep!"

Flore made to go to her and at the same time flinched away, with the effect that she seemed to wait for her mother.

"What happened to me?" Bonne demanded. "Gully won't say."

Flore told her about the bees; the blue pimpernels and their application by Gully and the visitor to the house; the mystery of Vigorce lodging the priest in the horse-trough; and the killing of Solomon by the serfs.

"The bees, eh?" Bonne said, not much concerned with the rest of it. "They die when they lose the sting; they'll be mostly dead. I wonder how many are left and what of the queen, did she sting me too?" Her hair, that glowed darkly in the house, burned with a ruddy flame when the sun was on it, but her eyes were gold in all weathers. She was as lovely as this morning's dawn, for her beauty was not dulled by the long sleep, and she was much refreshed to find she had accepted and survived the sacrifice of a thousand bees. "It will have been proper for the queen bee to stay in the nest," Bonne said. "She will not have come out to sting me. Now she will not have enough bees left to attend her, and that will be the end of her!" She produced a resilient smile. "A hecatomb of bees all to myself!" Now she laughed, a little shy. "You don't know what a hecatomb is, poor Flore!"

The daughter, who had looked chaos in the face that morning and still lived, opposed at last the mother's shameful habit of mocking for ignorance the child whom she had left untaught. "I knew something like that was coming when you laughed," Flore said (trying herself out).

"Rude!" Bonne said snappily. Her long eyes gleamed: she was a lynx that has just had its tail pulled.

"Father told me I *am* educated!" Flore said gallantly.

"What! While I slept! Grown wise and learned while I slept?" Bonne scoffed steeply down at her, extinguishing the upstart.

Flore reviewed the events of the time specified, and nodded. "Yes," she said, "while you slept." She knew herself that she did not know what she meant, but she knew that she meant it.

So did Bonne, who shifted at once to other ground. "I cannot think how poor Gully is to manage with the Jew's body. It will fall to pieces as soon as touched. Really, where is everybody? Where's your father?"

Flore looked about her and saw that they were quite alone in the yard. (She saw her father on top of the keep, but she let him be). "If it were me," she said, "I'd wrap Solomon up in plenty of straw and a corn-sack or two and tie it all together with old rope, and dump him in the shade. We'll bury him tomorrow, and get the rope back then."

Bonne took these practical proposals as an *amende*, as the resumption of ordered relations after Flore's show of pique. She turned and walked back to the house, an act which assumed that the child would follow.

Flore had a glimpse of Gully, red to the elbows, starting on the mess in the doorway, and ran with winged feet towards the gatehouse, towards the outside, towards herself.

*    *    *

Tall Caesar from the tower looked down.

He saw his daughter run off and away. She flew with the passion of an uncaged bird, and he felt her joy of it rise inside him where it lifted the heart between his shoulders. His hands moved a little in response but he made no great gesture of his own—not the vast and sympathetic stretching of his limbs that the endless air up here tried to win from him: for he knew the air longed to tip him from the parapet, and when it had hold of him would coax his spirit out. He had been above himself today already and not yet come completely to the earth. It was because he felt his spirit still volatile within him, still excited by its ascent to the rafters, and in the hope that he might satisfy its sudden ardour for height, that he had climbed to the roof of the keep. He did not want his spirit to learn the habit of quitting him, and leave him stranded on the earth.

He stepped back and put the parapet at arm's length. His object now was to keep calm for a while and nip excitement in the bud, until his fleshly self had recovered its grasp on the more flighty elixirs of his being. So, though his blood leaped to see Flore's heart take wings and waken to the air, yet he made himself be still.

Instinct had told Bonne at once when her daughter sneaked off behind her back, but she refused fully to believe it until she heard the

teeth grate in her mouth and felt, in consequence, a pang of tooth-
ache. She disciplined her chagrin, compelled her jaws to relax, and
had already spun on her foot to call Flore back, when instead she
heard herself say crossly, "Let the brat go!"—but not wholeheart-
edly, so that she looked and leaned in a number of contrary directions
all (as it seemed to the onlooker) at the same time. The onlooker was
Caesar, and his impression of her—swithering in that yellow silk
while the coppery hair flickered round her head; yearning after the
runaway but held to the spot by more insistent purposes—was of a
candle flame abruptly forsaken by its moth.

For each instant that she hung suspended there irresolute Bonne
was conscious of Caesar on top of the tower. His watching presence
laid such a weight of menace on the back of her neck that the skin
tingled with panic, as if it lay bare to a falling axe. She shuddered,
from the collarbone down and far into herself. She let her rebellious
daughter from her mind and summoned her internal forces to confront Caesar.

When Bonne turned round she found herself closer to the great
keep than she expected, so that it reared into the sky above her with
sudden violence. She stepped back like one brought face to face with a
giant. She was not so taken by surprise, however, as to step on the
hem of her yellow dress, for she lifted it cleanly from the ground just in
time to avoid tearing it with the same cool astonishment that had
allowed her to skip across the gory doorstep of her house—though she
had emerged that self-same moment from her Great Sleep on the
table—without a single fleck of Solomon's blood attaching to the
lovely silk that had come to her all the way from China.

This fastidious footwork owed nothing to health. It was not an
athletic, but a neurotic gift, and was a response to Caesar's habit of
conducting most of their shared life in silence. It was since they had
come here, or since the castle had stopped building, or at any rate for
a long time now, that Caesar had been out of the way of talking to
Bonne. He would speak to her occasionally, as he spoke to the rest of
the world, but it was as if the husband had lost the voice to use to the
wife. The offer of his presence had sunk to the submerged form of long
silences: he would sit there, in a conversing attitude, and be silent.

Sometimes he effaced himself with silence, and was inert, impas-
sive and invisible. Bonne might be sitting at peace, or working in the
kitchen, or out walking, and realise with a jump that Caesar was with
her, and had been secretly her companion for she did not know how

long. It was to meet the shock of these abrupt materialisations that her feet had learned to keep her upright, however suddenly Caesar might break upon her sight.

At other times there was such an intensity in these silences! A good-going one would last an hour or more, and after a while Bonne would recognise that Caesar's intensity had effused from him an air not quite domestic—not quite as between man and wife—but something more elevated, as it might be (though not wholly that, either) religious. Eventually she would in herself experience an emotion part personal and part theological, and a reticent harmony would prevail until at length Caesar had exhausted himself by whatever effort it was he put into these unsatisfying interviews: and he would depart, disappointed once more.

Plainly he had wished that they might converse (she would tell herself this each time) yet to anything that she might offer for discussion he would say nothing, but glower at her, and concentrate against what she was saying—for all the world as if he were still waiting for *her* to speak, and could not hear *her* for the sound of her own voice! "There will be no eggs," she would say. "The hens are going off the lay," and he would frown until she had finished, and then listen at her harder than ever.

What might it mean, that her husband sat beside her, seething with unspoken fervours to which he expected a reply?—a silent reply? What more could she do than reciprocate, which was to say, be sympathetically silent back?

There was one day he nearly had it out of her, whatever he was after. She had been as good as gold, sitting diligently speechless under his intense silence, submissive to his esoteric need, when she felt the soul start in her body. She saw her hands, one on the needle, one on the tambour, go pale while the blood from her face ran back to her heart. She was dying, she thought, and therefore looked at Caesar.

He sat as he had sat before, but he had seen—or he knew. She sat cushioned on the floor and Caesar was above her, leaning down upon her from his window-seat; tilting his whole body to her like an ear, the way he always waited, wishing at her with that hardly human but scarcely spiritual force; hunting in her for that hidden, insubstantial voice which—if she had it in her—kept itself a secret from her tongue.

He did not move, that moment when he knew her soul had shifted in her. He was breathless and still, the very heart of a stone for stillness. She thought, "My eyes are golden and my hair is like the sun. He has killed me with his silence, which he has made ours!" She saw the bones in her fingers that held the needle, while still—for the hand was up before her face—she looked at Caesar; and still he did not move.

She watched the silence in him put forth its strength: flood the marrow, fortify the sinew, heat the blood. The air between them twanged. She watched him struggle either to keep or to let go the silence. His face flushed purple and the veins cracked open round the sapphire-blazing eyes. She saw through her hand as clear as water. Now she was nearly dead, colder than snow. She closed her eyes.

When she opened them he had begun to move. His body yet leaned, stooped and tilted, there opposite, but it seemed to her as if it had leapt from a cliff and was whistling through the air towards her. Caesar's face contorted, the brow arched into surprise, as if someone had stuck a broad knife in his back and were turning it against the spine. The body stood—without ceasing, be it understood, to fly through the air—and was a claw curved to strike. ("My soul!" Bonne thought, "Did my soul go?")

Then, though her neck and throat shivered as if stroked with ice, her breasts were piled with warmth. There must be blood in her lips again, for she felt them smiling. There was a red spot on her fingertip. Her voice spoke, Bonne's customary, familiar voice. "*Zut!*" she heard it say, "I have pricked myself!"

Caesar fell on the floor then, from the top of his precipice.

*     *     *

Bonne stood in the yard between the old house and the new tower and called back her memory. It might well be that Caesar was disappointed of an imagined voice he hoped to woo from her—some hidden inner beauty to which its owner was insensible, and so did not deserve. Was this not an insult to her? Was the Bonne *she* knew, worthless to Caesar? Or was it otherwise, that she was so fine and fair, so beautiful and good, that he could not make do with that and turned greedy—a man who has found gold demanding better metal?

Bonne leaned against the stones of the great tower. She put her head back and looked straight up the wall and saw a blur of Caesar's head and hat between her and the shining sky. He seemed farther from her than from the sun. She spoke upwards to that height.

"Profound, exalted fool!" she said. "How do I love you?"

A tear thumped on her cheek and came to the corner of her mouth. She took it on her tongue and tasted the salt of it. It was Caesar's.

## Chapter 13

# CONFESSION

FLORE, still running, found Amanieu upon the bridge. She slumped onto the parapet and her lungs clutched for breath. He stood with his hands resting on the butt of one of the short javelins she had found for him, and gazed into the distance. She followed his look. It was aimed, she thought at first, on the village, a community whose homes were scattered over a wide spread of ground, each with its own patch of land. By the time Flore subsided from her fit of gasping, Amanieu had not even glanced at her—though she had learned enough of him by now to know that he would have heard the arrival of a mouse. She edged along the parapet to bring herself more definitely within his vision, and saw that his eyes were on the distance, back along the way he had travelled here from his wars.

He was quite the warrior, Flore thought, leaning there on the spear and with Caesar's sword down his back. That pale face and that shorn head, hollowed out at the sides, she equated with the intelligence and quick-wit that separated him from everyone else she had known. Even when Amanieu was silent and still—as he was now—his quickness lived in his eyes, the deep, black, remembering eyes; watchful, untrusting, estimating eyes. She liked his lank lopsidedness (though which side was loppy, you could not be sure) because its half-formed look brought their ages nearer. The wriggling top lip, always whispering secrets to itself, she liked for the mysteries it promised. Also, since some of her was still a child, she liked him for being part of the day.

"What do you see?" she asked.

"Shall I tell you?" He birled the spear round on his fingers so that it was almost invisible. "I see a dead knight under a tree, with his shield on his face."

"Is he all sliced up, like Solomon?" Flore asked.

The black eyes played on her, a waft of that north wind which came over the mountains in winter. "No," Amanieu spoke with certainty. "He is not sliced up. He has a knife in his brain, through the forehead."

Flore looked at this picture for herself, and felt a little grim. Yet she knew that what she was being told was all in the day's work to Amanieu, and it was important not to be squeamish. She adopted a very literal view of the scene. "Does that mean," she asked, "that the shield is resting on the hilt of the knife?"

Amanieu replied with an absent-minded air, but with great distinctness in the matter of detail. "The shield would not rest on the pommel of the dagger, but constantly slipped off. I had to turn his head to the side, but that blow through the top of the face takes great force, and the neck was out of joint and hard to turn. Still, I had one cheek to the earth at last, and laid the shield on the other."

Flore had been thinking herself into Amanieu's predicament. "I fancy the knife was stuck fast," she said.

"Yes," Amanieu said. "How sensible you are for a small girl," he went on. "I'd have had to break his head up to get the knife out, and that sort of thing always takes too long when you're in a hurry."

"Why did you want the shield there?" Flore asked, frowning at "small girl".

There was not at once an answer. "The eyes would not shut," Amanieu said at last. "I did not want the vultures to pick out his bonnie blue eyes."

"Blue eyes!" Flore said. "That's unusual hereabouts. Caesar my father has blue eyes, but he's mad." In a moment she added, "Well, the magpies will eat up your dead knight's blue eyes; they poke their way in anywhere."

Silence set in, during which the blind woman came out of her house—it was closest to the bridge—and gave every appearance of staring at them. Three serfs came down the way to cross the bridge, one hiding a billhook beside his leg, and one with blood on his breeks. When they reached the end of the bridge they stopped. They looked a little at the girl but mostly at the man. Flore looked up at Amanieu and saw that, wearing all these weapons and armoured in introspection, he looked like death guarding the bridge.

"Come on," she said. "He's not thinking about you."

They came quickly, while the safe-conduct was still fresh, and they came close by Flore, who had given it. She hardly felt that they had been part of killing Solomon, and might have killed her. Even now, she was in the middle of a lesson from Amanieu, in which killing seemed to be an essential part of living. She looked into the eyes of the man nearest her as they passed, the blood-stained man. "Good-night to you, Papoul," she said politely.

His face beamed wide, as if she had assured him that the earlier events of the day had been nothing very terrible. "Good-night, lady," he said. The three men went on their way to the village. The blind woman went into her cottage.

Amanieu had stopped brooding, and he watched them go. "Today has been more serious than you think," he said. "It is still serious."

Flore did not quite understand this, but she tried. "Is that why you are still so armed?" she ventured.

He nodded, and became at once abstracted again. She knew what that was about, however, and she thought carefully what to say to him.

"It's the dead knight's blue eyes," she said.

"They would not shut," he agreed, tamely.

This submissiveness from him astounded her, and she began to know a strange delight, which could have knocked her off the bridge except that she put most of it aside for the time being. "How did you kill him?" she asked. "Was it a good fight?"

"No, no," he said. "Nothing like that! I murdered him and robbed him. He asked me to do it, more or less." Amanieu sat himself beside her. "I was asleep on the roadside, famished, penniless, dressed in a mixture of rags and rust. I heard horses in my sleep—it was half a faint, that sleep: I was starving. You've seen the horses, a young German charger with his belongings on it, and this pretty-paced riding-horse carrying a big, fine-proportioned warrior. He was as tall as your father, but broad too, a strong fellow, and an absolute fool, the worst fool I ever met." Amanieu beat the end of the spear on the ground two or three times. "I sat myself on a rock beside the road and chewed a piece of grass, and looked about me. He was a knight. He had everything I wanted, I could see that: he had food, drink, clothes, money, arms and horses. I did not expect to get them. He was wearing the finest chainmail you'll ever see, his sword at his side and dagger in his belt. His axe and mace were lashed on the ledhorse and all I'd thought of was to try cutting loose the mace after he was past, and do what I could. It would have been no good, in fact—I was too weak to topple him with the mace, but I knew I couldn't manage the axe. Still, I sat on the rock and waited.

"He stopped. We looked at each other. We had no greeting to speak of, and he said to me—he spoke north French and his accent was

German, but I knew already he was German—he said to me, 'Man, I am absolutely lost. I travel by the sun. Am I far from the court of Roger Trencavel, the noble Viscount of Béziers?' I knew at once he was an innocent. He might have been a champion in fair fight, man-to-man: he was as mighty as Hercules, and with a big, confident face and big teeth and a big smile. He was as haughty as a tree standing over a mushroom, but he knew nothing of men.

" 'You should wait for your following,' I said. 'It is careless to travel alone.'

" 'Ach!' says he. 'I have no following. My squire stole my silver purse and ran off.' When he thought of his squire running off he looked puzzled. 'That man was well-born,' he said to me. 'He had come with me from Hohenburg to see his people. Their castle is at Ax, in the mountains—in the Pyrenees?'

" 'Yes,' I said. 'In the Pyrenees.'

" 'So,' he said. 'They have also a house by the sea, at Sète.'

" 'Yes,' I said. Sète is by the sea. They will be a good family of hill robbers in the winter, and well-born pirates in the summer.' I had to give him a hint about the world, before he left it.

"He looked at me then, and he almost wondered. He thought of it, but he was too snug in his own life to look outside and see it it was raining. He laughed a happy laugh; he laughed away his squire and his silver. 'No matter,' he said. 'I have still my purse with the gold.'

" 'Ah!' I said. 'You kept your gold and silver separate.' I nearly fainted then. Food and gold, two minutes off. My mouth began to run with water.

" 'Yes,' he said. 'I kept them separate. Am I not cunning?' He wanted me to approve of him. He was the most utterly damned, doomed fool that ever was. He wanted to be liked. I didn't like him one bit. I began to hate him. We had talked too much and it was time to get going.

"I stood up and scratched the small of my back, getting my knife into my hand. He thought nothing of it, my hand going out of sight." Amanieu sighed, but at which aspect of this story, who could say? "I swear the war-horse knew, the ledhorse. It came up on the other side of my German friend and had a look at me and began to stamp. The beast was wasted on him. I'm glad it's mine now.

" 'It's Béziers you want?' I said 'Béziers is only—' and I went into a convulsion, I groaned with pain, and I bent over backwards (to hide my hand) and crouched a bit down that way. My knight looks at me a moment and understands I'm not well. 'What's up?' he says, and leans down. I cracked that knife into his forehead up to the crosspiece. He never knew he was dead. As far as he ever knew, he was still on his way to the court at Béziers.''

The tale was told. The mischief was out and in the open. However it might reckon up when she had time to think about it, Flore knew she must not fail him now. "Not bad!" she said. "Not bad at all! Whack into the brain-pan!" Here she allowed herself some concession to the shuddering that wanted to take her over altogether. "I'm glad it wasn't me!" She made a pause but Amanieu said nothing. Apparently more was expected of her. She thought quickly and said, "It will not be an easy stroke. How do you do it?" She looked him in the face, where he sat beside her on the low wall. A peculiar smile ran along his mouth towards her, but he said nothing. "Show me!" she insisted. "Show me!"

He stood up. "Stand in the middle of the bridge," he said. "I don't want you to fall over the edge." He unslung the sword and propped it against the parapet with the javelin beside it. "This is his dagger," he said. "Look at it." He took the long knife from his belt, and gave it to her. "Take care," he said, "it's razor sharp!" She was nervous. Maybe she was afraid of him, now, but she took the weapon from him. She held it by the hilt in two hands. She held it in one hand and took the weight of the blade on her other forearm. The steel had a black cast to it, and it was dank on her skin, rather than cold. The sides of the blade ran from the hilt in straight lines to the fine point. She fingered it and bled, and felt more at home with it.

He took the dagger back and gave her in return a silk scarf he wore under his collar. "Hold that in your two hands, that far apart"—a head's width, was it?—"now hold it as high as you can; a little this way. Good. Are you well settled there—firm on your feet? Don't move! Be still! A statue!"

Flore was queasy in the throat and did not now care for the game. She wanted to shut her eyes but refused to allow it. She was firm on her feet and as still as a statue, and felt perfectly safe, but she wished to be alone, to go off along the hillside by herself. Where was her dog, Roland? She would take the dog with her. Amanieu stood in front of her. He did not look at all pleasant, now. His eyes did not look intelligent, either. One of them was wide open and round and seemed ready to pop out at her, while the other fell half shut as she watched, as if he had been thumped on that side of the head. He looked like a silly, overgrown boy, and not at all like an assassin, or a robber or a soldier. In a minute she would giggle! Also he looked like a man who was soft in the head.

He made a sound through his teeth and walked into her, right up to her. Her face was in the bosom of his shirt—in the hairs of his chest. She licked them, just to taste, very lightly with the tip of her tongue, so that he would not know. There was no taste, but there was nothing wrong with his smell.

"Let go!" he said.

What? Her hands, of course! She let go of the silk and he stepped away from her with the scarf pierced through, and draped over his knife-hand.

"I never saw!" she said. "Or felt it!"

"That's right. Neither did blue-eyes."

"When did it happen? After you reached me?"

"Before—a thrust of the arm, and a step in, almost together." He showed her in profile.

Something about it stirred her. She was deeply awed. "I never saw your arm, though!" She was upset, and bit her lip. She did not know why she was upset. She asked, "Can the men here strike—kill—as fast as that? Can any soldier?"

"Ah, no!" he said, for he understood her. "I can do it, and I've met an Italian and a man from Africa. No one else."

She breathed out, not knowing what was going on in her. "That's good, then," she said. (To herself she said, Did you hear that? he was being kind. Was he being kind?) "That's good," she said again. She had no command of herself. "Can we walk along the river?" She said it as if she had known him all her life. "Will you walk me along the river?" It sounded a little odd to her all the same, so she added, "We may find my poor old dog!"

He gathered his weapons about him and they went back across the bridge and began to walk upstream, high above the river. The great height of the gorge that was spanned by the bridge decreased gradually. The river looped its way round the rocks from pool to pool, its water sometimes deep and steady and sometimes running shallow, all foam and sparkle, down beds of shingle. They walked side by side, and Flore collected herself as she put her steps along the familiar path, with the ever-changing, unchanged river flowing at her side. Larks were lifting off the hill-meadow, all song and blue sky, and no bird to see. Vetch and thyme sprang under their feet, and grasshoppers carped on and on. Over the mountain peaks buzzards circled on the air.

Flore thought there were deeper places inside her than she had known, but that this was no wonder, what with butchery on the doorstep and the events of the week—meaning chiefly, even if she did not quite say so to herself: Amanieu has come. She calmed herself as they walked the meadow and the riverside, and she thought they would rest soon, and then go back, and she would find a quiet place in the house to settle accounts with herself.

They came to the place where the river bank was green with aspen and white poplar and threw themselves down in the shade. "I'm going for water," Amanieu said. "Do you want some?" Flore shook her head, and he went round a bend where the ground sloped down to the river. A wind passed lightly through the trees and turned up the silver undersides of the leaves. Flore lay on her back and looked up into them, at a roof patched of blue and silver and green. She wished she was alone, so that she could simply sleep for hours and hours. She pretended she was alone, and gave a great sigh, two sighs, and relaxed herself into all comfort.

# Chapter 14

## THE WATCHER

"COME!" a voice said. "Come and see!"

She opened unwilling eyes. Amanieu beckoned to her from among the trees. She rolled onto her front and stood up and followed him to the bend in the river. She stood beside him in the trees and looked down onto a pool splashed with the flickering sunlight that jumped through the shivering leaves, onto the three naked figures of Vigorce and the peasant women standing to their thighs in the river. There was no blood on Vigorce now, but he stood like a statue while the women threw water at him; skimming it off the river. He began to retaliate, smacking it back at them, the muscles of his arms and back rolling as he moved. He must be as strong as a horse, Flore thought. She envied the women their game. They were not thin, like her. They were full-grown. Their pale plump bellies and thighs glittered with the splashing water, their shoulders and breasts shone and sparkled, and the nipples stood out. They were all moving and quivering flesh, splashed and licked with waterdrops and light, the light that shook itself down from the fluttering leaves. Their brown faces gleamed and laughed.

The game came to an end all of a sudden. The two women stood up and panted for breath. One of them waded backwards and found the grass bank and sat there. She wiped the wet, blonde hair out of her eyes and stayed watching, speculative. She ran her tongue over her mouth and then rubbed her lips with her hand. The other woman was left beside Vigorce, some of the time moving her head from side to side, her large and lustrous brown eyes looking here, looking there, as if the man were not with her at all; and some of the time looking at him.

When she looked at him it was with her chin in the air, her mouth half-open and her eyebrows lifted high, but the rich, deep regard of the brown eyes slanted down towards the water. She said something and shrugged and laughed, and put a hand towards Vigorce. He had a smile, Flore thought, like a dog's. Her eyes followed the woman's hand to its destination, and a shudder whooped its way through her,

her eyes watered and her legs went loose. She came to the ground with a thump.

"Oh, the sweet Virgin!" she said. "What a day! Oh, the dear Christ! See what a great bull's pizzle he has made!"

Vigorce had such a growth of black hair on his broad chest that it overflowed, so to speak, and ran upwards full and curly right to the throat, where it became his beard. The ebullient hairiness was spattered with waterdrops and these winked and twinkled in the sunlight that fell out of the leaves and splashed up again from the surface of the pool. There was a ruddy tint on the skin as if it were filled with unusually bright blood, and the nipples showed purple and glossy; to Flore they were friendly and sympathetic, nestling tamely in the riot of that dark and furry front. The black hair flourished its way downwards, scarcely thinning on its passage over the stomach, to the bush it made between his legs. The belly seemed to be a wall of muscles; she watched them tighten and relax in time with the large, air-pumping breaths that now quickened in the mighty chest. The thighs that held up all this shaggy and tumescent manhood were wading deep in the river and hardly visible, but to Flore they were the very pillars of the world: she cherished them for what they held.

For most of all to Flore was that bull's pizzle which sprang out from Vigorce where those two columns, that were his legs, joined together. It was not only its size—this made her bite her lip, for surely it was thicker than her arm—but its own character of a fellow-creature that called to her. She knew that nothing constrained it from sharing its astounding friendship; from giving vent to the divine rage she saw pulse and throb there; from realising the unimaginable joys of its heroic lust except the being clasped (somehow) inside a woman like herself. Flore knew, with all her might, that here she had found a friendship she could trust.

She thought that Amanieu had whispered in her ear.

"Oh!" she said. "Hush! Do hush!" When she looked up, however, Amanieu was not there, and when she looked all round about her, she saw that she was quite alone. How long had he been gone? She was instantly forlorn, which was odd, since she had just accepted the companionship of her new dumb friend, vibrating out there above the water. Yet that is how it was with her: she felt herself a lonely lass, a solitary child, Flore all alone once more. Greatly fatigued she was, and now she thought of it, a little sick, and also, she noticed, trembling. She sat up on her heels and looked at her lap. She snugged the skirt of her dress under her knees, and sat with her back straight and looked down at the plain, sane linen within which her childhood was passing.

So, for a little she felt calm, but wildness leaped inside her, for she meant to see the coupling between Vigorce and the woman, to watch the woman take into her body that great bull's pizzle, and live. Summoning, therefore, her fortitude, she turned again to the scene. The woman now stood deep in the pool near the river-bank—the other woman, her friend, the other watcher, had gone, where or why?—and one hand held one of her breasts while the other rested on Vigorce's shoulder; she was holding him away for the moment, as if to rest from what they had been doing. Her black hair was plastered to her head. Her lips were puffy and a little parted and her breathing was fast and shallow. Her eyes looked into the man's eyes, candid and wide. She dropped her eyes to look at the breast she held and at her other breast. She looked down over her body, and then across at his, and then looked in his eyes again. She rubbed the big, erect nipple of the breast she held with the palm of her hand, up and down, watching him, and took her tongue between her teeth. She stopped and gave a shake and a sigh, and gently squeezed her breast. She threw a fleeting smile at him and dropped the hand from his shoulder to that ripe, straining weight that Vigorce carried before him. She touched it with malicious fingers and it reared up. Vigorce spoke and knocked her hand away. She looked down and watched the great creature bounce, and made a face and caught her lip in her teeth. Then she turned and waded to the edge of the pool. She climbed onto the grass on her hands and knees and waited there, crouched, with her bottom to him. She looked back at him, between her legs, and cried, "Come on, then!"

Flore blinked into a sparkling curtain of surprising tears. Her throat was clogged, her ears pounded. She wiped her eyes furiously with one hand—the other held her own breast, as the woman had, facing Vigorce in the pool.

"Well, come on!" Flore heard the woman cry again, and fall silent.

The colours of the rainbow now swam in Flore's watering eyes. On the far side of this iridescence she saw Vigorce behind the woman, he standing in the water and she crouching on the land. He put his hands round the fronts of the woman's thighs; he pulled her to him, and pushed himself at her.

A low, baying sound came across the pool and lifted until it became the woman's voice crying, "No!"

Vigorce pushed and pulled, and splashed, and pushed and pulled. The woman howled. She thrashed her head about, and stamped with her fists on the ground.

"That pizzle!" Flore said between her teeth, and shook her head, and felt her eyes start from their sockets so that she closed them tight, just in case.

There was quiet, and Flore opened her eyes again. Vigorce in the water was joined with the woman on the land, and in that moment they were still, breathing and waiting. The man stooped and spoke to the woman and she turned her face to him over her shoulder, displaying a lubricious and self-mocking eye, and smiled. Her big breasts hung below her and he weighed them on his hands and she laughed, softly and deep. He slipped a little on the river bed and leaned into her, his belly to her buttocks, and the laugh closed in a yelp. Then they were still again, poised and imminent, and to Flore's cleared vision with the rainbow gone from her eyes, they altered as she watched to share one nature, one spirit.

Ripples crossed the surface of the pool; the thighs of Vigorce had begun to move. As if the ground had quaked, Flore went empty within and hollow far below, far, far down into the earth. The woman's flesh convulsed and returned in kind, wish for wish, to the man's. Her voice threw out a song of monotonous, wide-spaced notes, of calls and exclamations that issued, not from herself, but from her body coupled with the man's—from the coupled creature that they had become, this creature with one pair of its legs standing in the water and the other kneeling on the grass, this creature pulled into life by its own tide.

Close to her, Flore heard another voice call out to the creature across the pool. It was her own voice! She pushed her fingers into her mouth to stifle it, but the teeth bit them. In the same instant she staggered where she sat—over her body had spread a flush of new and unknown feelings, and inside herself astonishing sensations budded and straight away began to flower. These discoveries were too much for Flore, who grew dizzy and faint, and afraid of losing the girl she loved. When, therefore, despite all she could do, that voice yipped out of her throat again, and although she had become extremely fond of the creature, made up of Vigorce and the woman, that was doing all these things to her from over the water, she turned her eyes away from

it and looked up into the dancing leaves and blue flecks of sky
overhead. She could still hear the creature, calling out now from both
its mouths, and she heard one of its pairs of legs splashing in the
water, and the ring of flesh on flesh, but she saw it hardly at all and
only from the corner of an eye. Gazing heavenwards then, she hoped
for a lull or respite, as one in a drought might pray for rain, or the
impending victim of a massacre might try to think of something else.

*    *    *

At the age of three Flore had seen the white Atlantic waves break
from the blue ocean and hurl themselves onto the beaches of Gascony.
They ran towards her up the flat shore, in foam and fury and churning
sand, but by the time they reached her they were clear warm water,
that trickled sweetly to the end of its journey among her tiny toes.
Moved, no doubt, by some recollective effect of the shifting silvery
leaves and agile particles of blue sky to which we have just seen her lift
her eyes, Flore now recalled herself to that far-away coast.

She did not quite recognise her own image, paddling there in the
shallows. For one thing, she had expected to meet herself in the
long-lost age of three, but the girl on the beach was the Flore she knew
now: for another, the girl was milk-white, so that she looked like a
statue of white marble walking the shore. Still, affairs here on the
riverside being what they were, Flore hesitated for only an instant
before she accepted the white vision by the distant sea as herself, and
once this was done, she stepped easily into her marble limbs and
found that, sure enough, everything fitted perfectly.

Alone and loitering on that strand, naked but adamantine as she
was, Flore epitomised those provoking maidens of mythology who
roused desire in passing gods, disappointed them, and were spellbound into trees, or stars, or sad and snowy mountains in the north.
So it is no wonder that as she watched the white horses leap and
plunge a furlong off, she spied one of them separate itself from the sea
and gallop towards her across the shining sand. On he came, and the
spray broke like shivered crystal from his scudding feet. His tail flew
like a plume and the wind of passage flourished his rippling mane.

Flore looked upon this portent with a pale, unfeeling gaze. The
stallion raced past her up the beach where he pranced back and forth,
kicked up gouts of sand, arched his neck and threw his head about
dramatically. Flore understood perfectly that the marvellous horse
had been hastily run up, out of salt-water, by some pagan god as a
terrestrial guise from which to slake upon her his unearthly lust. The

knowledge left her unabashed, however, and as the god in the stallion now bore down upon her, she faced its coming with equanimity.

For one thing, she had wished herself here—the situation had no existence outside her imagination—and she could wish herself away again in a moment. For another, she was made impregnably of stone, and need fear nothing from the ivory hooves that reared over her, or the teeth that snatched at the air above her head. She need fear nothing from the god-crazy eyes—but, alas! what was this?—whose red burning glare melted . . . no, no, not melted!—yes, alas! melted, melted!—her enmarbled bowels into, presumably, gravel.

Flore, vanquished equally from within as from without, face to face with the obstreperous divinity, made the best of it.

"Ah!" she said. "Be quiet. Try to stand still, and I shall kiss your nose."

The next thing she knew, she was hanging round the stallion's neck, her feet locked desperately on his withers, while he dashed straight into the turmoil of white breakers. They received her with a roar and whirled her about. The red eyes of the horse stabbed heat at her. Her throat was clogged, and her ears pounded. Her eyelids burned and would not open and she rubbed them furiously with one hand; the other clutched her breast as she had been shown. She was sick and giddy; she was bound to faint now. She fell through the breakers to find the sea far, far below and she went on falling, down and down, turning over and over, to the green ocean which closed over her with a splash.

*     *     *

When Flore's head rose through the surface of the pool, she found Vigorce and the woman rejoicing each other to the very mountain-tops of happiness. They were too exalted to have noticed Flore tumble into the water, or to see her climb out again. They had worked hard for their oblivion, and the leaf-blown sunlight on their bodies shone in a flowing varnish of sweat while the creature that they made climbed its last pitch of joy.

To this ascent it brought a cacophony of yelps and barks, of groans and hisses and suckings and splashes, and then there was a lull, during which the world stood still: at the beginning of this lull Flore, who had melted yet again into those responsive exhilarations from which she had, so recently, fled to the seaside, heard herself growl like a bitch on a bone. She shuddered, but now she stayed. She leaned her back against the trunk of a white poplar tree, and wiped her face, and smiled as well as she could.

Suddenly from the creature burst an outcry of unbelieving gasps—the crack of sinew and the creak of muscle. The open mouths snatched and bit at the air. A cascade of ululations poured from the woman, who seemed to be lifted above the earth as though levitating; and from Vigorce—who now emerged miraculously from the water—came a hullabaloo like a man being struck a succession of ill-aimed but cumulatively mortal blows. Even as it realised its triumph, the creature ended and became the man and woman thrown apart, blowing and panting on the grass.

Flore also—Flore's own trunk and limbs, her head and hair, her eyes and ears and mouth, her hands and fingers and feet and toes, her small and growing breasts, her heart and liver, stomach and spleen, kidneys and copious intestines, and all those secret passages whose doors had been found only today—this entire corpus of Flore lay effete and feeble on the ground: and on the very brink, once more, of the river.

Sometimes on the walk home Flore's legs went soft on her and she stumbled along. Sometimes she skipped like a lamb or fell into a dance the children played in the village, and sang. Sometimes she threw herself down on the meadow-grass and rolled about, or rested in the heat, spying out the skylarks that sang down at her from the blank blue of the sky.

At last she sat down and wept, which was the truth of it, after all, for though she had been enriched by the great copulation of Vigorce and the woman, a sense of affliction had since grown and swollen inside her: she was desolate and separated from herself, as if she had been possessed by that spirit in the dream.

No sooner did this idea enter her mind, than the dream vanished into memory, leaving her to wonder—why she had seemed to remember a spirit? Surely, all she had seen was a horse?

Flore commanded her tears to dry up and peered backwards into the haze, determined to decipher the dream, exorcise the spirit, and preserve unsullied her affection for the creature in the pool.

She asked herself, first of all, where the dream had taken place? By the sea, she remembered. She was by the sea, and she saw again the white waves curling. Then she saw something come towards her out of the waves . . . No, not by the sea! Certainly not by the sea—nothing to do with the sea! In a garden, that was it. Definitely in a garden, a peaceful palace: yes, in a garden. She had the grace to be rather surprised. A moment ago, she would have sworn . . . but, of course, it had been in the garden. Flore felt better already. Then what? Someone came into the garden. Who was it? It looked like a white horse, but she knew it was *not* a white horse, by any manner of means. What would a white horse be doing in a garden? She peered into the garden. It was a white . . . a white . . . a unicorn! A unicorn! It was a shy, nervous, gentle unicorn.

Flore cried aloud with happiness, for now she remembered it all perfectly. The unicorn picked its way among the laurel-hedged paths, and came up to her where she sat on her stone flower-box carpeted with thyme, in the shade of her mulberry tree. The air was full of scent, from her carnations and sweet-williams, heliotrope and pansy, and from the damask roses on the trellis. Colour filled her eye and in her ears the birds sang sweetly, and the fountain sweetly played.

The unicorn walked straight to her, regarded her with eyes as blue as asters, and laid its horned head kindly on her lap. Flore went to sleep, and so passed the next hour in her garden with the unicorn.

Later in life, she remembered it as if it had truly happened to her, and used to tell the story of the unicorn in the garden to her grand-children. It became a legend in the family.

## Chapter 15

# VICTORIES

ON his way down from the top of the tower, Caesar smelled ripe fruit, and the sweet, luxurious stench drew him from the stairs into an empty room. A tall slit window laid a bar of light across the floor, which cut in two a basket full of pears, grapes, apples and figs, all combining to produce a syrup whose heady gas, close to, sang like strong drink in Caesar's head.

He put his face to the window for fresh air. With his right eye he saw their young visitor climbing up the hill from the bridge. Amanieu came slowly and at his ease, like a man who has done a good day's work: Caesar wondered why—the boy had played no great part in quelling the mutiny! With both eyes to the opening he saw Bonne, who moved about aimlessly in the middle of the yard, in the slow dance of a child passing an endless hour on her own. It was a poignant sight, to see a grown woman so distraught. With his left eye, Caesar could see behind the house. The serfs he had sent there were fishing the unhappy priest out of the horse-trough.

Bonne looked utterly disconsolate, and Caesar wished he could distract her from her sorrows. She had slept through all the fun of the peasants' revolt, and then, of course, she had woken to find Solomon's butchered corpse on her doorstep; though it was true to say she had skipped over the body almost as if it were not there. Was she truly awake, or was she—as she had done often enough before—sleep-walking? He must go down to her. He was already back on the stairs when a happy thought came to him and he returned for the basket of fruit. Just the thing to cheer up Bonne!

Caesar stepped out of the keep and walked towards his wife. Round the corner of the house came the rescue party from the horse-trough, carrying the priest on their shoulders. They were heading for the gate-house and their road home when the priest saw Bonne and let out a yell. He waved a furious arm at her, which his many-legged steed took for a sign, so that they brought him up the yard and presented him to Bonne as if he were on a pulpit. Caesar was amazed to see that the wretched man's legs were bound with rope; doubtless his arms had also been tied (or he would have released himself) so his rescuers had freed the arms but not the legs. What could you do with these people?

"Harlot!" the priest shouted down at Bonne. "Adulteress!" he cried. "You are poisoned with lust, Bonne Grailly! You are as promiscuous as the rabbit! You tempt me but I defy you! You brandish your vile body before me, but I do not see it! You entice me with your smiling lips, with your lewd eyes and your brazen hair, but I do not perceive them!" He paused, shivering either from the cold of the horse-trough or the heat of his imagination. Spittle moistened his thick lips.

"Brazen, mind you, is a good word for your hair," Caesar said at Bonne's ear, and noticed with regret her nervous start of surprise. To soothe her, he held out the basket of decaying fruit. She peered at it first with disbelief and—could it be?—indignation, but all of a sudden delight gleamed in her face and her golden eyes smiled at him.

She took a fig from the basket and just as the priest opened his mouth again, she threw the ripe fruit. It broke on his sharp nose, and Bonne at once hurled a soggy pear into one of his big brown eyes. The priest's martyrdom had begun, for the crowd whose original war-cry had been "Give us back our priest!" were so happy with his predicament that they held him up higher than ever, while Bonne deluged him with sopping and splashy fruit. Soon the man's face was covered with the maggotty slime of the corrupt flesh. When he bowed his head the crowd cried "Shame!" and stretched up to crack him on the chin until he lifted it back into the line of fire.

At last there was no more fruit, and Bonne showed them the empty basket and accepted their applause. "Duck him in the river!" she said. "Get him clean—he can't go to his prayers like that!" The serfs whooped with joy and galloped away with their battered but indomitable burden. Faintly to the ears of Bonne and Caesar came his parting word, little more than a wail but fighting still: "Whore!" it proclaimed.

"Well done, Bonne! Well done!" Caesar exclaimed, when he was able to speak through his laughter.

Bonne herself was wild with hilarity and triumph, laughing like a fishwife or a goddess, her hair wild and her face flushed. When she was able, she said, "It was your idea, without the fruit I could hardly have done it!"

Into this harmonious scene came Amanieu with a wide smile

crossing his thin face. No doubt he had just met the persecuted priest on the way to his ducking. As he drew near to the exhilarated couple, a desperate figure burst from the doorway that led up to the room over the gate-house; with a bundle under its arm, it shot out through the arch.

Quicker than you could see him do it, Amanieu turned on his feet and hurled one of those javelins from Gascony, that Flore had found for him earlier. It took the serf through the heart and tossed him on the ground. Amanieu loped off to where the man lay, stilled and shrunken, and picked up the bundle that was clutched in the dead hand. He put a foot on the peasant's back and pulled out the spear, and shouted down the hill. As he returned to Bonne and Caesar, two of the peasants came and carried off, with no more said, the victim of Amanieu's peculiar art.

"He was stealing my money!" Amanieu reported cheerfully. "It's a good thing, really. A serfs' mutiny is a serious business, and that'll teach 'em a lesson! Besides, they killed your man Solomon."

"Solomon was killed hours ago!" Caesar said crossly. "This morning!"

"What a priggish young man!" Bonne said to Caesar, as they walked towards their house. Even before they reached the threshold the laughter they had so recently shared—whose sound had hardly left the air—rustled like dead leaves in their memories.

## Chapter 16

# THE FEAST

THEY sat down six to dinner, the family behind the long board of elm and the soldiers at an old plank laid on hurdles. This was a feast of celebration, because it was clear to the rulers of the house that each of them today had won a victory, and that between the two of them they had (for once in a way, and instead of fighting each other) triumphed over a common foe.

They took this as a reassurance that their private quarrel was not, after all, so far gone; that theirs was a vigorous union potent to contend with anything that came against it. Therefore it was only sensible, the mood of the people being so disturbed, for the lord and lady to advertise that, however far their uniquely complicated sorrows might carry them from the ways of ordinary mortals into hitherto unexplored regions of behaviour, they were nevertheless an effective alliance in the affairs of the world.

Again, while it was true that Amanieu, by equalising the casualties, had seemed to deal a decisive blow against their enemies, it had not been strictly necessary to skewer that serf. An eye for an eye, Caesar had said laughing, and in the same breath the javelin flew. Now, the atmosphere of a congratulatory feast would commemorate the particular style—so different from their young visitor's literal-minded usage—with which Caesar and Bonne, the true victors, had won the day.

Here, then, sat the family with its back to the wall, Caesar and Bonne side by side, flanked by Amanieu on Bonne's left and Flore at Caesar's right. Down there sat Vigorce and Mosquito at their humble plank, curiously close to the floor, for Vigorce was on Bonne's footstool and Mosquito on the milking-stool from the byre. Mosquito found that this perfectly suited his tiny stature, but the hired captain was put to much art in disposing of himself, for it seemed to him that an effect of this damned low table and this cursed—no, this blessed!—stool of Bonne's, was that his joints grew out of him in different places from the usual. Yet Vigorce was well enough pleased, for was he not sitting on his lady's stool and feasting in her hall; and above the salt at that, for Gully, pernickety to the last, had put a bowl with a careful amount of salt in it, between the captain and the common soldier. Mosquito, for his part, was delighted with it all, and cared nothing whether he took salt with his left hand or his right, so long as he had it within reach.

Though the company was small and the house had fallen on hard times, a few simple effects helped on the mood of festivity. For example, the first fire of the autumn had been lit, it being late September now and the night chilly. A supply of oak billets as long as your arm, from the pile that leaned on the north wall of the house, were stacked inside the door. There was an added significance to the fire in the excellence of the fire-basket—a prize piece of furniture. It was a square basket of iron, and its great beauty was that the legs at the four corners stood on small iron wheels, so that with the iron-hooked pulling-pole that leaned against the wall you could heave the fire to anywhere in the room.

"I've never seen one of these," Amanieu said to his hostess. "What an ingenious contraption!"

Bonne was not at all sure of this unprepossessing creature, to whom she had been formally introduced only this afternoon, but that opening remark of his went down well. She considered the fire-basket with pride. "It is one of our great possessions," she said, and went on without a pause, "I have to thank you for completing my cure. I believe you must have rubbed your blue pimpernels right through the skin into my blood."

Amanieu looked at the table-top and then at her. "It was nothing, lady," he said.

"Nothing!" Bonne sounded offended. "Well! Let me see your hands!"

Amanieu showed her his hands. "I mean, madame, that it was a pleasure."

"A pleasure?" Bonne said, making it a question, and smartly returning to him those hands which she had just turned palm up and scanned intently for a moment, as if to see if she could remember anything there. "A pleasure, do you say?"

She was charmed to see that her companion was a little put out. He had turned a purer shade of yellow, which with that complexion she took to mean that he had blushed. "A pleasure!" she said a third time. "Why, I was so ill that when I saw you in my delirium, I thought I was with an imp in Hell!"

Amanieu entered her esteem at a stroke. "If we had been in Hell," he replied, "I would have said it was an unexpected pleasure."

Bonne tilted her head down to a secretive angle and glanced at him from the side of her face, her eye following precisely its own level so that it looked him in the cheek. Her lips were closed but her mouth had gone as far back as it might without quite smiling. Then she touched his arm and gazed about her.

They were dressed all in their finest. She herself still wore the yellow dress of Chinese silk and over it a white silk tunic, embroidered with gold. She wore also her jewel, which Caesar had taken from the hiding-place along with his gold cap-badge. The jewel was three stones in a gold pendant, though the chain had been sold and she wore it on a ribbon round her neck. The stones were set one above the other: the top stone was the green peridot, next came the jacinth with its mysterious colour of a blood orange, and below them flashed the blue darkness of the sapphire.

Caesar, for the first time in many a year, had put on his lordly clothes. He was dressed all in red, except for his black cap. He had on a pair of woolly breeches that had been made for him when the style see-sawed between loose and tight, but these baggy breeks were of the true, nobleman's crimson. He wore also a long robe of scarlet with huge sleeves, and on top of that a vermilion jacket of Spanish wool, cut with armholes so that his wide scarlet sleeves could wave about in all their glory. His golden hat-badge was rimmed with twelve pearls, those at the four cardinal points being black. On it was enamelled a most unusual representation, apparently a phoenix falling—for it was shown head downwards—into the flames. The black velvet cap and its badge Caesar had just laid on the table in front of Flore, at her command.

"I've not seen it since I was little," she said. "I didn't know we had such grand things left." She picked up the cap and tilted the badge at the firelight. "What does it mean?"

"Something rather gloomy, unfortunately. What it is not, it's not the Phoenician bird, you know, phoenix for short, that burns itself to death in the fire—and suddenly a new young bird flies up out of the flames. That's in Africa, that happens. I must say, I'd like to go to Africa and see things like that for myself."

Flore felt a great sense of well-being. The firelight jumped here and there on her father's always-smiling face so that it turned from one expression to another, and another, suggesting sympathetically that to be indistinct and wandering in thought and mood was natural, not necessarily a weakness. His bright blue eyes were away in imagined Africa, watching bonfires for rejuvenated birds. While Flore waited for his return she studied the badge. The bird that was not a phoenix was in black enamel, and fell into yellow flames. There was writing cut into the gold under the picture, but she did not read well, and this was Latin, too.

Caesar returned from his travels with a whirring, as it were, of his scarlet sleeves—he threw himself about in his chair and flapped his arms, as if by way of making sure that he was where he seemed to be. "Where were we?" he said. "I do beg your pardon! I was thinking of something."

Flore said, "You were going to explain the bird on the badge."

Her father's rough pink skin opened into the woeful ditches and potholes where his deepest sorrows were buried. He turned to Flore and made it that there were just two of them in the room. He slanted over her his sad but love-kindly face, and curved one red arm round her shoulders while the other spread its billowing sleeve on the table, with the black velvet beret in its fist. "I told you about the pheonix?" he asked.

"You told me," Flore said. "The bird that flies up from its own ashes, born again."

"That's well put, Flore. I noticed earlier today that you were becoming a well-educated young person. Yes, well. The bird in the badge is not the phoenix." He stopped, and breathed heavily into his daughter's face as if he were drunk. He was quite sober, and she knew it. He simply did not want to go on.

"You'll have to tell me," she said.

"Quite right," he said. "I must. The bird is not a phoenix, but a crow. As you know, our name Grailly is a word for crow, or as near as makes no difference."

"Yes," Flore said. "So it is."

"Very well!" he said, and it was a kind of cry, and he flopped the fist that held the cap and its badge, on the table, like a deliberately ineffectual smite. "Well, the badge was my grandfather's. I don't know if his father had it before him. He had it, and then my father had it, and then I had it. My grandfather cut that motto on it, and made it our emblem, the family emblem. It was the time all the families began to choose emblems for themselves, and my grandfather chose this picture and made *that* our motto. Ever since, the family's gone downhill, and no wonder!"

Flore looked at the badge again, at the white, lustrous, promising pearls and the secret, tempting, black ones. She looked at the black crow, which she thought very beautiful, falling into the fire (which was also very beautiful) to be burnt up. She thought it dismal and perverse that so lovely an ornament, and indeed, one so costly, should depict a bird forever on the point of making a sticky end. Then she thought that all the same, it was a thing of such art, and preciousness, and so wonderful to see the more you looked at it, that she must try to come to terms with it.

Now, therefore, she asked, "What does the writing say?"

Caesar looked at the badge. He held it up to his eyes and into the light, as if it might have changed since he saw it last. "*Non phoenix*," he read, "*sed corvus*. Not the phoenix, but the crow."

Flore at once hated her great-grandfather. "What a scoundrel!" she exclaimed. "What a scoundrelly thing, to say that we are not phoenixes, but crows! Who's *pretending* to be a phoenix? We're not crows, anyway, but even if we were, even if we were exactly the same name as crows, it's not fair to say we're not phoenixes, but crows. Who's even trying to be a phoenix, who even wants to be—to fly up all newly born, and fresh from the flames, and the old and wrong and bad things left behind clean in the ashes? Oh! Oh! Oh!" and she threw herself weeping bitterly on her father's neck, her poor father's neck.

He hushed her and shushed her and petted her. "Even at your age!" he said. "Even you can see how it makes aspiration suspect and hope a mockery! How it annihilates ambition and makes it impious to do anything but slide wretchedly downhill! My poor Flore, how quickly you saw it all! Ha!" he said. "But you are your father's daughter, my dear child! It made my father a gloomy man, you know. He kept trying to throw the badge away, but he couldn't bring himself to do it. In the end he left the badge behind, and threw himself away instead."

"How did he do that?" Flore asked, her crying fit being over, and picking up this tactful offer to extricate herself.

"He went down to Spain and got himself killed by the Moors. He got killed on his own account, and I—", he stammered, "and I—," and Flore drew off from him, though still in the circle of his arms, and put a hand up almost to his mouth to stop him, but nearly voiceless he said it, "—I killed my own son." He looked at her, appalled. "I am that man," he said.

Flore dried her eyes with some of a scarlet sleeve. "You have no right to talk to me like that," she said, "and it was not because of the crow and the phoenix. It was a misfortune."

"Yes," he said. "You are right. I should not have said that. It was a misfortune, that's what it was." He held his silver wine cup to her mouth. "Drink with me," he said, and when she had drunk he drank from the other side, and they repeated this, and he put the cup down. "Flore," he said, very solemn, "do you recall the story of Icarus?" He was so tensed and serious that she merely nodded without speaking. "The vile thing is," he said, "that this picture of the deluded crow throwing itself into the flames, is the story of Icarus upside down. It is the story of Icarus spoiled."

"I expect I'm too young for that one," Flore said. "All I see, is that the poor crow thinks it is a phoenix."

There was a lengthy pause, and at last Caesar said, "It's a joke, in one way."

Flore made a face. "In an evil way."

"Yes," Caesar agreed, "in an evil way, then, it is a joke."

With one of those dire attacks of perception that dart in and winkle out the joke from the mess it has made round itself, they began, together, to see the funny side of it. In a bout of strangely mixed tones of merriment, Caesar's hearty gusts and Flore's giggling treble, they paid tribute to the black wit of great-grandfather Grailly.

"When it's mine," Flore said, "I'll sell it."

Caesar was astonished. "I never could," he said.

"I know," Flore said, "but I could."

"That's your mother in you," he said cheerfully.

Flore blinked, and successfully masked her annoyance. Caesar was still cheerful when he said, "I'd like to go to Africa, all the same, and see a phoenix for myself." His blue eyes flared at her over the steep smile and then began to grow vague—to recede, as it were, to Africa again. Flore had had enough of that.

"I like you in your red clothes," she said.

He whizzed back across the Mediterranean to her side. His head bumped as if he had been sitting in a boat, jolted when it beached. "Do you, Flore? Do you? That is kind, that's a very pleasant thing to hear. Thank you!" He was marvellously pleased. Flore thought, they should have a feast every night. She said so.

"They don't work, every night," Caesar said. "I remember that, quite well. You can celebrate some of the time only. Occasionally.

Not often." He covered her with a bright, down-bending face, all pink and far too alive.

Flore thought, it was only by the chance of the shared moment they were in that he had happened to see her clearly. It was as if the time he normally lived in had, just now, cracked open to show him a glimpse of her sitting there, being his own daughter Flore beside him—he noticed her, knew her and loved her as if she were the one orange on a tree in the desert, and he great with thirst. She was thereupon stark with loneliness and leaned forward out of her father's volatile ben-evolence, looked past her mother's beauteous splendour, and was rewarded with a glint from Amanieu's ever-roving eyes, those black, basaltic eyes. They offered her rapport with a basilisk, and she was warmly comforted. As Flore turned back to Caesar she fleeted a wary smile at a point near her mother, who had begun to descend from some aery Africa of her own.

"What did you say?" she asked Caesar.

"You look very fine yourself," he said. "Very fine, and lovely, and very much the lady. Are you really a child, still?"

He still glowed at her, full of a father's love, of mutual self-esteem. The moment apparently continued in which she was the orange of his desert tree. Yet an ill note sang in her ears. What had he just said? Was she still a child? Why did he ask that, all of a sudden? But, why shouldn't he ask it? Her face grew hot while she waited to remember why the question disconcerted her. Still a child? Yes, presumably. She felt herself, all the same, grow hotter still. She tossed her head, crossly, and her glance fell like a lightning-bolt (so far as she was concerned) upon Vigorce, her first conscious sight of him that even-ing. Her glance stuck there, smouldering, as if it was deep into its object. Vigorce brought his wide, dark face from his cup and his mouth, rich and glistening with wine, greeted her with its familiar generous smile. The smile soon curved into a grin, warmed by the good-fellowship of the feast and the fact that Flore went on look-ing at him. For she lacked—how could she not lack, remember-ing all at once the whole event of Vigorce in the pool!—the self-possession to nod and move her head away again. Instead she sat there smiling shakily—she felt her lips tremble—until Vigorce lost *his* smile and took on a worried and baffled confused expression.

So that, when at last she turned to face her father and was reminded (which in the panic of her encounter with Vigorce she had forgotten)

of his question—was she still a child?—she flushed up to the very
scarlet of Caesar's ceremonious sleeves.

He, still magnificently the father that he had hardly ever been
before, or was likely to be again, swooped intuitively to her aid. "It is
too warm!" he said. "Look at you!" He put the back of his hand to her
blazing cheek. "Feel that!" he said. "You are far too warm. I shall
have them move the fire!"

*     *     *

Bonne said, "Do you like my jewel? It is a talisman."

She made Amanieu take it, still strung on its ribbon round her
neck, to hold on his hand. Therefore he leaned into the smell of her
body, which was first of stale sweat, then a pungent odour that was
her own, and lastly an aroma that hung already in his mind—the blue
pimpernels.

The silk dress was in the fashion, close to her body and pulled tight
over the breasts, which even as he put his eye to the jewel began to rise
and fall more quickly than before, and made a landscape of impas-
sionated yellow behind his scrutiny of the red, green and blue stones.

At the same time, he had a sharp sense of being under her face as if
she had got him there on purpose—to examine him unseen while he
was occupied with the jewel. He felt her quickened breath now on the
top of his head, then on the nape of his neck, and again on his right
ear. He could not help looking up.

An inch from his right eye was her mouth, the lips just parted, the
lower quite turned in and paled, as if it had long held itself stiff against
vexations, the top lip luscious and full of history, turned up at the ends
and then at the extremity down, far down. This lip, enigmatic and
secretive, could not hide everything, and it lifted in the middle fat,
suggestive and promising; yet on all its hopes of luxury the strict
underlip kept a close rein.

The same tale of ardours restrained was told on the face itself. The
side of it that filled Amanieu's view was set in long flat lines and
carved planes, as if an impersonal, sculptor's beauty had been determined on: but when the cheek turned with sudden grace to the
straight nose (where he saw the hairs of one nostril blowing in her
breath) there came a channel shaped into a perfection of well-
resolved turns, and waiting at the end of it, Bonne's eloquent and
golden eye.

Through that unguarded orb he spied the turbulence which raged inside her. Griefs and angers blazed there brightly, furies howled for vengeance, and on the bedrock of her being an army of frustrated hopes encamped (warmed and eased a little, maybe, by these fires and war-cries) and waited with a bitter, inveterate patience.

His recognition of this caged ferocity was so immediate that he clutched for safety, in a sudden superstitious grip, the talisman she had laid on his fingers.

"Let go!" Bonne said at once. She spoke, since his grasp on the amulet had pulled her to him by the ribbon round her neck, with her mouth against his ear.

He let go the amulet. He sat up and his eyes, now meeting both of hers, saw deep inside the fires and furies glimmer and dim, as if behind the golden surface she had spread an infiltration of defensive magic, a baffling smoke, to keep him from forbidden knowledge.

"The jewel is mine," Bonne said. "It is *my* talisman."

She restored it complacently to her already almost tranquil bosom, and smiled at him with a clear and candid gaze. That affable mask bewildered Amanieu. He might have dismissed his recent insight into her tormented interior as a fit of imagination, but then he saw again the lines on face and mouth, drawn there by the discipline of ruling the emotions which seethed inside her.

"What are you staring at?" Bonne spoke again. "What do you think of my jewel?"

Amanieu came with an effort out of his thoughts. "Yes," he said. "It's your jewel I am staring at. You call it your talisman. What does it guard you from?"

"From epilepsy," Bonne said, "and other evils."

Amanieu was inspired to provoke her. He had an absolute need to make that smooth surface break open and discover some sign of the violent pressure it encased.

"From what other evils?" he asked. "From madness?" He glanced past her at Caesar. "Perhaps you are afraid of catching his madness."

"No!" Bonne exclaimed, and in her turn she clutched at the jewel so that it quite vanished inside her hand.

"I do know," Amanieu went on, "that the ointment of blue pimper-nels, spread upon the body, is a remedy against madness."

"How do you know?" Bonne shouted.

"From Gully."

"I shall have to tell you," she said swiftly, "that madness is not a topic of idle conversation in our house." She threw herself to the back of the chair and sat as stiff as the board against her spine. The gold eyes flashed at him and then glared into the fire.

Amanieu, whose nasty purpose demanded that he should aggravate her to such a pitch that the molten tides seething (as he supposed) within her burst out like the erupting of a volcano, jumped from his seat to perch on the edge of the table, and leaning over her exerted an irritating technique of pompous impudence.

Since he now sat between her and the fire, Bonne found that she was looking at his knees. She lifted her beautiful face and showed him eyes lustrous with venom. "Mountebank!" she said raging. "What do you think you're doing?"

Amanieu smiled down like an archbishop on a heretic. "Don't upset yourself," he said. "It is obvious that you got yourself stung by the bees in the hope of being cured with blue pimpernels—which is also the specific for madness." He waved a hand at the oblivious Caesar. "Are you afraid his madness is infectious? Or do you think you have madness of your own, growing in you invisible?"

He knew only a thudding blow on the face, then a fall and a crack on the head. He lay back thankfully into the embrace of darkness, to be jerked wide awake by a searing pain on his cheek, and he rolled over and over to get away from it. He came to his senses to find himself crouched on the floor with the smell of burning hair in his nose. He beat at his scalp with his hands, and sat up, and carefully opened his eyes.

He saw Vigorce and Mosquito in front of him, laughing as if they would die of it: embracing each other, falling apart to throw themselves about, babbling and yelling. There was merriment on the right, also. He stood up, slowly and staggering, for his head swam and hurt. He moved himself round towards the table until Caesar and Flore came into view, and saw that they were too deep in some private matter to share in the common exhilaration. He realised now where he had fallen, and at once the burning pain ripped into his cheek with redoubled vigour.

"My God!" he said. "I nearly went into the fire!"

These words, spoken as he turned now to look at her, refreshed Bonne's enjoyment of the joke. She made an odd sight, having her legs up on the table and her head and shoulders crammed into one of the corners of her great chair. This made it hard for her to laugh, but she repeated, with bouts of laughter in between, the sound "Oh!" She brought it out over and over again, rounding her eyes each time she spoke it, as if to match the shape it made of her mouth, and as if it were a useful word.

At last the happiness of the audience diminished, and Bonne was able to speak intelligibly. "Oh!" she said. "Oh, dear me! Oh, God help us! Oh, come on; come and help me up!"

Amanieu was, by this time, in a fuller possession of his faculties. The pains on his head had separated into their individual locations. He felt the most significant hurt to be on the back of his skull, and it throbbed with a slow, deep and sharp ache as if someone was pulling at a fish-hook that had lodged well inside his head. His nose felt nastily crushed (but seemed not broken) and it had bled copiously. He could see now out of only one eye, which meant the other had swelled itself shut since he began to recover. His cheek burned scathingly where it had been branded on the fire-basket. He counted that to be the sum of his injuries, but their cause still mystified him. He used the table as both crutch and guide, and steered himself back to his place beside Bonne, whose laughter, reduced by now to the last fits of crows and chuckles, faded a little more as she saw him close to.

He was in no case to help Bonne sit herself up and she did it on her own, with a sequence of ungainly, spasmodic shifts from one position to the next. He sat down, therefore, and when she had recovered her proper state, he asked her what had happened. She smiled brilliantly. Her mouth twisted and flickered as if it was too tired to laugh any more.

"Oh, my God!" she said. "I kicked you into the fire!"

She helped herself to wine and passed him the jug. "Don't look so belligerent," she said. "Cheer yourself up! Gully will fetch a bowl of water and we'll wash the blood off you." She smiled admiringly to herself. "Who would have thought I'd do that—kick you right into the air! You flew straight at the fire. Next time, my dear young man, I'll have you into the middle of it!"

Next time! Amanieu's good eye blinked into the glowing heat and leaping flames of the fire. He saw himself sizzling and screaming there, going up in smoke out of the hole in the roof, while Bonne howled with laughter. She would do it, too, callously and in good-fellowship.

"You're mad!" he said to her.

Gully trundled in and planked down a bowl, and retired.

"If I am," Bonne said tartly, "it's what you wanted to find out."

These words brought him to meet her face to face. Now he saw nothing mysterious inside her eyes. He saw there no bland external show hiding the wilderness within; no cunning and deceitful overlay masking the Gorgon's horrid soul. Now it was all perfectly visible on the surface—so far as he was concerned, she was mad all through.

"First I routed the peasantry," she said, "and now you. I'll have armour made and be a warrior."

"You will do what you like," he said. "I'm going to my bed."

"No," she said. "Don't!" She covered his fist, clenched on the table, with her hand.

He could not believe it, but now a warm kindness from her golden eyes poured honey on his outraged manhood. Ignominy was embalmed and irritations mollified, by the mere touch of her golden gaze on his one unwounded eye. Was this magic, or simply a mystery of the woman? He would not succumb, but go to bed this instant! Despite the resolve, however, he did not move. Was he spellbound? If she was a witch, and had a fluence on him, there was nothing to be done about it, and there were still his wounds to be mended.

"That's right," Bonne said.

With water and vinegar she wiped his face clean of blood. She made him blow his nose, though it hurt, to prove to him that he could breathe through it. She said the kick she fetched him had changed its shape, but it had been a nose of little character in the first place, so there was no great harm done. The closed eye, she reported, was already yellower than the rest of him, with other colours arriving, and it would certainly be black tomorrow. She thought the scorch-mark on his cheek would improve his appearance a good deal, when it had weathered-in, and in the meantime she applied olive oil to it with a touch like the fingertip of a moth. As to the bump on the back of the head (Bonne said) either it would addle his wits or not, and they would know by the time the scab began to itch.

Amanieu, fuddled or addled though he was, had begun to notice the paradox of a woman who could kick him brutally in the face one minute, and the next wash and anoint the resulting wounds with such tender care and so delicate a hand. He had even gone so far as to reopen his earlier idea of her, that she was made of two opposing natures, when events made a mockery of these simple equations.

The fingers whose lightness skimmed, like miracles of healing, the four painful patches on his head, began now to impart a sense of different purpose. Their touch was still kind, but it was kindness of another sort, and it was in a new spirit that Bonne set out to make friends with the three-fifths of Amanieu's head and face that had not been ravaged by her furious onslaught. She felt round the great crack on the back of his head, and passed her well-nailed strokes over the scalp and scrawny neck, ruffling up the bristles to make sure no gashes or contusions were hidden there.

Round at the front, her mouth made inquiries of its own. The right side of his face, since its borders were marked by the bruised eye, the crushed nose and the toasted cheek, was quickly written off. To the other side, however, both the sensual upper lip and its intellectual companion paid a lot of attention. Bonne now held Amanieu's head in a firm but gentle grip, so as not to aggravate any of its hurts, and put her tongue to exploring his left ear. If ever a bow was shot at a venture, you would think this was it: but it was soon clear that she had won Amanieu's lively interest. She came away from his ear and held his head while she caressed the two sides of his face, the broken and the whole, with a hot and misted look.

"When you are well," she said, "we shall make love."

A shiver whisked through Amanieu. He felt himself draw off and her spell begin to dissolve. In these simple words of Bonne's he had heard the mating of emotional riot and calculating intelligence, and understood with an intuition sprung from the recent whacking about, immediate cherishing and swift display of sexual promise that had been laid on him one after the other, that she was indeed a woman made of two forces and that neither would let the other alone. The wilderness of her spirit and the restless cunning in her head would not resign to each other control of an agreed territory. They shared everything: when one slept the other watched: when one rested the other walked: nothing ended, because everything continued into something else. When she spoke of love, her mind wondered what profit it might cull from that event—he had heard it, a mental overtone latching on like a parasite to the clear voice of carnal instinct. Here were two opposite characters that would not settle, each to its own business, but went along together joined in conflict, competing in common purpose, keeping up a running quarrel under the fair seeming, within the lovely head and behind the golden eyes of Bonne.

Against all this Amanieu closed his one working eye. At once the scene opened in his mind where Flore's astonished gaze lit on the great bull's pizzle (as she had called it) that Vigorce carried above the water of the river. He smiled. He sat himself slowly up and threw a glance towards Caesar and his daughter. When he caught Flore's eye earlier she was in deep talk with her father and wore for that moment a waif-like, solitary look; now by contrast she seemed to be harassed, caught on some cord that ran between her and Vigorce, and her and Caesar. She turned her head from one to the other and her colour was high. Caesar patted her on the cheek and stood up. She saw Amanieu then and rolled her eyes expressively. He could not interpret this beyond the plain fact that she was embarrassed, but it was a confiding so uncomplicated, the simple passage of trust between them, that it went home in him like food after fasting.

"My daughter is warm!" Caesar called out. "We must move the fire!"

Flore had recognised a familiar aspect in her mother's illuminated state. The shape of her mouth fell and she turned away again. Amanieu revolved on his bench and got up from the table. He stumbled with care past the blazing fire and out of the door into the night. He threw his arms about in the air, and when he could see in the starlight he danced, staggering with his wits afloat in his aching head, up, across, down the yard, in a circle. He clenched his right fist and shook it into the sky as if he were taking an oath.

"I will have the girl!" he said, and pointed to the orange doorway, so that there should be no mistake. "I will have that girl!"

He went back slowly to the house, and relieved himself onto a pile of stones against the wall. The stones gave a yelp and walked off with a sorrowful sigh.

"Who is that?" he said foolishly, peering into the darkness. "Hey," he said, "is that you? Come here, you great oaf!"

The creature came to him, not keen, but not shirking either. It was the mastiff that had not been seen since he kicked it on the head. He closed his hand round its muzzle and rubbed it a little, and then scratched behind an ear. "Listen!" he said to it, and the dog listened. "I'm going to have that girl," he said. "What do you think of that?" He peered into the darkness a second time. The dog was wagging its tail.

A great racket, the noise of a party coming to life, spilled out of the door. "Do you want to go in there?" Amanieu asked the dog. The dog hung back and made that husking and unhopeful sound in its throat with which dogs propose alternatives. "All right, then," Amanieu said. "Lead on!"

The dog took him up the yard, along the side of the keep, and sat down under the back wall. This was the north wall, and what shade there was during the day would fall here. It was the ideal place for a dog to sit out its differences with humanity.

There was a nook here, a dent in the ground at the top of the slope which backed the keep, and the two of them settled down there to rest; the dog agreed to serve as a pillow for Amanieu's battered head. Amanieu looked up. The stars glittered high and bright in the black sky. The air grew cold but the place was peaceful, even to the endless night-song of the crickets on the meadow. He would have that girl for his own. A beetle droned strongly overhead and flew with a thud into the stone wall, after which it limped off at a lower note.

"It's a harsh world," Amanieu said. "We must look out for ourselves: you, me and the girl. Trust nobody." He yawned. "Perhaps the midget," he said. "What do you think?" The dog snored, and he followed it into sleep.

# Chapter 17

# SNAILS AND GARLIC

"THE snails!" Flore cried out.

Gully came in, leaning backwards from the weight of a big iron pot. Her fists, which clutched it by the hooped handle, were bright red in the steam that rose about them like a cloud, throwing into the air an amazing smell of herbs and spices.

"Ah!" Bonne said. "The snails!"

Caesar, who was standing up when Gully entered, also exclaimed, "The snails!" and Flore hoped (since he dearly loved snails for his supper) that he would now forget the pinkness of her cheeks and his notion that the fire was too hot for her. No such luck!

"My daughter is too warm," Caesar said for the third time. "Put the pot on the table Gully,"—Gully had already done so, and she looked at him and sniffed, shaking her parboiled fingers as she set off back to her kitchen—"and we shall move the fire before we eat 'em."

"Rubbish!" Bonne said, returning to public life and seizing an initiative at a single stroke. "If Flore is too warm, and I don't see why she should be, she can change places with someone." She stared at her daughter through the steam, and by an ancient jealousy of motherhood saw what was up with Flore. "Why are you so pink?" she demanded rhetorically. "Really, Flore! Go and sit down there!" She pointed to the soldiery at their plank. "Captain, come and sit by me!"

"Certainly, captain," Caesar said, though it was not clear that he had been looked to for permission, and, "Do what your mother says, Flore," he added. Flore looked at him. He had receded from the moment when they touched as father and daughter, and he sat favouring his beloved fire with a sulking, lofty smile. The blue eyes shifted sideways but his glance did not land on her before it flew off again: a careful butterfly of a look. "Off you go!" he said to her.

Vigorce had risen from the makeshift table where he sat with Mosquito and which would now be Flore's penance for blushing, and for having cause to blush, and perhaps for getting on well with her father. It was in fact no penance to her to eat snails with Mosquito, who was her own height, an easy-going man and cheerful. To the captain, though, who was already bewildered from meeting her recent stare—in which, all blushing and trembling, she had seen him simultaneously as Vigorce here at supper and Vigorce in the river bared for love—to him she stuck out her tongue before she sat down.

As a defiance of all those who had brought about her exile from the top table, she talked busily with Mosquito, her animation suggesting, so to speak, that filial duty alone had kept her from his side. It had been an interesting day, she said. He thought so too. He thought the new young gent was very interesting as well. So did she, Flore said, but in what way interesting, particularly? More there than met the eye, Mosquito said cagily. Flora made a quizzical face at this reticence, and got a bland one back. What did Mosquito think of Vigorce? He thought highly of Vigorce. She thought Vigorce was better again, and so did Mosquito, it turned out. She had thought at one time Vigorce was going mad, and would stay there. Mosquito had been of the same opinion.

"I'll tell you what cured him," Flore said, "if you promise to keep it a secret."

"You can trust me," little Mosquito said, and Flore, surprised both at what she was doing and the composure with which she did it, began to tell him how Vigorce had made love with the peasant woman.

Vigorce himself was too preoccupied to hear any of this. At first he had been stunned when Flore stuck out her tongue at him. For what had he to do with Flore, that should lead to blushings and stickings-out of tongues? Then, having walked along the lord's board to the end where Bonne had summoned him, he saw that she was gone. Caesar, from the part-politeness that dislikes to see a guest standing about the place like a half-shut knife, said to him, "Sit between us, Vigorce! Bring that stool round behind my lady's chair and sit here! She'll be back in a moment, I daresay."

Vigorce did what he was told. He felt himself used as a puppet for any of the family to play with when the whim took them, but his spirit was weak from the early horrors of the day, and he was a leaf in the wind to the will of others. Accordingly, he dragged the bench on which Amanieu had been sitting into the space between the stately chairs, provided with sides and backs, which belonged to his betters. He found himself, by this arrangement, with his nose in the delicious vapours that rose from the steaming pot of snails.

"Set you up indeed!" This was by way of a stab in the back from Gully, addressed to the captain's having achieved a seat among the mighty. She had returned with a large bowl and a small, from which a stink of excruciating splendour jumped out to scar the atmosphere.

"Ayoli!" Caesar shouted. "My God, Gully, is that ayoli?"

Gully put the large crock of garlic-ridden mayonnaise in front of Caesar and delivered the small one to Flore and Mosquito. "Ayoli!" Flore sang, making a carol of it. "Ayoli, ayoli!"

Mosquito said nothing, but with the fumes of garlic tearing into his nostrils and the yellow surface of the mayonnaise gleaming into his eyes, he slobbered without remorse.

Vigorce had now, after so much psychological buffeting, fallen sceptical: he would dwell carefully within himself this evening, and eschew idle chit-chat: what did not occur to him from within, he would not utter. Sitting with his head in the aromatic cloud given off by the cooked snails; and when the stench of the ayoli bullied its way through these less substantial odours—ephemera such as fennel, thyme and nutmeg—he became therefore in silence no more than a little hopeful about his meal.

A face appeared to him through the steam. It was Mosquito, his head just reaching above the rim of the snail pot, a curious and indigestible portent. Caesar whispered into the captain's ear.

"Snails, Vigorce! Snails for my daughter and your army!"

Vigorce felt an object thrust into his hand, and saw it was a ladle. Mosquito thumped down a wooden bucket beside the cauldron, and Vigorce got to his feet and ladled generously—until the bucket overflowed, and Caesar's touch on his arm reminded him to stop. Mosquito withdrew and Caesar, setting the example to his captain, took some of the spilled snails off the table and began to consume them, richly anointed with the garlicky sauce.

"More!" Caesar said. "Snails on the table, and pour the juice on the bread!" Gully was back with her arms full of flat loaves, most of which she threw on the big table and the rest in front of Flore and Mosquito.

"Gully," her master cried, "you must have some!"

Gully stared at this foolishness. "I've got the best of it in the kitchen," she said, "and my own company forbye," and departed. She put her head into the room again. "Anyway," she demanded, squinting with heavy sarcasm at Vigorce, "who'll mind the goose, his lordship there?" She vanished.

As each stroke fell on him in this household Vigorce deteriorated socially, and grew more awry towards the company. "These snails," he said to Caesar, "are not a fifth the size of our snails in Burgundy."

Caesar was gluttonously employed in making up for this fact, of which nevertheless he had up to now been perfectly ignorant, and did nothing by way of response except add to the expression with which he chewed and swallowed a flicker of inquiring interest.

Bonne, however, was back, fresh-perfumed and ready for anything. "Well, captain," she said from behind, so that Vigorce choked for a moment but went on gorging himself, expecting and so no longer fearing, the worst, "I see that despite the wretchedness of the fare, you felt it ignoble to await my company."

Caesar said to Vigorce, "Give my lady some snails, or she'll chew you up where you sit."

Vigorce scooped snails onto the table in front of Bonne, who had sat down, and poured juice onto the chunk of bread that Caesar tossed there.

Bonne leapt to her feet again. "*I* have a platter, you fool!" she said wrathfully. "Look what you have done!" Her white samite was splattered with the beautiful juice that had cooked the snails.

Vigorce discovered that neither this fact nor Bonne's show of fury made any mark on his state of mind. He smiled to himself ironically— he was safe inside his shell! He scooped the snails he had dumped on the table onto her wooden dish, and reaching in front of Caesar he took the bowl of ayoli and gave her a good helping with the blade of his knife.

"Good God!" Bonne said, and sat down again, seeing nothing for it. "Have you gone mad?" she asked him.

"Almost," Vigorce said. "*Sauve qui peut,*" he added quaintly.

It seemed that he had become very literal-minded. Certainly, he was saying exactly what he thought. The woman who knew he had worshipped her for three years from, as it were, afar, bent to her snails.

Vigorce, hollowed out within by the calamity of Solomon's death; embattled on all sides by the petty violence of the Grailly family at play; joined, however, to reality by his love-making with the woman in the pool; and with his integrity, whatever that was—whether a virtue, a moral standpoint, a spiritual blessing or merely the invisible and pervasive cement of his character—with his integrity, then, fighting back on his behalf, Vigorce fell, once again, like everyone else in the room, to stuffing himself with snails, smeared with oil and garlic.

*     *     *

When Amanieu, woken by hunger, returned late to the feast, he found a listless company of revellers, half-drunk and utterly overfed. The geese were gone. So were the pig's head, its snout and tongue and brains. The raw ham unhung by Gully reluctantly—since it was one of only three—from the rafters, was now no more than a bone waiting to be boiled for soup. As for the black puddings fried in onions along with pig's liver and heart, and the rich and rancid pork sausages, and the rabbits potted with pork belly—nothing was left of them but crumbs and smithereens.

Silence and introspection had fallen upon the company while they ate that sauce made of garlic and—almost wholly—olive oil. This inwardness of disposition had deepened with the ingestion of fatty pig, done ten ways, and fatter goose. Now the feasters sprawled languid and swollen among the wreckage of their meal, picking at cold fragments and nibbling at such helps to the stomach as ripe goat's cheese and bitter grapes.

Amanieu stood inside the door and looked at Bonne, and saw that she was gazing at him with blank eyes, as if he were not truly present. Vigorce, too, was in a kind of trance. Amanieu looked at Caesar, and was mocked by the surface of those blue eyes, behind which as if they were a wall, he could retire at will. Mosquito was staring into the fire, caught by some thought already gone from him. When Amanieu turned his eyes at last to Flore, she looked up at him from the crumbs and grease and bones, from under her hair which fell down her face as she leaned over the table, as if she were trying to remember who he was. The whole lot of them, Amanieu understood, had drawn into themselves: the habit of that remote house.

*Part II*

WAKING

# Chapter 18

# NEWS

JESUS the Spaniard returned from his journey with a face like the conscience of God. Three days after the feast, in the middle of the afternoon, he rode into the yard on his little cream-coloured horse. Caesar and his family were picking the plums, and taking the shade, of the sour plum tree. Flore climbed about inside the tree, while on the outside Caesar made enormously long arms at enormously long intervals—slow, deliberated stretchings that marked each plum on the circumference as a discovery, in which might lie the first taste of a new truth.

The garnerings of this conceivably interminable harvest went into a basket at Bonne's right foot, where she sat against the wall of the house. With a sharp knife she stoned the dark fruit and dropped the filletted flesh in a pot on her left. Amanieu sprawled across the threshold (where poor Solomon had died), his legs in the sun and the rest of him in the cool of the house. The mastiff, still subdued by the happiness of their new friendship, lay beside him, lavishing the heat of its body on the flagstones.

Swollen with news, Jesus brought a ceremonious air to his arrival. He walked his little horse under the arch and then caused the tranquil creature to passage up the yard, as if it was the custom in his country for great tidings to come home sideways. No one paid any attention, and since the horse capered by the plum tree with its tail to the company, Jesus could not at once tell—without spoiling the effect by peeking—how far he had stirred the familiar self-absorption of his patrons. He therefore continued to arrive with style, guiding his steed in a wide and elegant circle to come face-on to the house. There he bowed in the saddle, took off with a flourish the wide hat Solomon had lent him on his departure, and held it out to one side. His own length and the smallness of the horse put his feet quite near the ground, and the effect of this along with the worn and patched state of his clothes—even to the tatty old straw hat—was to present him as a ramshackle copy of some heroic monument waiting for applause.

Jesus soon felt this himself, for Caesar continued to scrutinise the periphery of that commonplace tree, and Flore to fossick about in the middle of it, with no sign that they had noticed him. Bonne, of whom he had an unclear view through the leaves and branches, did look at him for a moment, but then she simply went on stoning those meagre plums. Jesus closed his eyes against self-ridicule, put the hat back on his head and stepped to the ground.

"What!" he said, picking up a fallen plum. "You have let the frost get them!"

This spontaneous expression of rustic outrage won an immediate response, and from the whole family.

"Frost!" Bonne said. "Don't be insolent!"

"Hallo, Jesus!" Flore said from inside the tree. "You've missed yourself this week—we had a feast, with snails! We're only just better."

"Been away?" Caesar asked. "Look here, the frost has hardly touched them, you know, and it is still so hot during the days."

"What's that got to do with it?" Jesus demanded, as if the plums were his. "The harm that the frost does, the sun won't undo."

"How dare you talk to your lord like that?" Bonne scolded him. "Come round here! I can see you have news."

Caesar put a hand on his shoulder and pressed him chummily round the tree. "Have you got news, my dear Solomon? Bonne will be excited."

"Not Solomon—I'm wearing his hat. My name is Jesus."

"Of course! How could you be Solomon? I forgot!"

Caesar pushed him gently at Bonne, who still sat against the wall. To her Jesus bowed, hat on breast, and this time received a decent nod of the head in return.

"Tell me this news," Bonne said, "that you are so proud of."

Jesus looked at Amanieu, who had risen and was leaning now against the doorpost, and then the Spaniard turned away, pointing his nose over the downhill, faraway country from which he had returned. "Madame," he announced, "the Viscount is making a progress through his land!"

"Aha!" Bonne said, and cut herself badly on two fingers, "Roger has remembered us at last!"

"Trencavel!" Caesar said. "Coming here? Hell and devils!"

"What!" Bonne exclaimed, gesticulating for a hand from Jesus to pull her to her feet. "Is this your welcome for my cousin, our over-lord?" She brushed her skirts down with one hand and sucked the bleeding fingers of the other. "How does he travel?" she asked Jesus, a little anxiously. "Is he supplied, or is he living off the country?"

"He has a vast train, madame, and travels well supplied, and sends cooks and food before him, wherever he stops for the night." Jesus was now much mollified. It was true that the news he brought was weighty in itself, but it was his delivery of it that had drawn blood.

Besides there was more, and to speak it Jesus resumed the awe-striking face he had worn on the way in.

"When is Roger coming?" Bonne asked, failing at once to notice this foreboding visage. "How long have I to prepare?"

"A week," Jesus said snappishly. "You've got a whole week yet." He glared down on her like stone-faced Jeremiah silenced, on the very brink of divine revelation, by some garrulous dairymaid.

Bonne went edge-faced and narrow-eyed. "Don't get on your high horse with me, my man. We are a small household now, but these times will soon be over! Gone! Past! My cousin knows what is due to me and my husband. You may flourish with us or take your destiny elsewhere, as you choose. Meanwhile—you think a week's enough time to be ready for the Viscount Roger? We shall be at it day and night, you fool! Flore, finish the plums! I'll have a council of war with Gully."

Jesus kept his prophetic countenance until she had gone, dropping her knife here, flicking froplets of blood there, and tripping over the slow-witted mastiff—"Damn dog!"—that lay in the sudden darkness inside the house.

Then, the Spaniard approached near to Caesar. "My lord," he said, in a tuneful but ominous tone, like the first rush of wind that hymns the imminence of the storm, "I would speak with you privately."

"Privately?" Caesar said. "You want to speak with me privately? You bring this dreadful news about Viscount Roger coming here—" he gestured with despairing eloquence at the keep, representative of the half-finished castle, and mimed with a cunning that would have supported him as a professional, the fact that his clothes, in their more exalted degree, were apt companions for Jesus's own tattered rig-out—"you tell me Roger is on his way, and then crave boons of me! Bah!" Caesar's blue eyes gleamed blankly, but he was too depressed to make them glitter with rage. They failed, therefore, to discompose the Spaniard's sophisticated balance of gloom and optimism, while in

Caesar's words Jesus discovered an invigorating slight to his personal humour.

"I do not crave boons, my lord!" he said, almost matching heights with Caesar, so much did pride assist his elevation. "It is our family motto, '*Non rogo, capio*'—'I do not ask, I take.' "

"I have Latin, thank you," Caesar said testily, and then smiled wittily. "I don't want to offend you, my dear chap, but either your family motto was chosen prematurely, or your family has outlived it! Ha-ha! Ha-ha! Ha-ha! Rather quickly, too, if I may say so. I was pointing out to my daughter, just the other day, that family mottoes only came in during my grandfather's time." He fell pensive again. "Cause nothing but trouble, family mottoes." He now regretted mocking the Spaniard's dignity, and said to him, "I think perhaps I shouldn't have said that, about mottoes. What can I do for you?"

Jesus understood by this that his lord had begged his pardon, and had forgotten almost everything they had said to each other. "I have something important, my lord, for your ears alone."

Caesar was extremely pleased. "Something private, eh? Come round the corner."

They went along the front of the house and round the corner, where Caesar hoisted himself up onto the woodpile. This was still high, since winter had not yet begun, and Jesus saw that he must either confide his secret to Caesar's feet, or bawl it out aloud.

"My lord," he said, and dashed back to peer down the front of the house where he saw that Amanieu was now leaning against the wall, a mere three yards away, "My lord, you will have to bend down. We must whisper."

"Must you, by God! I don't know about that!"

"My Lord!" Jesus was in a fever. If ever a voice had craved, that was what his voice had just done.

"Oh, very well!" Caesar said, and bent himself double, and more.

Jesus grabbed his shoulders, partly to hold him down, and partly to stop him falling off. "My lord," he said. "I have found out where our visitor came by his rich clothes, and armour, and fine horses! Two days from here he waylaid a young German knight, and killed him, and took everything he had!"

"Capital!" Caesar whispered carefully. "Two good men meet on the road, break a lance together. It's quite the vogue now. I've heard of it. Spoils to the victor."

Jesus spat, to clear his throat, no doubt. "No, my lord! They broke no lances. He ambushed him like a bandit, and put a knife in his brain. I had a struggle to get it out. See, here it is!"

Into the small space between their eyes he thrust a danger with a rotten smell coming off it, crusted with blood, and fragments of brain and chips of bone. Caesar's eyes stared at it, and his nose twitched.

"That's bad," Caesar said. "Killed and robbed, eh? Murdered? A German, though. Still, it's not good. I wish he hadn't done it."

"There's more," Jesus whispered intensely.

"I can hardly hear you," Caesar said, "You're very faint."

Jesus clutched his master closer to him, and whispered into his ear with a muffled, shouting voice. Caesar gritted his teeth to listen as hard as he could. "After I'd found the body, and worked it all out, I rode on as far as Olonzac. That's where I heard the Viscount was on his way here. I met one of his messengers in a wineshop. He said there's a German knight travelling with Trencavel's court. A giant warrior. A German lord. He's looking for his young brother, and they were to meet at Béziers. It's the lad I found dead. All that gear, and those horses, your young friend has brought here with him—it's all German. It's this big knight's brother he's murdered."

"Oh," said Caesar dolefully, seeing the whole picture, past, present and imminent, with frightful clarity. "Oh, God, my God!"

"Aye!" the Spaniard said. "There is trouble on your house, my lord! There is trouble coming!"

"You were quite right to tell me," Caesar said, still whispering. "But don't go on about it. You can let go now!"

Jesus still hung on to his collar, and shook it in the violence of his emotions, whatever they were. "It is bad news, is it not? I think it is the worst news I ever told—is it not?"

"Let go, you jackass," Caesar cried, but in a strangled way, being now partially choked.

"My lord," Jesus shook him more, and insisted with profound seriousness. "Is it not dreadful news for you to hear?"

"Yes, damn you! Hellish news! Soul-destroying news! Let go of me now!"

Caesar wrenched himself free at the same moment that Jesus let go of him, and fell violently into the air and onto the Spaniard.

They made a noisy fall.

"Jesús!" Jesus cried.

"Wagh!" Caesar exclaimed, striking his head on the ground, and hurting one knee while kicking the other into the forearm of the same side of the body, and giving it such a pang when they struck the ground together, that he thought it was broken. He leaned on all fours for a few moments, and recovered.

"Father!" Flore called out, and descended nimbly from the plum tree to come to his aid.

"Jesús!" Jesus now shrieked again. "María Madre . . ." he prayed sadly.

"Pull yourself together!" Caesar said, feeling rather better at the sound of the other man's aches and pains.

"It is too late for that," the voice of Amanieu said, with a hint of sanctimonious reproach. "See, you have killed him!"

This astounding speech drew Caesar to his knees, so that once again there hung before his affronted eyes that guilt-laden dagger. This time, though, the blood on it was fresh and steaming.

"Oh, father!" Flore said.

"I can't have killed him!" That was true, and he felt better. How could he possibly have killed him, without knowing it. Unless . . .

"Father!" Flore said again, and began snivelling.

"No!" Caesar breathed. "No!" he shouted. "No!"

He wept. He slumped to his haunches, sitting on his heels like a boy playing in the dust, and wept. Flore stood behind him and put an arm round his neck, and rested her chin on his child's curly locks. She had stopped snivelling and though she wept a little now it was in sympathy with Caesar, and while tears fell from her eyes her face was calm. Her father clutched at the circling arm and tucked his eyes into it. Titanic shudders convulsed him and forced his face to the daylight again. His shoulders threw off the consoling arm. He howled at the sun. He shook his fists at Heaven. He clawed his hands and tore at the air. He held his head with great care, and grew still.

Flore had placed herself in front of him. She threw a look of urgent appeal at Amanieu beside her, and said to her father, "Why don't you tell him?"

Amanieu said, "Yes, tell me!" He waited, completely in the dark.

## Chapter 19

# CAESAR'S TALE

"WHEN I was young, when I was young!" Caesar said. "I was a perfect hero in Guyenne when I was young. I was the coming man. I was the captain they all wanted to follow. I was the Captal of Yon, the war-chief *par excellence*! Ah, Christ, Christ! I was a chief man in the Council of King Louis when I was twenty! I was a tactician of the first skill, a fortunate commander, a champion in combat! My wife was the most beautiful woman in Anjou! I was putting my poor father's house together again, for he was unsuccessful in life and went to die among the Moors in Spain. I had a daughter and a *son*," and he said the last word very quickly, as if it burnt his tongue.

Flore had moved closer to her father's side, to give him the sense of companionship, and so that there should not be two of them confronting him, like judges. Also, so that she need no longer see, beyond her father's shoulder, the bluebottles feasting at the Spaniard's throat. Amanieu was poised on his toes, drinking the story in. He had waited to hear it since the day he arrived.

"My son was eight or nine. I had small armour made for him to take him to the wars. Not to fight, you understand, but to get the way of it. War would be his trade, as it was mine, and he should start early, have the advantage! It was a short campaign, the end of summer, and we were set on by ten times our number. The fight was the wildest I ever fought, the highest joy I ever knew, ever! I killed and cut and broke and hacked—I fought with the left arm when the right grew tired. Yes, I had taught it that. What a day that was! The blood-lust was like wine from Heaven. I killed more men that day than some men—soldiers too!—kill in a lifetime. Men in steel I broke open, faces flew apart, eyes fell out, bellies spewed their innards. How the horses shrieked and stamped and trampled on the wounded! And how *they* shrieked, the wounded and the dying, with their ribs springing out from the cracked armour, and heads cut half away! All that day the sun grew brighter and brighter on us. As for blood—we were blood to the knees, to the thighs, it made pools and puddles where the ground dropped. I waded in blood that day, and I went mad at last, as you see me now. I killed our own men, everyone I saw I killed. I killed my own . . . they turned a waggon onto me at last and kept me there till I slept. I slept like the dead, the dead."

Amanieu scrutinised that weary face, worn with emotion rather than the passage of life, with its high, vapid, fatuous smile. The blue eyes watched him back, as shifty at this moment as the dead Spaniard's eyes had been in their lifetime. Amanieu saw that Caesar was cheating him. He had not told the whole story.

"What happened to your son?" Amanieu asked.

Caesar's face stretched smooth, pulling all the cracks and crevices to the surface. His chin fell and his forehead climbed until the face seemed half as tall again as in its normal state. When the face began to twist and its bones to creak, Caesar had at last found words to say what he could not bear to hear.

"Well, of course, I was a laughing-stock after that. I'd cut the boy in two, two bits clean as a whistle in that little armour. Yes, I was a laughing-stock all right! Well, for one thing I was no more use as a captain, once I'd turned on my own men. Who'll follow you then? That was that! Those who weren't killed thought it was a good joke, afterwards, but they wanted to stay on the laughing end of it. Well, of course they did: to stay alive! So I was a laughing-stock, you see. Men who were there, they were kind about the boy, kind enough. They couldn't look at me—how could they?—but they were as kind as possible. To people who weren't there, that was part of the joke as well. I'd shed my own blood and killed my own heir. That made me more of a laughing-stock.

"He was just a little boy, out for fun, and I killed him!"

This last line came in time for Amanieu to understand that the repeated statements of self-pity were as a screen to stop the outsider's eye, a blanket hung between (in this case) himself, and the sorrow that Caesar woke to every day. From this cause, too, the perpetual smile.

"My overlord separated me from my estate and moved my brother in, into my place. They offered—my overlord offered it, and my brother did, and the Church was agreed—that my . . . my . . . my-my-my- lady should be taken from me also and married to my brother, and she would not, she would not do it! By God she would not, is that not wonderful?"

"Wonderful," Amanieu agreed. "Absolutely. Why would she not?"

Caesar found the question natural to ask and easy to answer. "For love of me," he said. "For hate of them, too, since she did not like to be trafficked like a cow at the market. She thought also their view of the thing was narrow and penurious-minded, to suppose that my killing of the boy could be tidied up and put away, be over and done with just like that. My killing of the boy would surely go on while we lived, Bonne said, and being unmarried from each other would not separate her and me from that."

Amanieu frowned at himself for being so much startled by this speech. He saw that he had quite failed to interpret Caesar and Bonne. It was true that he had not been fool enough to take either of them at face value, but he had been nowhere near showing the discernment that would have revealed to him that Caesar's expiation for the slaughter of his son, and Bonne's undying vengeance, had been combined, by subtleties of thought beyond his imagining, into this one, demented, life-long act of reconciliation. It was now apparent that the outward signs of this infernal game were merely a few symbols of a pattern unwound over years, and understood by the game's two players in a deeply complicated way that denied access to outsiders. They had grappled themselves to each other with hooks of steel.

Since, however, Amanieu found his understanding sympathetically attuned to Caesar's, he plunged on. "That's why you lost a wit?"

"Yes!" Caesar said, thumping his knee with satisfaction. "Exactly for this reason. I went mad in the fight, but that was a fit. It was soon over. It was afterwards I lost the wit. Why, it was essential to lose it! If my killing the boy was to go on like that, day after day throughout my life, I must lose a wit or be consumed with madness, burned off the earth like a pine tree!" He tapped Amanieu on the knee, and amazed him once more. "Where would Bonne be then, if I was whisked off in a puff of smoke?"

Amanieu felt like a swimmer who has been holding his breath in deep water. He lost patience, and began to return to the surface. To kick his way upward, he asked roughly, "What about Jesus? What about the Spaniard?"

Caesar drew back into himself and stared, trying to remember, of that death still stiffening on the ground behind him, only as much as he could stomach. He stood up gradually to his height, and stared to the front, carefully upon the mountain.

Flore put her earnest face close to Amanieu's. "Be our friend! Be kind to him! When you said he'd killed the Spaniard, he *knew* he hadn't—so he thought he had gone mad again, like the day he killed my brother."

Her brother! The boy had been Flore's brother, and he had failed to see this. Well, no wonder, for the whole story was such a celebration, however tragic and crazed, of Bonne and Caesar, that there seemed little room in it for the existence of a daughter of theirs, never mind a sister of the slaughtered infant.

"I've upset you!" Amanieu faced Caesar and spoke his piece like a man. "A slip of the tongue! When I said you'd killed the poor devil, I meant only that when he fell and pulled you down with him, he drove the dagger he was holding into his own throat. It was his own fault. He brought you down on top of himself."

Caesar's eye abandoned the distant cliff and focussed on Amanieu.

"It was bound to happen sooner or later." The young man kept going. "He was always a fellow to bring down trouble on himself."

"He did that, all right!" Flore said helpfully. "He brought Father down on him like a ton of bricks!"

This phrase evoked an involuntary laugh from Amanieu. Flore giggled, and went on giggling behind her hand. Amanieu laughed a succession of quiet, almost spoken, laughs. Caesar's smile became less mad and more real, until he joined in, with a pleasant and reproachful laugh of his own.

"Now, now!" he said. "The poor man's dead!" He frowned and twisted his face. "He brought hellish news—Viscount Roger's coming." He cast a wonderfully dark and cunning glance, like a statesman reaching a thought, at Amanieu; then he hastened to laugh some more.

Onto this cheerful scene Vigorce and Mosquito walked, leading their horses. They came to an ill-made stop, and peered past the merrymakers at what lay behind Caesar on the ground. The two soldiers did not at once believe their eyes, but then the Spaniard's cream-coloured horse came out of the shade of the plum tree and spoke to Mosquito's skewbald. Vigorce resigned his own horse to Mosquito.

"It *is* Jesus!" Vigorce exclaimed, trying to be in doubt but already sure. "Dead! Killed!" He glared at Amanieu with eyes both murderous and afraid.

Amanieu said quickly, "Jesus fell on the knife. He killed himself by

accident, the lord Caesar will tell you." He held out the knife, all
bloody, and the captain took it with a long arm.

"Whose knife?" Vigorce asked. "Because it is not his."

"Mine," Amanieu said. "He was using it to make a point to the
lord Caesar. He was excited and pulled the lord off the woodpile, and
fell beneath. Jesus was holding the knife himself."

"I simply fell off," Caesar said, "like Humpty-Dumpty."

Flore, whose giggling had stopped, now put both hands over her
face and ran to the task her mother had left her. She began stoning
plums with her head bowed and her back turned to the impromptu
inquest.

Mosquito shook his head at Caesar's sublime illustration. "I'll
water the horses," he said.

"Wait!" Caesar said. He made another of those marvellously
sinister and subtle glances, dividing it between Amanieu and the
Spaniard's corpse. "Don't take away the Spanish horse. I have things
to explain to your, captain, things to discuss. Perhaps my young
friend will kindly take the poor man's body down to the graveyard.
Put him on his horse for the last time, the poor chap! That will be the
proper thing. Nice little beast too!"

So Mosquito went off to the well, and Amanieu walked Jesus down
the hill to the church, on the tired and thirsty little horse.

## Chapter 20

# THE THINKERS

CAESAR led Vigorce to the great keep, and climbed the stone steps to the first storey. In that room, which was the captain's, Caesar told him all that he had heard from Jesus. "My wife has great hopes of Roger Trencavel's visit," he said. "Poor lady! She deludes herself! But whatever hopes she has, this young murderer being here, and known to have been our guest here, will not help us with Roger!"

Caesar heaved out of his depths a long, sorrowful sigh. Poor Bonne! For his wife, infatuated with the hope that energy and ambition could wrest from this bare patrimony of hers a wonderful restoration of their fortunes, was fixed in the belief that since he was vaguely her cousin, Viscount Roger, being also her overlord, would give them a leg up.

For his part, Caesar saw it as less a visit than a visitation: as the lord inspecting his estates after a long war, to see what revenue they would bring to repair his decrepit finances. It would be the last thing in his mind, to subsidise the completion of this superfluous castle, merely to oblige a forgotten relationship.

When Caesar had explained all this to Vigorce, he sighed again. "Where are the energy and ambition to come from, after all? A woman's tantrums are not energy, and her wishful thinking is not ambition. Still, that is not the point. We must get the miserable assassin . . . the young man, out of here: over the horizon, gone and vanished. We must think of a way to do that."

A bad look came onto the captain's face.

"No, no, captain!" Caesar said crossly. "We will not kill him! For one thing he has been my guest, and for another it would spoil the place. It's not much of a place, but that would spoil it."

"Yes," Vigorce said. "I can see that. I like this place, myself. I could live here for years, doing nothing more than we do. I like it as it is, too, though I would also like it if the lady found some of her hopes come true." He coughed to clear his throat, and went on to make a statement, looking with determination a little to one side of Caesar's face. "I value my lady's contentment," he said.

"I thank you," Caesar said haughtily, "on her behalf. Now, we

must tax our brains, and if it is any spur to your wits, I will say freely
that she is much struck by the young man, in that way of hers. I do not
deny Bonne her honest pleasures, they are few enough for her up here,
but she is much struck by the young man, and so for all our sakes—
eh!—and for good reasons, we must somehow tempt him away from
here. That's the way to think of it—tempt him away!"

They climbed now the wooden steps to the top of the keep, and
went out on the roof. They came from the stairhead facing north, and
stood together to look over the meadow, cradled in its rocky cliffs, that
rose to the stone desert where Caesar was so much at home. Out of
breath from the climb, by common consent they rested silent. Caesar
leaned on the parapet and grew reflective.

"Eternity is before our eyes," he said.

"What do you mean?" Vigorce demanded.

"Eternity and chaos!" Caesar said, rejoicing.

"What do you mean?" Vigorce asked again.

"There!" Caesar said, stretching an arm whose open hand offered,
with a flourish, the excellent view before them of the high stone
wilderness.

The afternoon had begun to end, and the sky, though it must be
blue for an hour yet, was already rippling through its brilliant evening
variations of that colour, prelude to the chromatic ecstasies it would
enjoy when, at last, the sun took it to bed. The thinning light was
radiant on the meadow whose flowers, undeceived, were now closing.
From the cliffs came the fluty call of a rock thrush, and from the air
descended the same call answering, where her mate took his last flight
of the day. On the ramparts a flock of sooty-black birds chattered and
fussed. The longer view, stark stone to the horizon, was softened by
the first wisps of evening haze. The scene was harmonious and
affecting.

"Very well!" Vigorce said, and waved a hand of his own in uncouth
parody of his master's. "I know you mean—there! But why do you
call that, there, chaos and eternity?"

Caesar's smile met the captain's glower. "I do not object to chaos
and eternity," he said. "I dwell in them! In their very midst!" he said
triumphantly. "Now, up at the end of that meadow is the end of our
world. Beyond, that empty place up there stretches on and on to God
knows where! Nothing will be found there but chaos, to the edge of the
earth."

Vigorce squared himself to the supposed vista of eternity and chaos. He held his arms up before him and sighted between the palms of his hands. "I can't follow your reasoning," he said. "I don't know this south country as well as you, but if I were that thrush singing up there, I would undertake to fly up that line and find Berri and Champagne and Flanders; and if I shift a little, to make sure of the whole . . ," and he swept a hand over the space in front of him, "then I undertake to fly to Maine and Normandy. The desert out there does not go to the edge of the earth. It is between here and these other places."

"Good Heavens!" Caesar exclaimed, while he stooped and smiled strenuously upon Vigorce. "I know that. I could walk to Albi over these stones, in three or four weeks. It's not the same thing, though. It's not what I mean at all."

"It never is!" Vigorce shouted, who detested these crazy man-to-man arguments with Caesar, where he was coaxed by some trick of plain speaking to believe that they were to converse on level terms. In these frank, philosophical tête-à-têtes Caesar, when opposed, just cheated. His fancy soared into a vast private empyrean where irrational whims flew from nowhere to nowhere with the speed of lightning.

This evening, on that tower, Vigorce rebelled. "If," he said, "I had an eye sharp enough to pierce that mountain, in that direction, and if it could see far enough, it would light on Burgundy."

Caesar began to speak. "I—" he said.

"Burgundy is green," Vigorce said. "I can see it now, through that rock and all the rocks beyond. It is September, when the rain has been, and when the sun has returned to ensure the vintage."

Caesar said, "Ah! When—"

"In this beech wood," Vigorce said, quite carried away, "The rooks are cawing, and in those elms, I hear the squawk of the jackdaw." He had started to believe himself. "On the plains of Auxois the granaries will be full—I mean, are full—and on the round towers of the farms the red roofs will glow in the sun: I mean they do glow, I see them glow. Along the south slopes of the low, low hills, from Dijon to Beaune, I see . . ."

It was clear that Vigorce was going to talk gibberish until the cows came home. Caesar left him to it and took a turn about the roof. It was rather a small keep, really, and the castle would be commensurate, a miniature. No more than a fort, but enough to secure their status, for Bonne's sake. Perhaps Roger Trencavel would renew the licence to build the castle, and lend Bonne the wherewithal, in a burst of cousinly feeling. Pigs might fly! There was Flore, still pitting the plums. She might have been a happier child, if their lives had gone differently. She might have made the three of them into a family! A good girl, all the same. His little tour brought him back beside his captain, who was still at it.

"The rivers," Vigorce asserted, suddenly self-conscious but still game, "run full of roach and bream, the lakes of pike, the ponds of carp—"

"The puddles of minnows!" Caesar sneered nastily.

There was a curious silence. At first, it meant simply that Vigorce had lost the place. Then, out of nowhere, an illumination more glorious than the sunset fell upon the captain. He leaned on the parapet and looked south into the purpling dusk. "Lord Caesar," he said, "I have the inkling of an idea that might send young Amanieu on his way." He jerked his thumb over his shoulder. "Northwards, to chaos and eternity."

Caesar gave him that one. "How?" he asked. "What is your idea, my dear captain?"

"Hush!" Vigorce said. "I am pulling it out of my mind." He snapped his fingers. "There!" he said.

Caesar peered down, through the dimness inside and outside his head. "You have, truly, an idea?" he asked.

"I have," Vigorce said. "What you must do, lord, is make sure that the young man will show you his fine armour tomorrow." He nodded. "Yes, tomorrow in the morning. Listen, lord!"

Long after sun and sky, rapt in glory, had gone to rest, the two conspirators whispered on.

# Chapter 21

# FAMILY LIFE

"THESE joys will kill me," Flore said, unless there are more of them."

"You have seen too much," Amanieu said.

In her mind, Flore saw Vigorce and the woman, mating on the riverbank. "You showed it me," she said. She stood at arm's length from him, held lightly between his hands. "You showed it me," she said again, "Now I am obscene before my time."

"It is a gift," he said. "It can hardly come before its time."

"*My* time," she corrected him, "Before *my* time. Early or no," she said, and did not stop looking at him with her eyes that glowed like dark chestnuts, "It is a gift I'll have to thank you for."

"You need not," he said, sly.

"Oh, I need," she said with scorn, "I do need!"

She took one of his hands into hers. She stroked her cheek with it, closed her eyes and opened them; closed and opened. The mouth sloped on her face, drooping to complaint at one end, lifted at the other by hope. She kissed the hand, and bit it and licked it, and let it go. She stepped away. The whole wealth of her rose to her face and showed itself to him. The chestnut eyes grew round with her candour of wanting him.

Amanieu looked back at her, at that small, true creature buoyant with awakened lust who offered her original innocence to him. From his weasel's face and his serpent's eyes, from his twisted mouth and his deformed spirit; but also from his heart, for which he had never yet in all his life found a use: he accepted.

\*       \*       \*

"There he is!" Caesar said to himself. "There they are!" He waved both arms at Flore and Amanieu, who stood facing each other on the roof of the gate-house, and did not see him. "Like a pair of statues," Caesar muttered.

"Ho!" he shouted. "Hoy!"

They looked down at him.

"Good morning!" he called up at them.

Amanieu came to the edge of the roof and leaned on the parapet. "Aha!" he said, with only modest cordiality, and withdrew.

Caesar was much nettled. Here he was, up early and brisk in the wits, ready to inveigle Amanieu into a pleasant conversation that would lead, in no time at all, to the young man's departure—and rebuffed at the outset. Caesar was now at the door of the gate-house. Bending double to save his head from the undersides of the stone steps, he pounded clumsily up the stairs. He climbed one floor, puffed and blew, and set off again. He turned up the second round of the stairs into a violent blow on the chin.

This threw him upside down on the spiral staircase, with his feet far above his head. The briskness of his wits was much blunted by this cataclysm and he lay there unable to move or think. His head rang and his senses reeled.

"Father!" his daughter's voice cried from the blurred dimness beyond his feet. "What are you doing down there?"

The question was cogent, even to Caesar's disordered state. He fought to clear his sight, blinking and stretching his eyes. The young man was perched over him, no doubt on one of the steps. He was rubbing his kneecap.

"You have surely broken my knee," Amanieu said merrily.

Behind him, and higher yet, a pale shape wobbled in the gloom, like a daughter precariously poised.

It seemed important to Caesar that Flore should not wobble head over heels, in imitation of her father, and land on top of him. "Take care, Flore!" he said, with a weak and husky utterance. "Do not hurt yourself! One of us is enough—God knows how badly I have fallen!"

"Come along!" her voice now said in his ear. "I shall push and Amanieu will pull, and we'll soon have you out of this. You're like a sheep that's got stuck on its back!"

The rescue that now followed composed for her father a deeply irritating event. Caesar, after a downfall that had left him inverted from the true condition of man, would gladly have lain there for hours to discover the metaphor that was certain to be lurking in a predicament so curious and rare. Such intellectualisation of misfortune had become, failing all else, his life's work. Bonne never denied it him. She would denounce it with sarcasm or contempt, but she let it take place—and she would let him lie there a week, even though she had to tramp over him twenty times a day, if that was what suited him.

Flore and Amanieu, far from regarding him as a philosopher who had, by turning turtle, taken up a position of enigmatic significance, treated him like a silly old man who had fallen downstairs. His daughter giggled and the young man was facetious. They were ignorant that there was anything inside him. Their ears were deaf to him and their eyes blind. They neither turned to him, nor away. They pushed and pulled him, they tilted, propped and tugged him through a series of ignominious postures and dumped him, at last, on a bed.

What bed?

"Where am I?" he demanded crossly.

"Where are you indeed!" Flore cried blithely. The impudent brat was jollying him along. "You are in the gate-house, of course, in Amanieu's room." She added, "There, there!" and after that she giggled fatuously again.

This child of his would trivialise him down to nothing, until his very shadow hunted for him in vain.

A dull pain encircled Caesar's head. He lay flat on his back and flogged the vaulted roof with wild strokes of his too-blue eyes. In despair he found cunning. "I am hurt worse than I thought," he said. "It is true I fell on ten steps at once, and slid and bumped. The noise was hellish! I heard my bones break. Go away. Leave me, I am dying. Get Bonne. Send my wife!"

Two peals of laughter filled the air with discord. There was a creaking noise like pigs revelling, and that was not at all pleasant, but it was the shrill treble that stimulated the ring of pain round his scalp.

"Oh!" Caesar cried. "My head, my head!"

"Oh, Father!" Flore exclaimed. "I shouldn't think you've cracked as much as a fingernail. You are wearing your armour," she said. "That's what all the noise was about, when you fell!"

Wearing armour? So he was. Chain-mail and the padded leather beneath it had taken the brunt of the fall. Caesar was so struck by this discovery that he forgot one of his hurts was real. He sat up and at once fell back, crying out, "My head! Oh, my head!"

Amanieu creaked like any number of jubilant porkers. "That's the funniest part of it," he said, and Flore tittered obligingly. "Your helmet's got knocked down almost to your eyes. Let me try it!"

He tried it. The head burst open with agony. "Ach!" Caesar shrieked. "Oil!" he croaked.

"That's right," Amanieu said. "Oil will get it off, sooner or later. It's good old armour, all the same. Why do you have it on?"

Caesar now remembered why he was wearing all this iron—that he and Vigorce had made a plot, the night before. "Oh," he said carelessly, "to see if it still fits me, in case Viscount Roger wants a bit of a tournament. He likes a bit of sport, Roger. Eh, ah, bring out your own, let's have a look at it, when I've got this thing off my head."

Done it! Caesar fell back, feeling so faint and gallant that he almost passed out.

"Why did he suddenly look so wily?" Flore said.

"God knows!" Amanieu said. "Plotting something, probably. Let's get him outside."

*       *       *

Bonne sat in the sunlight mending worn linen. She was enraged. Every so often her fingers shook and she could not see straight, so that the work fell to her lap in palsied hands, and she stared at the sky, or a stone, or a suddenly self-conscious beetle trudging through the dust. This bright anger had come upon her first thing in the morning, when she saw her husband parading about in his armour: the armour that he had not worn since the day when, wearing it, he slaughtered her son. She was confident that by noon the heart would have perished in her body, and she would be able to get on with the housework. After all, Roger her great cousin might be here tomorrow or the next day.

Meanwhile, sometimes her mind was empty and sometimes it seethed. The enormity that she found in this latest stroke of Caesar's was that up to now all his torture of her had been subtle or devious. By the sudden surprise of this coarse cruelty, therefore, he had brought finesse even to clumsiness. By this paradoxical conjunction she was as stricken as if Zeus had dashed into her one of his exquisitely sharp, but also shattering, thunderbolts.

Round Bonne rose a cloud of dust, and some of it climbed up her nose so that she sneezed. Awakened out of herself, she was aware of a vigorous commotion: a pleasing contrast to her gloomy private thoughts, to be sure, but—she sneezed again—an unconscionably messy one.

"What do you think you're doing?" she demanded.

Vigorce looked at her through the dust with as much reproach as his policy of inflexible adoration allowed. In fact, the two attitudes seemed to get on very well together, and appeared quite comfortable on his face sharing a single, harmonious expression. So, thought Bonne, in a moment of unwelcome intuition, would Vigorce show his allegiance to the Holy Virgin, brushing his worship with a tinge of indignation and complaint. She knew an incongruous sense of sympathy with the Queen of Heaven, a shared vexation with the self-deceit of men, but then she put this agreeable comparison aside and returned, blushing a little, to the secular world.

Vivacious with insight though she was, Bonne could not explain to herself what she now saw. In front of her, among the settling dust, was the great elm table from the house. She could see where they had been dragging it along the ground. They were only three—Vigorce, Amanieu and the tiny Mosquito—and to lift that great board it took eight men. She had never seen it out of the house before. Who would give her a straight answer?

"Mosquito," she asked the little man, "what's that for?"

"It's for my lord," Mosquito said. "It's for the lord Caesar to lie on."

"Thank you, Mosquito," Bonne said. "Why?"

"Gully wouldn't let him do it in the house, with the Viscount Roger coming any day now. She says we'd be spilling oil over the flagstones, and it takes months for the stone to drink it up."

"She's quite right," Bonne said.

"I expect she is," Mosquito said.

He really was a most agreeing man, Bonne said to herself, and the only unquarrelsome member of their small community. She felt herself to be insufficiently instructed by Mosquito's explanation, but it sounded as if the rest might be worth waiting to see for herself.

"That table must have been a dreadful weight," she said. "Rest yourself."

Mosquito sat on the doorstep. Amanieu had disappeared. Standing up and advancing one and a half paces, Bonne dusted off a corner of the table with her apron and put the mending down on it. She turned for her stool and Mosquito pushed it forward with his foot. They might have been familiar friends. She sat down at the table.

There was a jangling and creaking sound, and here came Caesar, dressed-up as the son-killer, armed cap-à-pie, but with his steel cap hard down over his eyebrows. Bonne had lived among battles, in their youth, and she knew why Mosquito had been talking about oil. Her face gleamed for an instant like a jewel turned to the sun, before she sat down and became intent on her darning. Her fingers had become nimble, and her eyes clear.

Caesar's eyes were half-closed between his pounding temples, but he recognised in Bonne's face what he had until this moment forgotten—so intent had he been on plotting with Vigorce. In playing the decoy to coax Amanieu's armour out into the daylight he had forgotten that it was from within this very chain-mail, and from under this damned helmet stuck on his head, that he had cut his little boy in two.

"I fell downstairs on my head," he said, by way of apology.

"Of course!" Bonne said, her needle twinkling capably in and out among the threads with which she was strengthening an old napkin.

The morning had come forward to that vivifying hour when the sun's warmth, though still mopping up the dew, now grows to heat on the skin. It is the fervent hour when strong men vow they will today out-labour Hercules; the hour of bliss when drunkards and sinners resolve to be bad for one more day; and above all, it is the hour of solace for the distraught spirit, when yesterday has certainly gone past, tomorrow will be another life, and today has not yet begun to take place: and may still be turned into a dream.

In this hour the last of the summer's flowers bloomed full-blown and gaudy along the front of the house. Bees and wasps buzzed in the depleted larder of the old plum tree. Swallows switched and swung in the air and through them flashed a yellow oriole, making the mad dash for the downhill woods and home. Into the blue a hundred skylarks rose and sang.

In this hour, then, Caesar lay dull and armoured on the long table, like a crocodile on the altar (Bonne thought) among the joys of easter. His head hung down over the far end of the table, and on the red, swollen ring where the helmet met the scalp, Vigorce poured oil.

"I have done that often enough," Bonne said, chattering to napkin, needle and thread, "for Caesar and for others. Sometimes the pot is holding the head together, and when it comes off—pouf!—everything falls out!"

During this speech Flore appeared, and sat herself on the table. "Will it come off?" she asked.

Bonne said, "I don't know. It looks badly bent, doesn't it? Often, when it's like that, you must have the blacksmith take it to pieces." She called down the table, and down Caesar, to Vigorce. "Give it a twist!"

"A twist?" Vigorce asked. "And so soon? The oil has hardly had time to make its way in."

"Never mind that!" Bonne said. "Try it!"

"Aaaaaah!" yelled Caesar, and jangled and creaked, kicking his iron-clad heels on the table. Vigorce let go the helmet and picked up the oil bottle again.

Bonne laughed recklessly and bit her thread in two. Flore looked at her mother with some particles, which she could not account for to herself, of admiration. "You are cross early today," she said. "What's up?"

Bonne wrinkled her face. "Never you mind," she said. "Your father knows."

This was an accustomed answer, but Flore let it pass. "Father!" she said, and laughed heartily, from her throat. "What a sight he is! I've not seen him in armour since I was an infant. He looked odd even before his helmet stuck." She laughed again and said, "Poor man!"

Bonne said, "Poor man indeed! Oh, poor man! I expect he will live, however. Your father has not the tact to succumb to an accident."

Flore stared at her mother's fingers as they rippled nimbly across the tatty cloth. "You're cross with him," she said, "because of the armour. Why does that make you cross?"

"Are you my rather young daughter?" Bonne asked. "You are very free with yourself, all of a sudden."

Flore bit her lip, but the blush against which she had prepared herself did not come. The girl and the woman looked at one another with curiosity and surprise. Flore said, "People grow up."

"Some do, certainly," Bonne answered. "Therefore let me explain to you about the armour. It is simply that your father has not worn it since the day he killed your brother."

"Oh!" Flore said. "Oh, yes! Yes!"

Bonne said, "All the same, I am not so cross as I was."

The body on the table creaked and clinked onto its elbows, and from there ground its way up until it sat, propped on its hands. Down its face, which was made of red and white patches, the olive oil ran uselessly from the rim of the helmet it was meant to loosen. On that congested face the eyes were almost shut, but in the flashes of true blue could be glimpsed the comment of their wretched owner: woeful and unloved. He got his mailed legs off the table and stood solid, more or less, on the ground.

"I shall go to my desert," Caesar said. "The heat will draw this pot off my head." He lifted his arms a little from his sides. "Someone help me off with this gear. The heat will roast me in here like an ox in an oven."

"Wear it for penance!" Bonne said. "Roast for your sin!"

Flore gazed upon her mother with hatred, envy and yet more of that uncalled-for admiration. Bonne's beauty, at the moment when she issued this vengeful challenge to her husband, had plumped up in her as if she had been irradiated with ineffable grace. She now went so far as to lay down her darning on the table, and smiled kindly at that hopeless, hampered figure, which stumbled even as it did not move. When Caesar let his arms fall to his sides, she sighed with deep content and let her gilded eyelashes descend, skimming the sweet curl of her cheek.

"Yes," Caesar said. "I'll wear it." After a little silence, he spoke again. "I'll wear it for penance, since you put me to it, but in this heat, it may be my last!"

Bonne licked the next words off her tongue with a pellucid and exact diction. "We must hope not," she said. "There have been many before, and we must hope for many to follow." She picked up her darning and plied the needle. "Go fasting," she said, "and take no water. If a thing is worth doing, it's worth doing well."

Now with no more words Caesar set off up the yard towards his desert, crusted clumsily in armour, embarnacled by that old chain-mail in which Bonne's curse had rusted ever since he wore it last, the day he killed their son.

He went slowly and his course wandered, as if he were blind: as if it were dark and all the stars of navigation misted over. He stooped low, and you would have thought the steel pot jammed on his skull was hammering his bones into the earth, so far downwards had that tall figure shrunk. Bonne's needle flicked unfaltering among the sparse threads.

"Where's he off to?" Amanieu asked, and dumped two leather bags on the table. They struck the wood with a metallic thud.

"Aha!" Bonne said. "Now we shall see what a real soldier looks like!"

She pulled the edges of the napkin straight to keep the darn, with which she was prolonging the life of the napkin for at least a week, as even as possible.

Flore said to Amanieu, "He's going up to the desert. He says the heat will draw the helmet off."

To Amanieu this was senseless and he shrugged, but like all of them except Bonne, he watched Caesar make his crablike way up the yard into the heat of the day. The mailed feet dragged and turned up the dust, the limbs shambled, floppy and askew, only the head kept itself poised on top of that dishevelled hulk against the jarring of the helmet. At last Caesar vanished round the corner of the great keep.

At this moment Bonne burst into tears and began to toss into the air the pile of ancient linen that lay on the table, awaiting her ministrations. "Oh, see!" she cried. "See how hopeless it is! It is all rotted and worn to shreds!"

Everyone was startled, and stared at her.

"Well!" she wept, and tumbled the poor old cloth about as if it were dough, and she kneading it. "How can I show this to my great cousin Roger? How can I lay these old rags before the Viscount, our overlord?" She let the cloth be and sat with her fingers rubbing and smoothing the old elm-wood. The tears flowed from her eyes, and she sat there blubbering like a child of three.

No one had anything to say. Only the mastiff, and she had never been his friend, came running out of the house and put his black and tawny head on her lap.

"Oh, no!" she said, and bent to kiss him but afterwards pushed him off. "Oh, no! How can *you* help? What can *you* do?"

Bonne bent her head. The lovely face was puffy and the golden eyes blurred by tears, but though their look was cast upon the ground, it seemed to Flore that she gazed with longing up the yard to the distant slope beyond the keep, the way Caesar had gone.

# Chapter 22

# THE TROUBADOUR

MOSQUITO had been to the well inside the house, at his chore of drawing water for the horses, and now he appeared in the doorway. "Who'll have the nice little horse poor Jesus left behind him?" he asked.

"Do you want the horse, Mosquito?" Bonne said. She had begun to restore order to the jumble of lamentable linen. Flore helped her.

"Thanks," Mosquito said, "but the beast is too kindly for my taste. I like a horse with a bit of wicked in him, like my Poison."

"Poison!" Bonne said. "That scruffy skewbald!"

"Yes," Mosquito said.

Gully came out of the house and joined the other women at the linen. "Lord!" she said. "What a sad old state that's in! Still, if it's the best, we must make the best of it." Mosquito fetched benches from the house and Gully pulled one up to the table. She sat beside Bonne and now two needles were set to the work of restoration.

"Your mother sews a neat darn," Gully said. "You'll never come up to that."

"I daresay not," Flore said, and sat on the table and revolved, coming down on the other side. There, Amanieu had opened the bags, and drew out burnished steel. The armour had a mournful gleam on it, like a flat winter sea.

"What about the horse?" Mosquito said, and sat on the step. "Who'll have it?"

Flore said quickly, "I am the only one of us without a horse of my very own: well, except for Gully."

Gully said, "Don't mind me."

"Good God, Gully!" Flore said. "Cooks don't need horses."

"Don't be rude to Gully, Flore," Bonne said.

"Oh, come on, Mother! Gully hates horses. She screams if she's put on a horse. Can I have him?"

Bonne nodded, but while she was fitting thread between two teeth for biting, Amanieu opened his mouth.

"That creamy horse will suit you," he said. "It goes with your hair."

"Her hair!" Bonne said, biting like anything. "Flore's hair!" She threw her own tawny locks about so that they jounced and flowed with beauty. "What do you mean, it will go with her hair? That's the last thing Flore would wish for, to draw attention to her hair! Such a sad and nothing colour, I have always thought it."

Flore was so busy expressing silently to Amanieu her contempt for his intervention, that she evaded her mother's insult with ease, and picked out of it only what was useful to her case. "I don't care what I look like," she lied blithely, "so long as the horse is well-behaved."

She was bouncing up and down on her toes, willing her mother to agree, when another interruption took place. Vigorce, who since the mordant dialogue between Bonne and Caesar and the latter's unhappy departure, had stood almost like a statue—a statue chiselled to show a figure in a state of suspended animation, and brooding simultaneously over love, pity, loyalty and grief, and set in an attitude of worship harassed by doubt—Vigorce stepped from his plinth and said to Bonne, "Shall I not look after the lord Caesar?"

Bonne laughed. "My poor husband!" she said. "Even if his little grey brains are lying loose inside that helmet, we shall see no difference in him at all." She rested her sewing and preened her head; a brief display for Vigorce.

Flore saw that if she was to be sure of having the horse she must strike without delay, for her mother was ready to throw her beauty about, and once she had begun her daughter would be invisible to her. "Dearest Mother," she said, wooing shamelessly, "may I have the Spaniard's old jennet, to learn my riding on?" The horse was four years old if it was a day, and Flore could ride like an Arab.

"Of course, my child," Bonne said. "Are you backward at that too? Is it not too late for you to improve? Well, take the old horse and make what you can of it."

"Thank you, Mother," Flore said, and with great wisdom did not rush off to see her very own horse, but waited quiet till her mother had lost interest in the subject.

Bonne put herself, first of all, to beguiling Amanieu. She recalled through something of a haze that she had enslaved him at the feast, but saw now that she had been neglecting him since, quite carelessly. Bonne had always said, in the old days, that the way to a man's heart was through his armour. "That's fine gear you have there," she said. "Where is it made?"

"It is German," Amanieu said. "I killed a man for it."

Vigorce sat down, suddenly. Gully had gone back to the house, and came out with wine and bread, which she set on the table.

"A gallant deed, doubtless," Bonne said to Amanieu, remembering how bored she had been in the past, by gallant deeds being told her.

"No," Amanieu said. "A dirty trick."

Vigorce stared at him.

Bonne was deeply intrigued by Amanieu's words, and therefore ignored him at once. "My dear captain," she called down the table to Vigorce, "what do you think of that for a suit of armour? Flore, give the captain this cup of wine!"

Vigorce drank two cups of wine, more or less from Bonne's own hand, before he said anything. When he spoke his voice was deep and rich with respect for that supple steel laid out on the table. "It's the best I've seen," he said. He looked at Amanieu, almost with approval, and said, "I'd kill a man for that."

There were two ways to take this, and Amanieu noticed them both, but nodded pleasantly, and drank from the cup Flore had filled for him. "It is German," he said again. "I think it had hardly been made—two or three months—before I emptied it of its owner."

"My God!" Bonne said. "Young man, you speak bluntly."

"When it is convenient," Amanieu said, "I like to speak of things as they are. Is that bread?"

Flore got him some bread. "He only kills people on purpose," Flore said.

These words, which would have sounded oddly in other company, were easily understood to be a tribute. Everyone thought of Caesar, who had killed his son by mistake. Flore saw, however, that she had rashly exposed her friendship for Amanieu, and resolved to say no more.

Vigorce now remembered that Caesar was sweltering in his armour only because he, the hired captain, had promised his master it would bring about the departure of Amanieu. He set out, therefore, to move their plot forward. "Do you know," he said to Amanieu (and over his dark, Burgundian face came such a look of cunning that the young man glanced all around, and especially behind), "do you realise that in the north, you can make your fortune with armour like that?"

Amanieu asked him, "How?"

"In the joust. Jousting is all the rage up there. There is money in it; prizes. Winner takes the other man's horse and armour, just as you did this." Vigorce looked at the new steel shining before him. "On a good day a knight can overcome five or six others. That's more than you'll get by the roadside." Vigorce was chancing his arm there, but Amanieu just lifted his eyebrows and laughed. "Most of them buy their gear back, the same day. There is an Englishman made five hundred pounds at it last year."

"Five hundred pounds!" Bonne exclaimed. "Dear God! That would build our castle for us." She thought again. "And in one year!"

She regarded Amanieu in a measuring way, but then so did all the pairs of eyes round the table. Money like that was the money of kings and princes. The breakfast became silent, but for the sounds made by swallowing raw wine and chewing stale bread.

"I have not the build for it," Amanieu said, "and I am not a knight."

"You have the cunning," Vigorce said. "You have survived three years of war. If you wanted to win, you would win."

Bonne threw her darning aside. This was damned nearly exciting! "Caesar can knight you," she said. "He knighted men in the old days, when he was a great soldier, and he can knight you now."

Flore, however, did not want Amanieu knighted, and gone jousting in the north. "If you are knighted it will spoil you," she said. "Knights are virtuous."

Amanieu smiled at her. "That is a rumour," he said. "Knights are as much rogues as the rest of us."

Despite herself, Flore asked, "How is it done?"

"He spends tonight in the church," Bonne said immediately, "and tomorrow when Caesar comes down from the desert he'll gird that sword on him. Confound it!" she said. "It is absurd to have armour like that and not be a knight when you get the chance." She fixed her glaring eyes on him, and she was certainly a little tipsy. "Heaven, boy! Will you stop us all being rich? Caesar will make you a knight, but I shall draw up the financial arrangements: you will owe us something for it!"

"Then I must keep my armour bright," Amanieu said, and with Flore's help he returned the German chain-mail to its fine bags of leather. He had said neither yea nor nay, and more wine went down the throats of the breakfasters as they tried to figure out where they had got to.

Amanieu slung the bags on his shoulder. "Come and show me your horse," he said to Flore, "and I'll tell you what I think of him."

When they had gone, followed by the mastiff, a moderate perplexity settled on the breakfasters, the centre of their interest lost to them. They huddled round the table, for it was common ground, and palpable.

"Throw the mending to the other end of the table, Gully!" Bonne said, ebullient, defying she knew not what. "We're going to get drunk, and spill wine."

They should have moved to the shade, for it was noon and the sun was hot and bright over their heads. Slowly they grew stupid, and hardly spoke. They did not guzzle their wine, but drank steadily and with a kind of attention, and expectation, as if there were some hidden and serious thing to be found in the rough, pale red wine: that might be in the next mouthful, or might be still waiting on the tongue, from the last.

It was too much for Gully, who went underneath the table into the shade, and slept, snoring. They grew languorous in the beating heat, absorbing the warm wine. Bonne laughed now from time to time, though she said nothing, and tossed her head with a slow, sleepy motion and looked at Vigorce. The captain's heated face looked back at her. Mosquito looked at both of them, and would have preferred to be with the horses; but he wanted the wine, while it lasted. It was rare that a bird sang or an insect hummed, that noonday. It was hot and still silent. They were like three people caught in a painting, to be held there evermore.

Into the painting stepped a little donkey, that stood beside Vigorce and considered Bonne from intelligent eyes.

"Where have you come from?" she asked it. Before it answered, she saw a man behind it, sitting high up on a tall mule.

"In God's name," Bonne said. "Who are you?"

"I am Saturnin of Cucuron," the man said down to her, as if he spoke from the sky.

He wobbled in her vision as if he was being thrown from one of her eyes to the other, and back again. She fought this equivocation, and got him to be still. He was a thin, straight figure in sombre browns.

"Why are you so thin?" she asked.

"For gloom," he said. She thought he smiled, but her eyes were not clear.

"Come lower down," she said. "Who can see you up there?"

He came down from the mule and tied the reins to a ring in the wall of the house. "The creature runs away," he explained, standing now at the head of the table. He cut a bow to Bonne, sure of grace, and turned his head by way of salute to her drinking companions.

"Am I welcome?" he asked.

"For what?" Vigorce demanded, rising half-way to his feet, getting a knee onto the bench, jealous of all this confidence and style. He lurched and the donkey kept him from falling. He grabbed at the pack on its back for support, and elicited a musical sound.

The newcomer laughed and addressed himself still to Bonne. "For my music," he said. His voice had a warm but bitter tone that spoke deeply to Bonne. "For my verse," he said.

"Ah, Heaven!" Bonne said, and now she stood up. "You are a troubadour!"

"Yes, I am," he said.

"What happiness!" Bonne cried out, and threw her arms round his neck.

When she had welcomed him, she kicked Gully out from under the table and sent the poor biddy to her kitchen. "Meat for my guest, Gully!" she cried. "And better wine than this!"

"There is none," Gully said grimly. "More's the pity!" She put three fingers to her head and off she went.

"A better jug, then!" Bonne flung after her. "So there!" She filled her own cup with wine and gave it to the visitor. "You'll be thirsty," she said. "Drink from my cup!" She was full of mettle again, burning off the alcohol in her blood so that her face purified itself of drink before his eyes. "Am I beautiful?" she asked him. "No! Don't answer!" She turned to Vigorce, and saw that he was sat on his bench again, his elbows on the table, his face concealed, his thatch of black, greying hair clutched in his fingers.

At the door of the house, Mosquito was unpacking the donkey. He held a small harp, with care.

"Troubadour," Bonne said, and took him by the hand, "bring your wine, but come with me!"

She took him under the arch of the gatehouse, and some way along the hillside, until they were above the oak wood that dipped towards the distant plain: that plain which she loved to watch, dreaming herself there; the plain that shone in the sun and ran to the haze of the far mountains. He gazed out over all this and sighed.

"Why are you sighing?" she asked. "Is it not beautiful, does it not call you?"

"I hope it does not call me," he said. "I have just come from there. I told you—I am a melancholy man. That is why I sigh."

She looked into his face, and said, "Your eyes are different colours."

"One is grey," he said. "What's the other?"

His mouth was strained, perhaps with sorrows, but it was full enough to be kind. She ran her finger along it, while she considered the other eye. It was all colours, black, grey, brown, red, blue, green and yellow, confused into a dark and smoky gloom. "It is the colour of shadows," she said.

He was pleased. "Yes," he said. "That's good."

"Does it see?" she asked.

"Yes," he said. "It sees." The eyes were set far in, under black brows, and from their caves they smiled at her, seeing.

"I ask you again," she said, standing before him in her old green housekeeping frock, with the fresh afternoon breeze licking the coppery hair off her face, the golden eyes wary, but a little hopeful. "I ask you, do your eyes tell me if I'm lovely?"

His face was disconsolate, but she took in how handsome it was, with a straight nose and an intelligent brow, those deep-laid disconcerting eyes, and skin of a marvellous golden brown. Great God—the man himself was beautiful! And a troubadour to boot!

"More than my eyes," he said, "do tell me you are lovely."

A small sound escaped her, cawing in her throat between a sob and a cry of pleasure. "Then will you," she said, "will you," she repeated, and then with a rush, "will you make a song of me?"

"Yes," he said.

"Of *me*?"

"Yes," he drained his cup and looked forlorn.

"I mean, will you make a song of my beauty?" Surely there was great sadness written on his face, but his smile that came now, for being sad was all the sweeter.

"That is what I mean, too," he said.

"Oh!" she said. "Oh!"

"However—" he said.

"Yes!" she said.

"I must study your beauty, since it will not be enough simply to say it is incomparable: I must say what it *is*. Therefore I must learn it. You will have to sit for me, as for a painter. I shall have to stay here some considerable time." The grey eye met her eyes, but the shadowy one she could not find. "Also," he said crisply. "I must have my fee. Cash down, full payment on completion."

Bonne was radiant. She was a sunburst on the green hillside. She was joy incarnate. Her beauty excelled itself—she gave off beauty! The poet stared at her and light glowed inside the eye of shadows.

"I am fortunate to have come here," he said. "You may be the most beautiful woman in the world. Your beauty will bring an excellent song out of me. Each of us will be immortal. We must settle the fee accordingly."

Bonne was bathing in these pleasant words, and she closed her eyes for bliss. "I accept your conditions," she said happily. "You shall have my fine jewel for your fee—it is three stones set in ancient gold, and has magic. As for staying here, you may live in my house forever." She opened her eyes and the gold in them seemed fresh from the stream. "I will sit for you day and night, for you to know me and my beauty. Oh, I shall sit for you stark naked, if you will make a song of me!"

"That will be a start, certainly," the dismal troubadour replied. "You should, however, wear for the sittings your jewel of three stones set in ancient gold, and I shall have that and your beauty to tempt forth my best powers. There was some talk of food?"

# Chapter 23

# VENUS

EARLY that night the new moon rose low to hang suspended from a single star, and sank before midnight. The star was the planet Venus, which continued to rise.

Before the moon went down, Caesar was woken by the mastiff's tongue washing his face. When he cursed it, the resilient dog showed its delight by standing one foot unsteadily on his chest and the other on his nose. It slipped and with one of its floundering paws pushed the jammed helmet from his head.

"Aha!" Caesar crowed. "Ah, estimable beast; intelligent hound!" Then, "Get off, however! Good dog! Sit!" He sat up himself and put careful fingers to his bruised scalp.

"It is not happy," he told the interested mastiff, "but the night air will do it good." It felt as if his ears, which had been squeezed double under the helmet, had not sprung back into shape, but it was hard to tell by touch alone. "I shall not need my coat," he said to the dog, "for it will be warm out."

The truth is that Caesar had not spent the day roasting in red-hot armour after all, but lurked instead on the cool floor of the keep. He had made himself what comfort he could, pillowing his neck on the hauberk and the jacket, so that there was no pressure on the vexatious headpiece. The only penance he had so far undertaken of his promise, was to fast. "I am famished," he said, "But it will do my soul good. Come on, we're going for a walk." He pointed upstairs, where Vigorce and Mosquito slept. "Hush, or we will wake the garrison!" They set out.

Caesar took twelve steps and then stopped. "Well," he said, "it seems I must do it!" He went back to the keep. There he encased himself once more in his old armour, while the dog whined impatiently through its teeth. "Hush," he said. "Hang on, don't make such a fuss." It took time, while he fumbled for straps and strings in the dark, but he had been used to doing this once, long ago, and he was in no hurry. When it was done he said to the dog, "I think we may be excused the helmet," and off they went again.

As they walked up the empty meadow (for the goats went home at night) the horned moon kept them close company along the crest of the mountains. At the top of their climb the moon left them. It waited at the edge of the stone plain while they picked their way forward into the desert, striding upon solid rock, stepping precariously from stone to unsteady stone, and trudging through crunching shingle. The mastiff did not share Caesar's intellectual faith that there was knowledge in this place, and would have stopped long before he did. All the same, it came with him to the wild olive tree where the bee had stung his hand and there, after a standstill of some minutes and seeing itself forgotten, the dog lay down and slept.

The moon was not long in following the dog's example. Its pale and virginal crescent slid decorously to rest behind the hills. Venus burned brighter. Caesar felt, from within, the cares that marked his face: the kiss she laid on them. The stone world pressed up against his feet and from the high plain skimmed with starlight he rose into the black sky.

He felt the brain against his skull, the blood sliding in his flesh. He saw the light and the darkness touch his eye. He heard the sound of the mountains and the night as if they flowed like the running sea. He thought, therefore, of Lucretius and the theory of atoms, but still he rose to the goddess.

He was tongue-tied before her. He sought to describe himself. "I am iron from my ankles to my soul," he said.

He heard no answer. The goddess did not kiss him again, and shone no brighter for his being here. Was she displeased? Yet surely she had drawn him to her, for he could scarcely have achieved this ascent on his own!

Had he mistaken his goddess?

Was not Venus the divinity who, but three days ago, hailed him upwards to the rafters, from where he looked down upon himself and Bonne, and saw a man held in brightness mourn a woman swathed in dark?

Now, above the wild olive tree and the dreaming mastiff, he hung suddenly unsure, one pale scintilla among the scintillations of the sky. He had begun to doubt. His faith swerved and sought a home.

If it was not Venus who raised him to these heights of adoration then who could it be? Could it be? . . . It must be! Hastily he revised the description of himself that he had offered to Venus, for now he must address one who knew how to sorrow and who knew even what it was like to be human, bandied about between Heaven and Earth. He must present her with a telling image of himself, nothing half-baked or self-pitiful.

"Blessed Virgin!" he prayed. Forthwith the planet vanished in a cloud, and he began to descend. "On Earth," he said, rapidly introducing himself to the Virgin, "I carry an anvil and I walk on eggs."

This explanation of himself ended in a howl, and with Caesar falling into a complicated friendship with the wild olive tree. From there, gathering in the by-going some small and bitter fruit, he found his feet once more on the plateau of rock.

Caesar was querulous and cross. It had been a rotten day, starting with the upset on the stairs and ending with this spiritual come-down. It was peculiarly annoying that he could not make out which of the two sacred ladies he had offended. On the whole, he thought it must be Venus. He should have been more patient with her. Above all, he should not have said that other name—that other word—for if it *had* been Venus who summoned him to these elevations of his spirit, now after so pointed an apostasy, it would never be Venus again.

The mastiff woke from nightmares and snarled, so they set off together companionably morose, and falling over their feet a good deal: for the night was now pitch-black and every star in the Heaven blotted out.

## Chapter 24

# NAKED TRUTHS

IT was an hour since she had bared her body to the moon, and when that bright sickle left the sky Bonne, kneeling, stretched her hands through the window to caress the starlight. Her arms gleamed wanly in the dark but at the sweet, soft sheen on them her eyes wondered. She stood up and on the very window's edge to let the veil of pale brilliance fall round her out of the night. She felt the stars light on her. She moved in her body to watch them touch her. Under the moon she had sat as proud as marble, but now she sighed and shifted and stroked her shimmering skin, and from being enchanted by the starlight on her body, grew enamoured of her body, starlit.

She stepped down into the room, a whisper of light in the darkness. "This body of mine is a marvel," she said.

Saturnin, that troubled troubadour, spat grape-pips at her toes. He huddled the pillows more comfortably to him and stored handily within reach the fruit, the cheese and the wine. "So far as I can judge," he said, "in this truly sympathetic murk, it is a very adequate body."

Bonne was so excited by herself that she did not frown, even in the dark, but said, "I don't mean its beauty. I mean its life."

"You are beyond me," Saturnin said. "I am a poet, not a philosoper."

"Where are you?" she said. "Give me room."

"Along the wall," he said. "There is plenty of room."

She threw the marvellous body on the great bed and stretched from one end of herself to the other. Long-slept ligaments awoke, crackling and creaking.

"Dear God!" Saturnin said. "Do take care."

"That's what I'm talking about," Bonne said. She sat up. "Pass the grapes."

When he had done so, he ran the knuckle of his forefinger down her backbone. "Oho!" Bonne cried. "He exerts himself, at last."

"You are impatient?" the troubadour asked.

"I'm not sure that I am," she said.

She was sitting on her heels now, and he stroked her unseen bottom in the dark. "Well," he said, "there are rules to be followed."

"The rules of love are public," she said. "We are private." She lifted slightly on her knees to let his fingers beneath her, and poised there she swayed like a charmed snake.

"Poetic rules," he said. "I refer to poetic rules: as, the song of unrequited love must come before the passion is consummated, not after."

Bonne put away his hand, which had not in any case come as far forward as she would have liked, and got to her feet again. "Troubadours have licence, though," she said, puzzled rather than cross, "and ladies have licence with troubadours."

Saturnin laughed. "Only in public. Only in company. In private, they would be as much sinners in their coupling as any other couple in their sinning." There was a waiting silence, until in deeply enervated tones he added, "That is to say, almost any other couple."

"What does that mean?" Bonne said, back in the starlight, and then, "It doesn't matter just now. Don't tell me just now." She stroked her body with her eyes, and it shone back at her, tempting her: her own flesh. "Why my body is a marvel," she said, "is because it has a life of its own. My body is a creature on its own, and with a life of its own."

"That is an excellent thing to say. That might be a song."

"Aha!" Bonne said, unheeding. "It wants *me*, that's who my body wants. And I want it."

"Go on," the troubadour said, "Go on!"

"My body is beautiful and perfect," Bonne said, "except that this breast is bigger than the other—you need not put that in your song," she added, and squeezed the erring breast gently as a punishment, or to make it seem the same size as the other.

"Of course I shall," Saturnin said. "Don't be foolish, and don't interrupt yourself."

Bonne hardly heard or cared. She squeezed her breast again, and again, and on and on, until she drifted to her knees. The last words she spoke, before she was transported to speechless ecstasies upon the floor and in the black (now suddenly starless) night, were, "I have the spirit of a woman, but my body is my master!"

The troubadour beat upon the wall and hissed, "Are there some lucky days at last? Food, shelter and esteem from a mad patron who speaks *lines*, and gives me an IDEA!" He was so moved that he left out of this catalogue (though certainly he thought of it) the precious jewel which he had not yet seen. In that moment he was as close as hope had ever brought him, to being a troubadour in all his parts: forgotten the fatal flaw, the stultifying misfortune. "Perhaps I shall tell her," he muttered, as he noted down Bonne's lines that had so worked on him. "She is mad enough to understand." He lay on his back and looked at nothing.

For some time the room was peaceful. Outside the crickets ranted in the grass and two hunting owls called to each other. The night kept pitchy black. Out of it, at last, Bonne spoke.

"Do I inspire you as you had hoped?" she asked, uncertain and a little shy.

"Much more," he replied. "More than I had hoped."

"Truly? I will make a song?"

"Truly, by God!" Fervour rang convincingly in his voice. "Truly, you will make a song!"

"Oh, good!" she said. "Then we shall keep up our vigil, despite the dark."

He heard a yawn, and the sound of scrabbling and rummaging, and then her languid passage through the room. Soon a glow of light came in the door and with it Bonne, carrying a candle: Bonne unchastened by the withdrawal of moon and stars, Bonne candlelit and wearing her jewel.

"A wax candle!" he said. "And your jewel!" he added, coming to his feet.

"I have six candles," Bonne said. "If we burn them two at a time, they will last till morning."

"Three stones—just as you said—and set in gold," he responded.

"Where shall I sit," she asked, "for you to see me?"

"Three stones—and one a sapphire!" he replied.

"Now do stand away, Saturnin! Let me light the other one!"

"A true, dark sapphire!"

"Get off!"

"The yellow's a jacinth, but what's the green—what's the green?"

"Jabbering mountebank!" Bonne shouted. "Stop pawing me!" And she put the candle-flame to his beard.

There was more stink than fire. Though Saturnin yelped at the first shock he was more indignant than hurt, and not long after that, to Bonne's surprise, he was more apologetic than anything else.

"I got carried away!" he said, rubbing the charcoal out of his beard.

"Yes, indeed!" Bonne said, and since her candle had not gone out, she lit the other one from it, placed them on the floor of the window embrasure and sat on the stone bench opposite, so being underlit in the best tradition. She looked up at him, where he stood on the edge of her candlelight. "Yes, indeed!" she repeated. "You were grabbing and chattering like a monkey. Not like you at all."

"It is though," he said, and retreated into the darkest places of the room, rubbing as he did so not only his frizzled beard, but his whole face, and sighing several sorrowful sighs. He paced up and down in the shadows and at length came to a stand.

"You were pawing at me," Bonne said, "quite carried away, as you put it, but it was not lascivious, was it? Not at all lascivious?"

He leaned back further into shadow. "No. I was infatuated with the jewel, which was soon to be mine!"

"Which *is* soon to be yours! You have not cried off writing my song, just because I lost my temper?"

He leaned into the light. "No, no! I have never wanted anything more than to make a song of you."

Bonne basked in this affirmation, and in her candlelight. She looked out of the window into the night. Moths would be lured from that blackness to perish in these flames. Their immolation would be a tribute both to her beauty and the art that was to make it immortal. She regarded herself, dressed in this new and intimate illumination, and felt the renewed movement of those deep tides of feeling that earlier, under the stars, her own body had roused in her. She saw that in the rich light of the wax candles, she was more intensely desirable.

The man stood on the edge of her pool of light. "Are you lascivious now?" she asked him.

He shook his head.

"Not at me? Not at my fine body?" She stroked her thighs. "Look," she lifted her breasts on her hands. "It shows now in the candlelight, how I have rose-tipped my breasts. I do not make you lascivious?" She shook her head, asking.

He came down from his high, distressful mood to kneel at her feet. He put a hand on her right thigh, and the other under her hand that held the left breast. "You are lovely," he said. "Your body is lovely, and your rose-tipped breasts are, as an idea, intoxicating. My song shall make all of these, as well as your name and mine, immortal. Continue to believe that!"

"I will!" Bonne said, and all her surfaces quivered with passion. "I do!"

He took his hands from her thigh and breast, and stood up. "Your hair," he said, sifting it among his fingers as he stepped away, "is, for the time being at any rate, beyond words. Now I shall walk up and down, and tell you everything. I shall put food and wine beside you, eh?" He made loping strides back and forward across the room, full of briskness and decision. "There!"

"I shall eat with this hand," Bonne said. "Shall I continue to hold up my left tit?"

"What? Yes, by all means. Does it not tire your arm?"

"No, no. I have this little shelf my elbow rests on."

"Good, good."

"I am sitting for you, after all," she said earnestly. "I want to do it well."

"Yes, I know," he said curtly, "but I am trying to tell you something."

"I do realise that," Bonne said, "but I honour you for the person you have been since you arrived, and I want to do you what honour I can, no matter what you are about to say." She sipped at the cup of wine. "I must take care not to stir the lees of my drunken breakfast! Now I am all silence."

Saturnin had been scratching at his face and fretting with his foot. Now he set off, very fast, to say his piece. "It is the business of a troubadour to attach himself—his affections and his desire—to a lady: some lord's lady. And to sing songs complaining that she denies him the kindness of her body."

"The kindness of her body," Bonne repeated. "I should not like to have lived without hearing these melodious words." She brushed her own body with a kiss from her golden eyes, to remember its recent kindness to herself. She bit some grapes off the bunch and spoke with her mouth full. "All the same, it imposes a burden on the lady that her body must be kind. Kind? Kind? Why must her body be kind?"

"It's only a poeticism," Saturnin said tetchily. "I am simply describing the formula to which the troubadour is compelled to work, and which vexes me, I can tell you, a hundred times more than it may irritate you!" All at once his voice came from a wider throat, freed of secrecy. "What does it matter to me if all the women in the world are cruel, or chaste—word it how you like!—and what shall I care if all maidens live immaculate forever?"

"What shall you care?" Bonne was uneasy with this question, which sounded like a proclamation. A sense of paradox held her back from understanding what she heard. She went after it. "How can your songs complain of being denied your lady's body"—she made a fine, unconscious gesture on her own body as she spoke—"if you don't care whether she will give it to you or not?"

"That," he said, "is my predicament."

"Do talk straight," she said. "My brain is dizzy."

"Listen, then," Saturnin said. "I was born to write songs. I've sung my own songs since I was three. Therefore I was born to be a troubadour. But, I do not love women, and so I was *not* born to be a troubadour."

Bonne feared that her rare happiness in this day and its night was about to be injured. "What do you love?" she asked huffily. Then without a pause she understood him and said, "You love boys."

"Yes," he said. He had emerged from shadow and leaned on the angle of the wall opposite her. His face was in the light. Her foot could touch his. She looked at the ground beside him.

"You love little boys." She looked at the candle-flame near his hip.

"Grown boys," he said.

She looked at his ear. "Sodomy," she said.

He said nothing.

Her mouth shook, but she did not weep. "Damn you!" she said. "You have cheated me all this day and night. How can you swear to make a song of me—of this body? You will not know how! Damn you for a cheat and a liar!"

Still she sat on the stone bench. She felt foolish now, in her body planted picturesquely to glint and glow in the radiance of the fine wax candles. Yet there are two of us in this folly, she thought, and no one else to see us. Why should I feel foolish? She looked him in the face, and both the grey eye and the clouded one met hers.

"You have not been cheated yet," he said.

"Christ!" she said. "Be quiet, and go!" Yet she could not stop her voice, which rushed on. "How was I to know? You looked so handsome, such a woman's man!"

"What does it matter how I look?" Saturnin came off the wall. "What matters is how you look, and who you are, and how your body looks, and most of all, who your body is! From these questions I'll make your great song."

Bonne, for once, could not look at herself. She kept her eyes at his face with a fleering, falling glance. She had so ruinously collapsed, was so hollowed-out and fallen-in, that she felt as clearly as if she saw it from someone else's eyes, her face gone drooped and blubbering like a mournful child's. She had been given a dream at noon and lost it at midnight. If now, the moment after, she was being asked to dream again, she did not know how to believe or disbelieve. Nevertheless, she got her ears to listen. She heard her own voice, jeering. " 'Who my own body is.' What sense does that make?"

"It makes new sense," Saturnin rejoined, conceding little to her mental state. He spoke slowly, however, and pronounced with care, like one trying to share a thought with a pet animal, or a bird in a cage. "It makes new sense," he repeated. "It is a new idea, and it came from you."

She shook her head at this, but his insistent, careful voice went on. "You said your body was a marvel, because it had a life of its own. 'My body is a creature on its own,' you said, 'with a life of its own.' "

"Did I say that?"

"You said, 'my body wants me, that's who my body wants.' "

Her eyes stopped slipping about and fixed on the scorched patch in his beard. "Wait a moment," she said. When she had thought a little about her body wanting her, she furrowed her brow for him to continue.

His patient teaching style went suddenly out of the window. He cried out, "Don't you see? Dear Bonne—dear lady—I may write a song in which I say that you want me, but your body forbids it; or that I want you, but my body forbids it; or that your body wants me, but my body wants your soul!"

"My soul!" Bonne exclaimed, startled. "I should think my own body will want my soul."

"Yes, yes!" he said. "I mean, though, that this idea you have made that your body has a life of its own, is one of great originality, and that the songs we make of you and your body, will be unique, and new, and famous."

She had heard him. "You mean that you might write a song saying, it is not the lady herself who denies you, but the creature in her body?"

"Yes. That's it!"

"Or it might be—the song would say—the creature in your body that denies the lady to you?"

"You have grasped it perfectly," the poet said, "though I think the second one might be too sophisticated to begin with, until we have established the idea, and made a vogue of it."

"A vogue!" said a Bonne she remembered well. "Songs about the lady Bonne—a vogue!" She had a thought and caught her lip in her teeth. "Does this mean that though you love little boys—I should say, grown boys—the originality of my idea is so strong that you can write a great song, songs you now say, about me and the beauty of my body?"

He stood up, for he had bent himself flat from the waist in his need to persuade her. "Exactly," he said, and wiped the sweat off his face with a sleeve.

Bonne sighed and gave a little laugh. "What a strain it is," she said, "sitting for one's song. Is art always like this?"

"Don't speak of it," Saturnin said.

"I too am pouring with sweat," Bonne said. "I shall sit here and hope to grow cool, now that I am calm again." She giggled. "I was almighty cross when you kept trying to get your fingers on my jewel, instead of my painted bosom!"

"You must know," Saturnin said, "that I am deeply avaricious, and I covet your jewel." He cleared his throat, and moistened a suddenly dry tongue. "I shall not take your jewel," he croaked. "The idea you bring me is the only poetical idea I've ever had off women. It is possible you have broken my bad luck. Bed and board, maintenance for me and my beast, and some simple present when the songs are sung—that is all I ask."

Bonne could hardly believe her ears. "I love my jewel," she said, "which is also my talisman, so thank you." She shook her head in sympathy. "What a predicament you have—a sodomite troubadour. I should be happy to think I had been the means of revitalising your career. I take it to be a considerable compliment to me, that it should be so, and to my body."

He had been well brought up. "I do not deny it," he said.

"Dear Saturnin," she said. "Go and rest."

He retired to the bed in the shadows, and Bonne sat on into the night, more than ever underlit by the descended candles, while the sweat cooled refreshingly on her body.

# Chapter 25

# ILLUMINATIONS

CAESAR came lolloping through the night. He was quite done up from stumbling over the stone plain in the darkness. He had strained his ankles and knees in a hundred attempts to keep from falling, and he had fallen headlong a dozen times. Even on the meadow and the grassy hillside he had staggered from one pitfall to the next. The dog had long since deserted him, declining to be the companion of so much incompetence and misfortune. Caesar had never known a blacker night in his life: black enough to quench a man's soul in his body. It was blindness complete, until at a turn in the invisible landscape a yellow light appeared before him, calling him to the end of his calamitous journey.

Caesar longed for home. Dropped cold by Venus, that fickle goddess, and failing to rebound into the compassionate arms of the Blessed Virgin, he had lost the spirit for divine aspiration. The last of his courage had been pummelled out of him by the number of croppers he had come, and feet he had put wrong, on the benighted walk out of his mountain desert. Now, when he saw the cheerful portent ahead—that guiding light which defied so much actual and symbolic darkness—he sat down and wept. His tears were manly tears, his sobs were outright guffaws of relieved woe and no mere whimperings, and when he had wiped his eyes and finished snuffling and snorting, he set off again with something hopeful and expectant in his mood. His legs, too, though they shook from the fatigues and errors of the night's wanderings, from now on placed their feet with unfaltering steps, and soon began to stride along. It was as if the far-off light had a mysterious power to guide them, long before it lit their path.

During his passage to the yellow light Caesar knew he was being drawn out of the chasm of despair into which the night had led him. Caesar did not do well in the dark: heart and soul he thrived on brightness, and these parts of his nature pointed him towards illumination like the hidden forces in a lodestone. Even now he could feel the very fibres of his soul knit themselves together—so quickly had they begun to heal—and the strings of his heart tighten like a tuned harp.

By the time he came to stand in the glow of that beckoning light, he was ready to rise once more to his fate. Whatever divinity this might be ahead of him—whatever goddess shining late, late and lonely in the long-stretched night—he was ready to offer her, from that sublime state to which for this third and last time he would exhort his being, to offer her . . . to offer whatever it was the Divinities in the sky, above the olive tree on the stone plain, had rejected. He could not recall now what that was or whether, indeed, it had ever had a name: no matter—any goddess worth her salt would be able to read it in his face. He crossed, therefore, the pool of light, and looked in the window from which it poured.

Gods! It was his wife! It was the goddess, but it was Bonne! For the thirteenth time that night he thudded to the ground. He landed on his knees and his hands clutched the window-sill: he was like a man on a prie-dieu and began at once to worship. He did not pray, but adored, and his devotion was inarticulate but exact. His soul worshipped the lucent apparition, his heart loved the beauty of the shining form, and his body rejoiced for the friendship of that human flesh, with the jewel breathing on the sweaty bosom and the grubby feet lying between the guttering candles.

He did not know what he might not have done, had she not sworn him to wear his armour.

## Chapter 26

# PLIGHTED

A MANIEU had dreamt himself into an irritating version of the Moslem paradise. A houri there was, certainly, but she was far off at her own end of the garden, playing like a water nymph on the edge of the river. For much of the time she was dressed down to her ankles in weeping willow, or up to her neck in laughing water, and the shifting glimpses of her—the voluptuous hints—that came Amanieu's way were themselves half-hidden by such interventions as the spray from fountains, high-grown rose bushes, a restless jacaranda tree and flocks of bright birds painting their colours on the air.

He could not call to her over the noise made by the river, and he could not go to her until he had identified the owner of the voice that spoke in his ear. It grew cold and a strong wind threw everything about. The doors of the garden flew back and forward on their hinges, slamming with a rickety sound. The girl was gone. Paradise was not what it had been.

The voice said, "My talisman; my talisman!"

Amanieu opened his eyes. He was shivering on the stone floor of the church. The first object to hold his sight was the plain cross of hollywood hung from the neck of the priest, whose scarlet and excited countenance hung close above his own. The priest jumped away and pointed the finger of denunciation.

"Anathema; anathema!" he cried. "Servant of Satan! You flew through the walls of my church."

Amanieu found that he had been sleeping on his sword as well as on the floor, and he sat up from these discomforts slowly. "Shut up, you fool!" he said to the priest. "I came in the door like anyone else."

"Demon!" the priest cried. "God does not let me be deceived by your cunning lies. The door was locked against you."

Amanieu rose to his feet, using for a prop his scabbarded sword, that symbol of good common sense. The priest jumped back again. "Listen, man!" Amanieu said. "The key was on the outside. I unlocked the door and came in for my vigil. I'm to be knighted today."

"Desperate imp, you lie!" the priest shouted. "Out of your own mouth you are condemned! God locked the door against you, and when He had locked it He left the key on the inside. You could not have come through the door—even I had to break it open to get in."

Three infants scampered in at the broken door and stood making large eyes at the grown-ups. Amanieu addressed himself to them, so keeping his voice and his language calm, and also with better hope of being understood.

"When I came to the church it was locked with the key on the outside. I unlocked it and brought the key in with me, and locked it on the inside." He smiled nicely at his little audience, one of whom had begun to nod as he spoke.

As soon as Amanieu finished the priest let go an ear-splitting screech. Two of the babes leapt into the air and the third clipped her eyes shut and stood petrified. One of the leapers came down running and left the church, but the other tripped and fell.

"Hear him!" The priest yelled exultantly. "Now he says he is God! He says _he_ locked the door! But we know—don't we?—that God locked the door."

The fallen child scrambled to his feet and taking the shut-eyed one by the shoulders, gallantly led her from this raging monster's cave. Amanieu started down the aisle.

"Blasphemer!" the priest said, in a voice that all his shouting had scraped to a husk. "Adulterer!"

Amanieu came back again. "Adulterer? Why do you say that?"

"The lady Bonne lusts after you. Deny it!"

"She lusts after something," Amanieu said. "Who knows what it is?" He considered the passion-scorched creature before him, the thick neck and fleshy face on the gaunt body, the round brown eyes and fat mouth with the thin sharp nose between. "You let yourself go, don't you? If you denounced a man like that in some town square, he'd be racked and burnt before you got your voice back."

"Do you think so?" The man was pleased, and smirked with gratification while he knelt to pray. He looked much healthier, as if he had been costive and purged himself with agaric.

\*       \*       \*

When Amanieu reached the bridge Flore was there waiting for him, seated on the parapet in the morning sun. "I dreamed of you," he said, "but I had a rude awakening." He told her about the priest, hoping to make her laugh, for she was a little pale.

She did laugh, too, though with a dry note. She stood up. "Come on," she said. "You've told the priest you're being knighted today and he'll tell the village. They'll come up to see the fun."

"Fun?" he said. "It'll be over in two minutes."

"Well!" Flore exclaimed, and the blood rushed into her face. "That will be a treat all the same. It makes a change for anything to happen here; it makes a difference. No one hopes for much, you know, but it can be cheerful for something to happen."

"Surely," he said, baffled but consoling. "Surely."

The tears streamed down her face. "Surely surely!" she said. "What will I do forever, when you are knighted and gone away?"

He pulled her off the track and down the slope until they were hidden in the trees. He kissed her eyes and face, ears and neck. She hung in his arms like the victim of an evil: held as if lifeless by a saint and waiting for him to administer the miracle.

"I did not know you were mine," he said. "I'm not the image of a girl's delight. I thought I'd have to win you, by fair means or foul."

"Foul means took you part of the way," she said. "The rest I did myself. We have met on the road." She stood free and faced him. "The Amanieu I met before"—she passed a hand over the few days since his coming—"told me you were on the way. Now you've arrived. I see you in your face."

"That's not to my advantage," he said.

"It is with me," she said. "You show your true self. You do not pretend to be who you are. This is your advantage, to me."

She put up her face and drew his mouth onto hers. Her kissing plunged into him and sucked them together. They swam in each other until they became the torrent. They shook: Flore slipped to the ground and Amanieu stood still. Her face was stricken and she cried out, "Dear God! I thought you would go jousting in the north."

The sorrow of that was still in her and she wept again with her eyes fast on him, flicking her head to clear off the tears. The oak wood rustled and creaked in the breeze, sunbeams and blue sky shone down and birdsong fell from the leaves. Despite all this, and the happiness the two of them were making, there was a darkness in the wood.

"Too much happiness," Amanieu said aloud. He had just shared his first confidence, and Flore beamed at him through her tears and bawled louder than before.

When she had quieted he stroked her hair and said, "I shall not leave you. It's a useful thing to be a knight, but I'm not going north, when it's done, to make a living with broken bones. That's what *they* think. Your mother's daft, and thinks I'll do it to grow rich and pour tribute in her lap. Caesar and that captain of his want me out of the way when the Viscount gets here with the German in tow, whose brother I killed. They know Roger won't think much of the place, and if he finds it harbouring bandits and murderers—I mean me—he'll think even less."

Flore heard the last words twice as loud as the others. "Roger will hang you," she said wildly. "You must go north, you will have to go north to hide. Let me come!"

"Listen to me!"

"Yes, Amanieu." Two tears stood ready in her eyes.

Amanieu tossed an acorn in his hand. "I'm going to play a kind of joke. It will begin with the knighting and if I'm lucky, it will put paid to the German and save my neck from Roger's rope. Dry those tears," he said, suddenly indignant, "and make no more of them."

Flore wiped her arm across her eyes.

"Now!" he said. "When I've been knighted, I'll set off as they expect—but I'll be back tonight. Look for me tonight!"

She watched him talk. She watched his clever head with its black bristle sheared close to the scalp: the black eyes that shone far into their depths because—and she knew it for the cause—he was telling her about himself. She watched his strange mouth. She watched the movement of his lank body with its overlong arms, that indefinably squint and even misshapen body which she loved for what it had said to her already, and considered askance for what it promised.

"We must go," Amanieu said, and his eyes stared as if only their look, fixed on her, kept her held to the earth. "There is no time for us now," he said. "There will be time for us later."

"So there will be," Flore said. From her dark, dark chestnut eyes he felt this new, impassioned need of his, wielded and returned. "Besides, you will do me more honour when you have been made a knight."

# Chapter 27

## ACCOLADE

"HERE they are at last," Bonne said. "Why is he not wearing his armour?"

"Because it's packed and in his luggage, for one thing," Caesar said crossly. He had woken an hour ago to find himself on the hillside, and he had been in the very moment of calling to mind a remarkable dream—it had been on the tip of his tongue: a vision, a revelation!—when the fool Vigorce thundered up shouting that it was time to make ready.

"I don't know why you're wearing yours," Bonne said.

"My what?" Caesar asked, still hankering after his vanished dream.

"Your armour."

"I fell asleep in it," Caesar said. It sounded absurd. "I've not had time to take it off since the captain hounded me out of my dreams. I can't take it off now, I should look ridiculous in front of the priest and the people."

Bonne gave half an eye to the priest and the people. She would not have felt ridiculous if every one of them had spent that night peering at her through the window. Someone had, she knew that. The curious thing was that she had known who it was at the time, but could not now put a face to her rapt admirer.

Suddenly she said to Caesar, "I am having a song made of me. There is a troubadour here who says I shall inspire such poetry in him, that I shall be famous."

From somewhere, Caesar said, "I can well believe it. I'd like to meet a troubadour. Cheerful chaps as a rule."

"Not this one," Bonne said.

"Sleeping still, I expect," Caesar said. "Lucky man."

Vigorce, who from his position of hopeless devotion to Bonne found such affable conversations between the alienated pair deeply confusing, now dropped the gold spurs that would enhance the heels of the new knight. He managed to keep hold of the lance and the shield.

Bonne bent down to pick up the spurs. "These will be worth something," she said.

Caesar first smiled and then laughed, with an amusement that perhaps only one of them there had heard before. Bonne looked at him in surprise.

Caesar frowned, as if he had disconcerted himself, and waved a beckoning arm. "Come on, you two!" he called over the heads of the little crowd. "We're all waiting for you."

Bonne knocked the gold spurs together to see how they sounded. "It's taken her long enough to fetch him," she said. "They shouldn't be coming up among all that rabble. The child has no sense of style."

For the most part it was the adult serfs who had arrived with the priest, and the children who were now crowding through the gateway with Flore and Amanieu. They were an excited and unruly little gang, and when they came on the scene the priest scowled and raised a maledictory hand, telling them to be quiet.

"Now, now, Father!" Caesar said. "We're all here to enjoy ourselves, I'm sure. Will you say a prayer?"

"No," the priest said. "There will be no prayer for this wicked man's knighting."

"That would be a shame," said the musical and sonorous voice of Saturnin. "I know a prayer for knighting. A poet may recite a prayer as audibly to God's ears as a priest."

Caesar turned to this gratifying arrival. "Now that is good news. You are Bonne's troubadour, I take it. I trust you slept well. Come up here, Amanieu, we must get on."

"God is not mocked!" the priest exclaimed, in a kind of half shout.

"You may not be the best witness to *that* proposition," Saturnin said, almost cheerfully. "Pass the sword," he added. Amanieu gave it to him.

The children quieted down, their elders perked up, the priest sulked. Flore went to stand beside her mother as a good girl should, and just when Amanieu took his place between Caesar and the troubadour, Mosquito led up the Mecklenburg charger and the packhorse, saddled-up and ready for the road.

Saturnin took Amanieu's naked sword by the blade and held it up to the sky, so that God could see it better. The sun struck lights off it onto the faces of the peasantry, who were agreeably affected by sharing, in this way, the great event. The priest shut his eyes and retreated into his spirit. Swallows cut through the air above the sword and the larks began their day's singing. Gully came out of the house. Near her the last of the marigolds smiled at the bright blue, but now thin and autumnal, sky. Bonne's coppery hair lavished itself on the light west wind, but Flore's creamy mane lay still upon her shoulders, heavy with peace. The black mastiff gambolled up to Amanieu and woofed, and sat down whining. The Mecklenburger, who had seen fancier knightings than this, stamped and shook the ground.

Mosquito said to it, "That's the boy!"

The troubadour declaimed by rote and at speed. "O Lord, deign to bless with the right hand of Thy majesty this sword with which this Thy servant desires to be girded, that it may be a defence of churches, widows, orphans and all Thy servants against the scourge of the pagans, that it may be the terror and dread of other evil-doers, and that it may be just both in attack and defence."

Amanieu knelt down. Caesar took the sword from Saturnin and slapped the flat of it on the bare neck bowed before him. "Put on this sword!" he said.

Amanieu stood up again and Caesar shoved the sword into the scabbard at the new knight's side.

"What's next?" Caesar asked. "I've forgotten."

Vigorce, who had been propping up twelve feet of oaken lance (not to mention the shield) for half an hour or more, said, "The spear should be blessed, and the shield and spurs."

He looked at the priest, who had opened his eyes again to see the ceremony enacted.

Bonne said, "You don't bless the spurs, I'm sure."

The priest said, "I'm not blessing any of it. I'll have nothing to do with it."

Flore, not quite snatching, took the spurs from her mother's hands and bent to strap them on Amanieu's feet. He patted the top of her head clumsily, like an uncle.

Bonne saw that this awkward gesture marked a private bond between the two of them, and easily understood that Amanieu had been coaxed to befriend the lonely girl in her quaint world of child's play and make-believe. Now, of course, by grabbing the gold spurs out of her mother's hand and putting them on the new knight's heels—usurping, with her baby fingers, the true woman's place— Flore had brought her sad little dream-world into the real world of grown-ups. It was too embarrassing! Plainly the young knight found it so, for his sallow skin had gone the jaundiced hue it turned in place of blushing. Even Flore was quite pink, silly child.

"Really Flore!" Bonne said, and saved the situation. She drew from her bosom a square of Chinese silk, left over from the making of the yellow dress, and which she had always regarded as a kerchief too elegant to use. She stepped smartly forward and tied her bright favour round his neck. "Wear this for me, sir!" she said, gazing at him with virtuosic alterations of eye and flickerings of eyelash.

Amanieu, with the daughter at his feet and the mother, so to speak, at his throat, addressed himself to the men. "Is there more?"

Caesar said, "I remember, you should be presented with lance and shield."

"What do I do?" Vigorce asked.

"Just give them to him," Caesar said.

Vigorce went up to the new knight, and the women drew aside. "Here you are," he said.

"Thanks," Amanieu said, and took the lance and the shield.

"They have still not been blessed," the priest said snippily.

"The lad I took them from was a knight, before I killed him," Amanieu said. "They'll have been blessed for him, if it needed doing. No one had blessed the knife I killed him with, that I know of."

He joined Mosquito and they set about tying the lance onto the rest of the baggage. The swifts and swallows were low overhead. The day had grown cloudy.

"It's raining," Vigorce said.

"Come," Caesar said, and offered his arm, stately, to Bonne. "You will be soaked. My armour will rust. We shall go in."

"Come, Saturnin," Bonne said, and the three of them went through the first rain of autumn, which was not heavy, towards the house.

The peasants, led by the priest, now began to drift away, but some of the children stayed to see the end, and drew closer to the horses. Vigorce rubbed noses with the warhorse, which bared its teeth to him as a mark of affection. "I've grown fond of this one," he said. "I'll be sorry to see him go."

Amanieu laughed at him. "Thanks," he said.

"No offence," Vigorce said. "It's been a hot summer," he added lamely, as if apologising for something, or someone. "I wish you joy of the horse."

Mosquito cleared his throat and patted the charger's neck. "I'm going with him," he said to Vigorce.

"With him?" Vigorce said.

"Yes," Mosquito said. "A knight needs looking after."

"I will be alone?" Vigorce asked himself.

While he spoke the four words unhappiness entered his voice as sudden and complete as the clouds that had covered the sun. "Och!" he said, and put a hand over his eyes and walked slowly away. The dog whined, not wanting to leave the party, but true to its nature it went off to console the bereaved captain.

"I'll come with you as far as the bridge," Flore said to Amanieu.

Outside the gateway they were brought to a standstill. Their advance guard of children ran into the flock of goats on their way up the hill, like a river meeting the incoming tide, and the two herds of small creatures eddied and turned. Flore gripped Amanieu by the hand when she saw the blind woman standing to one side, waiting for the confusion to repair itself.

"She's wearing Father's hat again," she said. "I wonder how she gets it. Perhaps Gully gives it to her, or my mother."

When the goats and children had sorted themselves out and resumed their two separate ways, Amanieu greeted the blind woman.

"You will walk in death's shadow," she said, "before three days are out, but help will come from above." She lifted her blind eyes to the overcast sky, and laughed with dry but well satisfied humour at what she saw there.

"You may be right," Amanieu answered her.

She followed after her goats.

The knight and his escort went down to the bridge. Mosquito and his skewbald pony, with the packhorse in tow, shepherded the children over the bridge while Flore and Amanieu made their farewell.

"Until tonight!" Flore said. "Until tonight?"

"Before the moon goes down," Amanieu said.

She believed him, but she wept to see him ride away.

## Chapter 28

# THE POET'S SUNSET

THE rain had stopped at noon. Afterwards the sky that had been stainless blue throughout the summer was fleeced with high white clouds moving slowly, all day long, towards the east. The freshened air poured an elixir of well-being into the lungs which only the most morbid spirit could resist. Caesar, though playing the polite host to just such a spirit, felt exhilaration bubbling in his blood.

"My word!" he said, stepping out on limbs no longer restrained by yesterday's chain-mail. "The air is as fresh as . . . as fresh as . . . ." He looked with an expectant eye at his companion, gracefully offering him this plum chance to express his poetic gift. "What would you say the air is fresh as?"

"The air?" Saturnin said. "Yes, fresh as anything." He sniffed. "That's because of the rain."

"No, no!" Caesar said. "I meant, is it as fresh as spring water, or as fresh as a child's laugh? That sort of thing."

Saturnin listened gravely to Caesar's problem, but did not seem to understand what he was getting at. "That's up to you," he said passively.

Caesar was walking his guest—Bonne's guest—up and down the yard after dinner. He did not take to the man. Since his first impression of Saturnin at the knighting ceremony, it had been all downhill. The poet's melancholy presence took up too much room. He was assiduously morose, as if to be so were a part of his stock-in-trade, and Caesar found the man's infusion of gloom into the air of his home, an affront.

Also, it was ill-timed.

It was not only the rain-refreshed air that had given new buoyancy to Caesar's mood. An instinct was growing in him, as clear as a voice, which said that the miasma between himself and Bonne—the blinding and poisonous fog that afflicted them like witchcraft—was beginning to melt and thin away. This mysterious hope had risen in him during the course of the day, a hope of happiness that had unbruised his bones, quickened his heart and brightened the seeing of his eye.

On one thing Caesar was utterly resolved: if he and Bonne were destined to emerge at last from the wild and stormy sea through which their life had battled for so many years, then he would not allow this self-indulgent pessimist to make a wreckage of their landfall. He would not let him stay here, for his insistent melancholy to keep alive in Bonne a habit of past sorrow: a habit that, left to itself, was ready to fly into history. One way or the other, the man must be removed.

Accordingly, Caesar went out on reconnaissance. "I expect," he said to the troubadour, "that you will depart with Viscount Roger's court, when he leaves us after this visit of his. How long will you take to write the song that makes my wife famous?"

Saturnin lengthened his face. "I have no truck with courts. Viscounts have no importance in my scheme of things. No, I shall not be tempted to serve Roger, and it will certainly take me months, many months, to write the number of songs that are to be made of your lady."

"How many months?"

"Well, really it is not possible to say."

"I see."

Almost, Caesar wished that he had not engineered Amanieu's departure. That young man would have made short work of this fellow. They had come to the foot of the keep, and stopped there. They looked up the face of the wall. Vigorce appeared at the top and leaned over the rampart to favour them with a dejected salute of both hands, like a sovereign with no largesse to offer his loyal subjects. Caesar waved back at the captain.

"Poor Vigorce," he said. "Nothing goes right with him."

He saw that Saturnin had turned pale and was shuddering, with his eyes fixed on the man on the roof.

"What's up?" he asked. "Not feel well?"

"I can't stand heights," the troubadour said.

"But you're on the ground," Caesar said.

"It makes no difference which end of it I'm at, if I see a man standing like that there."

He went on shivering and Caesar turned him round forcibly by the shoulders. "Off we go!" he said, and pushed Saturnin on his way down the yard again. "Get away from the place, that's the thing. You've got your troubles, I must say. Mind your feet!"

The troubadour took a grip on himself and his feet walked without stumbling back to the house. There Bonne sat by the door, mending her little store of linen in the last of the daylight.

"Don't tire your eyes," Caesar said.

The needle hovered erratically in the air for a moment, as if it were suddenly bewildered. Bonne looked up at Caesar. "I'll finish this one," she said, "and stop."

"I'll fetch some wine for our poet," Caesar said. "He had a fit of vertigo just now, seeing Vigorce on top of the tower. Sit beside Bonne; plenty of room on her bench."

"Vertigo!" Bonne exclaimed. "On the ground?"

"Ah!" Caesar said airily. "It's all one and the same thing, whether you're up there looking down, or down here looking up there."

Saturnin sat beside Bonne on the bench. "What are you doing?" he asked, peering incredulously at her working fingers.

"I'm mending the household linen," Bonne said, "what we have of it. Darning dead napkins back to life, that's what it comes to."

Caesar came out swigging wine from a mug. "Excellent needle-woman," he said. "That'll make Roger sit up. Here!" and he handed the mug to Saturnin. "Drink this, it might stop you shaking."

"Thanks," the poet said mournfully, and took the wine at a swallow.

Caesar stood with his hands on his hips and looked about him. "It's a beautiful sky, tonight. What colours! There's Flore on the gate-tower, making the most of it."

Saturnin said, "Can you take up tapestry instead? Mending old linen has a hopelessly domestic flavour. I could never write a song about you while you do that sort of thing."

"Fiddlesticks!" Bonne said. "I'm surprised, after that sitting I gave you, that you haven't written a song of me already. I'll expect you to sing one before Roger's visit ends. He's very likely to be here to-morrow. You should go to bed early and get up early in the morning, and start work on it."

It was borne in on Saturnin that the world of the day before had vanished. This was not the woman, despairing drunk, that he had met yesterday noon: nor the other woman he had watched at mid-night, eager to show her self-love to his objective gaze. This woman now beside him had laid aside her need of the unknowing stranger, the ephemeral alien, the talking mask of Apollo.

She had let the forces of her nature shift, during the day, and there was every sign that this was part of a larger upheaval in the deep shelves of rock which had been fired and fixed, long back, when the world was made between Bonne and Caesar.

Saturnin had lost, in this bilateral earthquake, his essential status of the reflective voice and the third eye.

Bonne would not want mirrors now, to know herself seen.

Saturnin felt the wine in his stomach turn sour, and tasted black bile on his tongue. He had come to the right place, but at the wrong time. He made a moan—a sigh that had been too heavy to fly. Where would he spend Christmas this cold winter? He put a check on himself. He must take care not to turn misfortune into disaster; and perhaps all was not lost. One thing at a time! He asked, "Where shall I sleep tonight?"

"In the gatehouse," Caesar said, "where the lad was. A tall room with a bit of bed in it."

"I've slept on it, when you had your nightmares," Bonne said. "It's very comfortable."

"The gatehouse it is, then," Caesar said in an encouraging way.

"Come inside, however," Bonne said. "It is not bedtime yet, not even *early* bedtime." This misplaced kindness irritated all three of them, since each of them wanted Saturnin to be alone.

"I will, then, just for a little," the troubadour said.

"Get out your fiddle," Caesar said, in the hope of easing the impending hour. "Sing us a song."

"I couldn't; not tonight."

Bonne gathered up her mending, with Caesar's help. Saturnin could not bear to touch it, so he carried the bench. The three of them went into the house, leaving behind them the purpling dusk.

# Chapter 29

# STORM

WHEN the sun set behind the mountains Flore said aloud, "He will come, he will come." Into herself she said, "But it is growing late." She stood firm on her heels with her arms on the parapet and stared at the farthest corner of the road. The clouds that rolled endlessly towards her still wore the colours of the fallen sun, though the crimson waned to pink and the purple sank to violet as night advanced its shadow. When there was no more road to see, when even the bridge was taken from her sight by the dark, she waited for the moon.

The clouds, now without light or colour, stooped low above Flore's head. The wind, that had been steady and continuous while she waited through the evening, hurled itself at her in gusts, fell off in flurries and rushed back at her through the air. She moved nearer to the shelter of the wall, and held her hair close about her neck. As if the wind had been let loose to run wild by the coming of night, its violence grew while the darkness thickened. Flore put herself into the corner that took the brunt of the wind and hunched down. There, huddled inside the familiar comfort of her hair, she began again to wait.

Walled-in on two sides by stone and on the third by night, and lurking under the roof thrown over her by the gale, there came a time when she felt herself as much shielded by, as shielded from, the storm. Therefore she stared into the dark. What enemy was there, watching to catch her unguarded? She shut her eyes and tightened her mind: but, sure enough, the black mood with which she had started the day crept home to spoil her happiness.

This was the sorrow that had said, even before she got out of bed to walk into her momentous day, that during it Amanieu would leave forever. Now it said to her: Your day has reached its other night, and though you have shared promises with him since I woke you so early, he has gone away and not come back.

To drive these words from her Flore stood up into the howling storm. This had reached such a pitch that it nearly tossed her down again onto the roof. She stretched her arms across the wall to clutch its far edge, and hung on for dear life, for dear Amanieu, for dear everything. The wind poured over her head like the sea. It filled her ears and scoured her face, it took the breath from her mouth and forced tears from her eyes. The long hair streamed out behind her, lashed at her face and blew off again. The gale rushed out of the empty air before her and flew upon the crags behind, where it shrieked and whistled its way up and over the mountains.

The girl shouted and sang, and cried and laughed, and panted and sometimes, when the wind in all its strength blew right through her, she shuddered. She yelled his name, and both their names: Flore and Amanieu, she yelled, and the wind took the words to fly off with it in the black sky.

The wind grew wilder yet, and so did Flore. She left the shelter of the parapet and gave herself to the madness of the gale, for Amanieu had not come and might not come, and madness would be better than that. She rose in the ascending riot of the storm to ecstasies of fear and hope, of loss and gain. The fury of the night came into her. She danced and stamped and shouted. She danced long after she was exhausted, but still she was whole, still she was Flore and remembered the brightness of her day, and the darkness now.

A creature with a wolf's head came out of the night and tore her from the grasp of the storm. He was stronger than tempests and more terrible than demons. He gripped her with claws of iron until the bones crackled in her arms.

"Sweet Christ!" she said.

The creature laughed. "Not I!" The voice was a bark.

The moon broke through the flying clouds to show the dreadful face. It was a mixture of man and beast, with the wolf's head on top of a human mask. From wide-spaced teeth it slobbered over her. From eyes as black as pitch, with red sparks flying about in them like spyholes in hell, it looked deep into her. Its lips writhed like elvers, and said, "Flore!"

"Amanieu!" she shouted.

He wrapped her in his wolfskin cloak. He filled her face with kisses. He carried her through the storm as if it were a beaten army in flight and he the conqueror, and rode downhill, deep into the oak wood of the morning.

When he lifted her to the ground she was still leaping with the fear and madness of the storm. He folded the wolfskin twice over and made her lie on top of it.

"There is none to cover me," she said.

He slapped the horse to send it thumping off into the dark wood. "I will cover you," he said.

"You will love me," she said.

She sat up and pulled her frock off over her head. He knelt beside her and held close her two hands. Here, in the bottom of the wood, wind and moon hardly touched their pale and questing bodies. Only, leaves and twigs and acorns pelted down about them, and above the trees the storm howled.

"Mary defend me!" Flore said.

Amanieu said, "I am raging. I must."

"I know," Flore said. "It scorches me, but—" Then she said, "I am not a child."

She screamed, for Amanieu broke into her as if she were his victim in a sacked town. Her screams rode on his shouts of exultation into the treetops. Flore screamed on and on, for Amanieu went on and on, as brutal as a warrior on the battlefield, and gave her nothing but pain.

When this rape, which was what it amounted to, was over, he sat beside her while the moans, that had replaced the screams, fell away to whimpers, and stroked her hair.

"I wish I could spit you out again!" Flore said.

Amanieu patted her head, as if she were a bitch.

Flore had stopped whimpering, and now wept for bitterness and pain. "Oh, you have hurt me!" she said. "Oh, I am sore! You are cruel and vicious. I should have remembered." She wept again. "That was rape," she said.

"That's what it came to," he said.

After a while Flore sat up. "Oh, my wounds, my blood!" she said, and wrapped the wolfskin round her shoulders. She watched the blur of movement in the darkness that was Amanieu putting on his clothes. "Do you know what you made me think of, while I screamed?"

"No," he said.

"My father, berserk and killing his own son," Flore said.

"There is something in that," he said.

"Amanieu," she said, "I am sore, sore!"

"There is nothing to do," he said, "but wait."

The noise of the storm had fallen, and bits of oak trees had almost stopped pattering down about the two lovers. Through the leaves Flore saw the moon, and in the moonlight she saw Amanieu. He looked fine-drawn but full of well-being, serious but without care.

"Amanieu," she said, "are you always cruel, making love?"

He said, "I have no reason not to be."

"My God!" she said. "That it hurts, is that not a reason?"

"It doesn't hurt me," he said. "It won't always hurt you. Most of that is because you were a virgin, and are so young."

A silence lay on this remark, which Flore lifted from it with a laugh and a sigh. "Does that mean, that *you* would not always hurt me?"

"That's what I'm saying," he answered.

Flore tried to discover, by listening again to this last part of their talk, what the future might be. She did not quite like the answer she found.

"I will wash myself in the river," she said.

She walked naked through the trees towards the river, with slow and careful steps. After a moment's thought, Amanieu gathered up her clothes and followed. He found her up to her waist in the stream, looking at a clear and starlit sky and the bright streak of moon. She had not taken in that he was there. Her eyes were great with fear and she stood stark, like a rabbit facing a weasel.

What inevitable death had he shown her? Death of childhood, of innocence? Something moved in Amanieu near the heart, and he received an intuition of her: she had hoped for happiness, and thought she had met sorrow; she had turned away from childhood, and now saw nowhere else to turn to at all.

"You will catch cold," he said, for the wind still blew a little, and she was shivering out on the water.

She moved her head round and he took the force of her eyes. He was the weasel in this tale, he knew, and felt it in himself under that gaze. Equally, however, he was the place where she must turn, not only because she had nowhere else, but because he wanted her.

"Flore," he said again. "You will catch cold."

She did not squeal and topple over, but came to life. "There you are!" she said.

"How is it?" he asked her.

"Not so sore," she said. "It's probably stunned. The water's chilly."

She rubbed away at herself under the water, splashed a bit and waded to the bank. "I've nothing to dry off with," she said. He gave her a cloth and she began to wipe herself down.

Naked in the moonlight, diffident with new wisdom but still graceful from a child's lore: with her long flanks, her body as slim and sudden as an arrow, the high round breasts and the cream-coloured hair that brushed them, she was a wonder to see.

"You are beautiful," he said.

"I?" she said. "This cloth is silk," she said. "It doesn't make the best towel." She wrung it out as well as she could.

"Yes," he said, "you. You are beautiful. Why doubt it?"

"My mother is the beauty in our family," she said.

Amanieu said, "She is a beautiful woman, but not so beautiful as you."

Flore looked at him solemnly for a while, then she skimmed her eyes over herself in the light of this fresh judgment, and smiled at him with curiously vulgar art through her eyelashes.

"Well, you must take more care with me," she said, and tossed her hair back fetchingly over her shoulder. "Perhaps you are not cruel," she said, "only callous."

"It's possible," he said.

"Are we to be married?" she asked him.

"Yes," he said.

"Oh, good!" Flore said, and burst into tears. She began to dry her eyes with the wet silk, and finding it fruitless said, "Give me my frock, and what shall I do with this?"

He gave her the blue dress into one hand and from the other took the wet handful of silk. He shook it out and she saw what it was, the yellow favour Bonne had tied round his neck. Flore collapsed laughing on the ground.

"I love you, Amanieu," she said. "Ah, but it hurts to laugh!"

"Love is the word for it," he said.

# Chapter 30

# JOY

THOUGH Caesar and Bonne, as usual, had lain far apart on the great bed that night, Caesar slept as dreamless as a stone. He woke bright and early the next day. Bonne was up before him, and he heard her early bird's prattle consorting with Gully's in the kitchen.

He went outside. It was a cheerful morning. White clouds flew high and fast across the blue sky, as if the winds that had fallen on the earth the night before had returned to their own region. The gale-washed air sparkled, and made the familiar scene twice as clear to his eye.

The ground below the plum tree was littered with leaves and rotten fruit thrown down by the storm, but in the centre of the tree Caesar spied a single plum that seemed whole. He worked his way into the tree and picked the plum and put it in his mouth. Except for being sour, it was delicious. He turned to emerge from the tree.

Here was Bonne.

"The mice," Bonne said, "have eaten the wax candles."

"They say," Caesar replied helpfully, "that where there are mice, there are no rats."

Bonne said, "We do not keep enough store to ingratiate ourselves with rats. Even the mice must be dissatisfied, to eat my candles. I have saved those candles four years against Roger's coming."

"Dear wife," Caesar said gently, "we do not keep enough store to ingratiate ourselves with Roger Trencavel, never mind the rats."

When Bonne laid her head on his chest Caesar nearly died of love, as if he were a sixteen-year-old boy. "Oh, Caesar," she said, "the mice did not eat the wax candles! I used them, all to myself!"

For the twinkling of an eye, Caesar had a vision of Bonne illuminated by candles. It was as if a mirror had been tilted down a wall and glimpsed a picture there in passing. Of this vision what stayed with Caesar was a speck of light, a spark of memory waiting to catch fire: a promise already in the bud, and soon to flower.

"What shall we do?" Bonne begged of him, among her sniffles.

Caesar cuddles his darling as if she were thistledown. Such closeness is a forgotten joy, and for each second of the embrace in which he holds it, he fears its end. He knows that when this meeting flies apart the cause will be that he has assumed too much, that he has held her too close, that he has forgotten he is a monster, mad and unforgiven. He fears at any moment to hear himself say something foolish, that will turn Bonne away. He holds back the wise and useful words he longs to speak, but which are sure to arrange themselves in meanings quite opposite to what he does mean.

How precarious, then, is this joyful moment! To Caesar it becomes a bubble which holds him and Bonne in perfect bliss, a bubble that any breeze may break or any whisper of his joints destroy. If he can keep still, if he can still his every nerve and silence his very mind, perhaps the moment will be enchanted into an aeon!

As things stand, however, Caesar has trouble sufficient unto the mere moment. He has been caught, when Bonne lays her bonnie bright head upon his chest, wrong-footed. He is, after all, inside the plum tree. Leaves tickle his nose. Broken twigs and the stems of picked plums are hazards to his eyes and vexations to his skin. In his ears rings the ominous song of a thousand intoxicated wasps, gorged but still guzzling on fermented fruit.

Meanwhile Bonne presses her face and her clenched fists against him, as a bad moment takes her. When it is past her hands loosen only a little and lie beside her pillowed head as if they are a child's, and she is one of those babes, already anxious in the cradle, who sleeps with infant fists curled tight.

It is from dilemmas like this that Caesar has been used to float up into thin air, letting the rough world get along without him: today he stands fast. He holds Bonne in his arms and keeps his feet on the ground, a prey to cramps, itches and the fear of sneezing such a sneeze that the bubble they are in will burst—this bubble which encloses them like the walls of a dream; from which the count of atrocities that tells the story of their love, is excluded; and where, with the quarrel of their two souls forgotten, they rest now heart on heart.

## Chapter 31

# THE CHALLENGE

THE clang of a trumpet broke the day in two.

Bonne's head, startled into life, struck Caesar a fearful blow on the nose. The trumpet shrieked again. Water gushed to Caesar's eyes and noise dinned in his ears. His arms were empty of Bonne, but when he tried to make his own way out of the plum tree he struggled blindly into a hedge of impenetrable twigs, that sprang up like magic wherever he turned.

A hand took him by the arm and a voice said, "This way, lord Caesar." The noise stopped and his eyes cleared. It was Vigorce who had hold of him and who, with his body and his free arm, made a space empty of leaf and branch, an arcade through which Caesar walked out of the tree.

Vigorce was in good spirits this morning. "See what we have here!" he said, positively merry.

Caesar looked at him. His appearance was odd, and struck a chord in the memory. He wore a woollen shirt, mail breeches and a sword. The mail breeches were loose and bagging heavily, ready to fall off any moment. Vigorce laughed at himself for the odd sight he made, and Caesar remembered: Vigorce had been wearing half his armour, and laughing his head off, the day Bonne sent him and Solomon to fight the bees for their honey.

Vigorce hauled up his baggy steel trousers. "I heard the trumpet in my sleep," he explained. "I thought it was the Saracens." He laughed again. In all this laughing, some of the old Burgundian wildness had begun to sound. He pointed. "See!" he said. "See what the trumpet means!"

Ceasar saw Bonne's copper head, of which he knew every hair, and the green housekeeping frock which had been her everyday dress for so long that hardly a thread in it was anonymous to him. Now Flore came out of the house, walking a little stiff. She stopped and shaded her eyes against the sun. Then Caesar saw the troubadour, who had started work early and been tumbled out of his lodging by the trumpet-call, for he had a clutch of paper in one hand and a fiddle slung from his neck. The three figures shaped an arc taut with expectation, all of them gazing up at the tower above the gate. When he looked at it himself Caesar was dazzled by the climbing sun, so he walked down the yard till he could see.

Up there on the roof a flag was flying. It fluttered gently in the soft breeze, a long banner of pale blue spotted with red, and it hung from a pole held by a child or—Caesar moved closer—a very small man. Mosquito! The wide-mouthed trumpet stood on the parapet, gleaming in the sun. It was as long a trumpet as Caesar had seen, and it was wonderful that so meagre a body could have forced so much noise from it. Now, supported by the shining brass on one side of him and on the other the fine bright flag, Mosquito issued a proclamation.

"Be it known!" he shouted.

"Not so loud," Bonne said pleasantly. She had always liked Mosquito.

"Be it known!" the small man called down to them. "The valiant knight Amanieu of Noé will from noon tomorrow defend this bridge against any knight who would cross it, to the breaking of three lances and twelve sword-strokes, to maintain the beauty and fair-fame of the loveliest lady between here and Africa in one direction, and between here and Asia in another, and between here and Bordeaux in a third, and between here—"

"Between here and Heaven!" Vigorce said sarcastically.

He was interrupted in his turn. "Let him go on," said Bonne, in a deep and thrillingly convoluted voice. It could now be seen that she blushed a fiery red and was inching towards Mosquito as if he held manna behind his back, and she meant to fly up and grab it.

"—between here and Russia in the last. And though Amanieu of Noé will not name this fair lady, to spare her blushes, yet in token that no other knight may look upon her without first defying him (the said Amanieu) with lance and sword, he (the said Amanieu of Noé) will defend the bridge from its north end, so that no other knight may cross save at his peril."

Each time what he deemed a period in this rote-delivered address, Mosquito brought the flagpole to his chest in a flourish, and then returned it to its station of rest. The effect was extremely pleasing. When he had done Caesar and Vigorce cried out, "Well done, Mosquito!" Bonne said only, "Thank you!" Mosquito bowed and started rolling up the banner on its staff.

"A joust on the bridge, eh?" Caesar said. "That's a good notion. Will it be allowed, though? Deuced dangerous, on that bridge."

"Who is there to allow it, or not allow it?" Bonne asked.

"That's a point," Caesar said. "Is it usual, to defend a bridge in honour of some woman? I wonder who she is."

Flore, slipping quietly past him at that moment, was betrayed into a squeal. Caesar recalled that she had been limping. "Got pins and needles, hey?" he asked her.

His daughter had flashed a smile at him as bright as a new penny, but on this remark, by an exceptional contortion of the face she swallowed the smile whole, and met him with a bland and hiding eye. She did not speak, but went out under the arch.

"Saturnin!" Bonne summoned the troubadour. "You ought to know. Is it usual to defend a bridge in honour of—some woman, as my lord puts it?"

Saturnin, for the second time on this visit, was stirred out of his melancholy. "No," he said. "I've never heard of it before. Absolutely new, a new expression of love in chivalry. It's marvellous, its history being made." He offered a slight smile. "And I am here to help make it!"

"Then it is the woman," Bonne said, turning pale as if *in extremis*, "who has inspired it."

"Who is the woman?" Saturnin asked her.

"Ah!" Bonne whispered, and looked modestly at her feet.

There was the sound of hooves. "Where's Flore off to?" Caesar asked.

Through the arch of the gatehouse they saw, as pretty as a picture, the little Spanish horse running down the green hill, with Flore riding bareback.

Caesar spoke again. "He can't mean to break lances for our Flore, surely! She's quite an ordinary child."

"I daresay he does," Bonne said, showing a resilience beyond most of the previous martyrs. "Children can be deceitful, you know, and they grow up when you're not looking. Have you thought what we should do about the wax candles, and the . . . the wretched welcome we'll be giving Roger?"

"Yes," Caesar said surprisingly. "Yes, I have."

Bonne put both hands on his arm with her wrists crossed, as if that would attach her to him more definitely. She led him quickly away in no particular direction. He felt her hands shake on his sleeve. He saw that her face was shaking. Some calamity had befallen her. "Caesar," she said, "please speak! Speak at once! Tell me what we can do about the Viscount."

He did so, but took time to notice that she had said simply "the Viscount," not "Cousin Roger" or "my cousin." The day was busy with strange portents. "We can do nothing about our poverty," he said, "so when Roger comes we shall just face it out, together. When the serfs came to kill us, we simply faced it out. It worked then; it'll work again."

"In God's name, Caesar, it's easy enough to lord it over peasants!" She tugged at his arm. "I must keep walking!" She shook it. "And please answer me, at once!"

These were extraordinary appeals, and though Caesar did not understand them in the least, that they were being put at all made enough sense for him. He responded instantly. "We shall not try to lord it over Roger," he said. "We faced the serfs out that way from above. With Roger, we shall face it out from below. We are not rich, our face—the face we shall present to him—will say; and that's that, it will say."

"What else? Quickly Caesar! What else will our face say?"

Caesar laughed aloud. Whatever this was, it was better than life in an enchanted bubble! "Very well—our face will say—you are here, Roger, but we cannot become rich just because you are here. It will be plain eating. You have your habit and we have ours—the face will say—and if our habit doesn't suit you, you need not stay for long."

As if she had made up her mind to a great and difficult act, Bonne now turned them about—they were wandering back and forth in front of the keep—and started them back down the yard. "What shall we do then, for his welcome?" she asked.

"What you have done already!" Caesar said. "What you and Gully have done, and not much more. You have spring-cleaned the house, although it is autumn. We shall bring out the great bed and air it for his lordship. We shall sleep in the kitchen. Are you proud enough to sleep in the kitchen?"

"I?" she said, half-way to hysteria. "I? I? I proud? I tell you, Caesar Grailly, I am haughty enough to sleep in the kennel, or the stable, so what care I for your kitchen?" But still she pulled at his arm. "Go on! Tell me more!"

They had entered the arch under the gatehouse.

Caesar told her more, gabbling a little now. "The house being clean, we shall have leafy branches in it and flowers and herbs. Our house is yours, we'll say, and what food and wine we have is yours too. Though it's likely he'll send his food and his cooks on ahead of him anyway. His following are not our concern—"

Bonne's clutch on his arm brought him up short. It rendered him speechless. He stood on his toes for pain and his body writhed as if it were a voice trying to make Bonne hear. He pried her fingers loose, and held her knotted hands inside his own.

When she spoke the sound was lifeless and shrunken. "Don't you think that is the *most* charming . . . " Her mouth had dried completely and for a moment or two, though her lips went on working, nothing came out. She stared and stared at whatever this was, so charming that it seemed in a fair way to strangle her.

They had come out of the arch and walked some way down the track that led to the great world. Far beneath them lay the plain. Alive and shining in the clear day, it stretched away to the blue distance where Pyrenees and the sky met under a shawl of cloud. This was the stuff that Bonne made dreams of. It was on this hillside that she liked to sit—when life was not so full as it had been lately—and imagine herself out on that inhabited plain, visiting this city or that town, and winning at last to the far-off mountains.

Today, however, Caesar knew at once that it was not the wide panorama, and not the long, long vista that filled Bonne's eye, but the pretty scene in the foreground, by the bridge.

It was a scene made of colours, and Caesar walked down to have a look, with Bonne dragging at his sleeve until he stopped, not quite entering the picture. The tent was pale blue embroidered with red teardrops, and it looked remarkably like silk. The guy ropes were of the same colours, intertwined. The edges of the tent were scalloped with gold.

"Just look at it!" Caesar said. "That's no campaign tent, that's your actual jousting pavilion. The German boy he won it off must have been as rich as Croesus." He whistled, as a memory came to his mind. "The Spaniard said the brother is a giant. Well, there's nothing we can do about it now."

Bonne came round in front of Caesar. "His brother?"

"Yes," Caesar said. "His brother is coming with Roger, breathing fire and vengeance: a giant, that's what Jesus the Spaniard told me—his last words, before he fell and killed himself. It was a pity about that, the poor fellow, but I will say that Flore looks extremely well on his horse!"

Flore's linen dress was the same blue as the tent. She sat half-sideways on the cream-coloured horse with one bare foot up on its neck. Her head was tilted over her shoulder and the long, thick hair flowed down her to show how close it matched the horse's coat. Amanieu stood beside her. He leaned over the neck of the horse and kissed Flore's foot, at some length. Her head tilted to the other side, making a slow, ecstatic span of motion.

Beyond her the angle at which the bridge crossed the gorge continued this movement, and the arch that held the bridge there, completed it. The moment in which Flore turned her head seemed, by its oneness with the long-shaped stone, not to end.

Caesar came to himself with a start. He set off happily to climb the hill again, going at a good lick to catch up with Bonne.

## Chapter 32

# ROGER

"**M**Y God, Grailly! This is a dead-and-alive hole up here! You've got the house nice, though. My dear Bonne! Adelaide sends her love. She wants to see you, but we'll talk about that later. Can I put my couch in with you and Caesar—we're cousins, you need have no secrets from me. I'll be with you two nights, I think."

Bonne sat and blinked at him. She could not move for pleasure. To call her cousin—just like that—and to bring his wife's love! Things might take a turn for the better after all. She managed to stand up, sustained by her yellow silk dress.

"Your wife's a beauty, Grailly. Kiss me frankly, my dear. Here's the daughter. You too child, kiss your old cousin. Oho! Why, my fine girl! Well, well!"

Roger Trencavel, Viscount of Béziers, Carcassonne, Albi and Razès, was a middle-sized man of forty with an active and muscular body, a round head with short ginger hair, quick green eyes, a nose with a dent in it, and a mouth where the confidence of experience joined natural arrogance of spirit. He was thick and compact about the shoulders and the energy in him gathered there, passed through the short neck, and was continually expressed by the poised force of his head and the life in his face. He filled the room with himself. The effect fell upon the three Graillys like the rays of a benevolent sun; but it was also, so sheltered was their existence, as if they had been thrown into a torrent of spate water chilled by melting snow.

This man, who had just finished a war of six years that was part of a war into which he had been born; whose father had been hanged by his own subjects in the cathedral at Béziers, but whose people were no more unruly to the Trencavels than the Trencavels had been to their overlords the Counts of Toulouse: this man ruled a lordship whose northern edge ran from Albi in the west to Montpellier in the east, and which stretched south to the Pyrenees. It was this land that had been devastated by the long war.

"I'm travelling light," Roger said. "I'm riding over my wretched territory to see what's left of it. I've a little army with me, mostly lawyers and money-men, but I've left them down in the plain. We've kept such a pace they've lost count of their sums. A couple of days apart from each other will do us good. I've a dozen men up here with me, no more. Are my cooks in there?" He walked to the kitchen and peered in.

"Gully!" he shouted. "I thought the buggers were quiet. No wonder!" He gave her a hug and kissed her on top of the head. "We're not growing any younger," he said to her, and "Ah, well!" he said, and shook his head as if to dispel reminiscence. Gully went back to her kitchen, perfumed, on both sides of the doorway, with historical speculation.

"Where was I?" this politician now asked. "Yes, I'm travelling light. I've a dozen men with me, and a German visitor, who tells me such a tale that I've brought my hangman into the hills with me." Roger sat on the table and swung a leg, and waited for the room to pick up its cue.

Bonne fell onto her chair again, and Flore held fast to the back of it for support. Caesar swayed on his legs, anticipating the impact of this message, for though his wits had not yet received it, his instinct told them it was on the way.

Amanieu came out of the shadows, attired with the relative simplicity of the day he arrived. He went close to Roger, presenting himself in the daylight from the door, warts and all. He bowed, not very low, to the man who might have him hanged.

"All right," Roger said. "Tell the tale."

"I met the German on the road. I killed him and took his armour, his horses and gear. I had beaten him," Amanieu said, "and it is the custom to take the other man's gear."

"Was it a fair fight?" Roger, sitting on the table, exuded force, a bow pulled to the arrowhead.

"All fighting is fair," Amanieu said, "between fighting men. He had his wound in front. He was a slow, stupid boy, fat already. I had not eaten for three days."

Roger's gingery eyebrows leapt with surprise. "He was fat, and you had not eaten for three days? Why tell me that—it makes you sound like a bandit!"

Amanieu said, "It does not prove me one, and it tells you what you want to know."

Roger sat square to him, swinging both legs and gripping the table's edge in both hands. "What shall I do for proof, since there were no witnesses?"

"I'll fight the brother. Let him accuse me to my face, and prove it on my body if he can," Amanieu said. "I am knighted–will he refuse me?"

"Trial by combat," Roger said, thinking. "No, he won't refuse, but wait till you see him. This one's not a baby. Hoy!" He sent his voice to the door of the house. "Ask von Krakken to join me. Tell me your name," he said to Amanieu, who gave it him. "I know your father," Roger said. "I don't like him."

Darkness filled the doorway and the lintel clanged sonorously. The darkness groaned, and stooped lower. It came into the room and reared up to its height. It was wrapped in chain-mail of black steel, armoured from head to foot, showing not a vestige of human tissue. Even its hands were covered with the steel gauntlets. It stank.

"He is vowed," Roger said, "not to take off his armour until he has avenged his brother. Before that, he was vowed not to take it off until he had found his brother. It's been a terrible few days."

Under the table the dog growled.

Bonne shrieked suddenly. "He has no face!"

Flore fainted where she stood, but she clung to the chair and whipped her senses back into action. This was no time to be squeamish.

"Nonsense, Bonne!" Caesar said, much interested. "That's one of those new pot helmets. Covers the whole head and face. You can see where he banged it on the doorway."

Roger said, "Ulrich von Krakken," and presented the steel-clad giant to the family. He was indeed a giant, and Amanieu came alive to the geometry of his own place in the room, and kept his feet light. There was four times as much Ulrich as there was Amanieu, and if Ulrich lost control of himself a line of flight must be in view.

"This is Amanieu of Noé," Roger said, "who killed your brother. He says it was a fair fight."

The room bated its breath.

From the steel head of the black giant emerged a hiss like the warcry of an angry snake. The figure stood still but rattled and clinked: a statue having an apoplexy. Then it lifted a fist among the rafters and took a step towards Amanieu. This was also, since Amanieu was where he was, a step towards the Viscount.

"Take care, Ulrich!" Roger said. "Not in the house, there's a good chap."

Ulrich stepped back and crashed the frustrated fist into its fellow.

Amanieu felt the hair bristle on his neck. Flore fainted once more, and once more pulled herself together.

The giant had a vast and resonant voice, as of one who sang well. It boomed cavernously from inside the helmet. "Foul piglet!" it said.

"He means you," Roger said to Amanieu.

"Yes, but what does he *mean?*" Caesar asked.

"He means rotten little swine, that kind of thing," Roger said. To the giant, he said. "Do you accept that Amanieu killed your brother in fair fight?"

"*Nein!*" It echoed like a drumroll about the room.

"Do you accuse him of murdering your brother, and will you prove it on his body?"

"*Ja?*"

"Will you fight him? As his accuser—a trial by combat?"

"Fight the piglet? *Ja, ja! Ja!*" Ulrich's voice boomed, and he bent down at Amanieu with a strange appearance of friendliness. "Wait! Is he *geboren?*"

"Yes, yes. He's noble. I know his father. I don't like him but I know him. And the boy's knighted. All right? Now," Roger said to Amanieu, "do you accept the challenge?"

"Yes," Amanieu said.

"I'd like it as soon as possible," Roger said. "I've formed the opinion that we must settle this before we get down to our own business. What about noon today, that's in two hours or so?"

Five thoughts moved across Amanieu's face all in an instant. His eyes were windows into a busy council chamber. You could see questions falling on the table and being decided, one after the other. Roger watched him curiously.

"Noon will suit me," Amanieu said. "I've a vow of my own, though, to defend the bridge against all comers. Can we make it on the bridge?" He smiled, almost. "Kill two birds with one stone."

"You're likely to," Roger said. "It will be hellish dangerous on that bridge."

Amanieu said, "From where I stand, it looks to be tolerably dangerous anywhere."

"Noonday at the bridge, then, von Krakken. You will want to prepare yourself. Hey!" Roger said sharply to the door. "Show him out."

Snuffling sounds came out of the black helmet and then the giant began to laugh with happiness. The quality of his joy was disconcerting—the laugh of imminent vengeance should have a bitter or sorrowful note, but this sounded as happy as the day was long. The effect of it, muzzled inside the steel pot, was strange and horrible. It was like a human spirit caged forever inside a steel body.

The last thing Flore heard and saw before she fainted dead away, was the clank of the black giant as he smote his armoured head a second time on the lintel: and his darkness that filled the doorway, and blotted out the sunlight from the day.

*Chapter 33*

# THE CHAMPION

"I KNEW you would want to arm me," Amanieu said to Flore as she laced the helmet under his chin, "but I overdid the brandy. You smell like a distillery."

"Mosquito did most of it. Where's he gone?" Flore's voice was desperate, as if an ally had deserted in the field. "My nerves are wrecked," she said.

"Believe me," he said. "I shall be with you in an hour. This German is as stupid as his brother."

"My God!" Flore said. "You are going to fight and I am no help to you. The gauntlets!" she cried. "Your mail gloves! Where are they?"

"I don't want them," Amanieu said. "Leather gloves will do best. I'm going to throw things at him. Remember how I skewered that peasant? Mosquito's found three of these javelins, and he's sharpened them to needlepoints."

"Will they go through his armour?" Flore asked, and there was a little colour back in her cheeks. "Is it allowed?"

Amanieu laughed, a short and tensed-up bark of sound. "They *might* go through his armour, but they won't. They will go into his horse, and if Ulrich doesn't fall over the bridge when the horse comes down, I'll put this stiletto in his eye and stir it in his brains."

Flore was squeamish. "I didn't know fighting was like that," she said.

"Fighting means killing," Amanieu said. "It doesn't mean anything else. I'm going to kill that big bastard to stop him killing me. It doesn't matter how I kill him. Once it's over, Roger will let it be."

Flore gripped his hands. "I'll bring you luck, won't I?"

"That's it," he said. "That's the stuff!" He looked at the white and shivering child. "Now you stay here," he said. "You sit on the doorstep, that's where you like to sit. When it's over, Mosquito will blow that trumpet of his. Come on, I'll have to mount up from the doorstep, with all this steel on me, and then you'll wait there!"

Flore said, "You're not so callous as you were."

"Not to you, maybe," Amanieu said.

*     *     *

From the roof of the gatehouse, Caesar and Roger watched the young people. "He can't win," Roger said. "The girl will be heart-broken."

"Will she?" Caesar was much interested. "Why?"

Roger stared at him. "She's your daughter, Grailly. Can't you tell?"

"She keeps very much to herself," Caesar said. "Tell what?"

"Poor little bitch," Roger said. He expended some of his temper. "Another thing, Grailly. If I were you I shouldn't much like the way that troubadour hangs around Bonne."

The two of them turned and looked to the other side of the roof, where Saturnin expounded to Bonne the idea of chivalry.

"I'm with you there," Caesar said. "I'd forgotten about him, with all this excitement. I'd meant to put a stop to it."

"Do it now," Roger said.

"Now?"

"Yes, now. Bonne!" Roger called to her. "Come here and see the young man mount up."

Caesar's mind moved like greased lightning. As Saturnin followed Bonne accross the roof he took the troubadour by the elbow and turned him round again. "Lord Roger wants to be alone with his cousin," he said. "We shall see the lad ride out under the arch here, you and I. Here, we must stand in the middle. That's it. He'll come out just below us."

"The German is waiting on the other side of the bridge," Saturnin said. "He leads his horse up and down every so often, so that they won't get stiff. I wonder what he looks like? Your peasants seem to be rather taken with him. It must be a pleasant thing to have a bit of an audience," he said jealously.

"Never mind all that!" Caesar said urgently. "If you don't look down you won't see the lad ride out!"

"What does that matter?" Saturnin said. "In any case, I can't look down or I'll fall over. I've got no head for heights."

"Nonsense!" Caesar said bracingly. "I'll hold you by the belt. A poet must see every detail that he can. Put yourself in the embrasure, there! And hold on to the sides, like that! Good man! You're as safe as houses!" Caesar said, "I've got you," and pushed him over the parapet as the hooves of the big warhorse came stamping through the gateway.

\* \* \*

When Amanieu came to himself, he was lying on his back looking up at Roger. The Viscount was far above him, leaning over the battlements like God looking out of Heaven.

"Sweet Christ!" Amanieu said. "Did I lose?"

"What does he say?" Roger shouted down.

"He says, did he lose?" That was Vigorce.

"You didn't begin!" Roger shouted, and broke into laughter and withdrew.

This rough humour was too much for Amanieu, who was passionate to know if it was over, and if he was to be hanged. He struggled to sit up.

"Take it easy," Vigorce said, and held him by the shoulders.

"God damn you!" Amanieu shrieked. "Let me go!" With a mighty effort he threw off Vigorce, lost all power of breathing to a whitehot pain in the arm, and left the world again.

\* \* \*

Saturnin lay winded against the wall, out of the way. He had landed belly-down, plump on the withers of Amanieu's Mecklenburg warhorse. The horse had thrown off both the troubadour and its rider, and begun to stamp and kick as if it was in a battle. It had kicked Amanieu on the head and trampled on his arm, which was broken.

"His sword-arm," Roger said. "Then he can't fight." He looked up and saw Caesar. "By God!" he said. "You have a short way with poets!"

Caesar joined the ring of people round the fallen knight, between Flore and Vigorce. He saw that he had completed the perfect circle. The idea came to him, of the symmetry of fate.

"If he does not fight?" He asked Roger.

Roger said, "If he fails of the combat at noon, he must hang."

At Caesar's side, Flore gave such a cry of grief as, before, he had thought of only in his mind. With his forefinger, he trailed the long hair over her shoulder, to see her face.

"I loved him," Flore said. She looked at Caesar. "He said he would win!" she complained. "He was going to win!"

Roger, Viscount and judge, said sternly, "God defends the right."

With this saying, in which he discovered that abstract questions could be settled on the lance-point or the sword's edge, Caesar felt parts of his being that had long been widely separated, unite in sympathy.

"What did you say?" he asked Roger.

"God defends the right," Roger said. "It is the essential principle of trial by combat."

Caesar looked at the ground between his feet. He waited for a sign.

On the bones and sinews of Bonne's face the skin lay close and tight, as if the day was pressing in on her. "When I was spring-cleaning," she said, "for Roger's visit, the last thing I did while the house was still asleep—" and she lifted her chin, since she was making a private gift in public "—I tossed your armour in sand, and oiled and polished it."

Caesar lavished so genuine a smile on her that she narrowed her eyes against it. "I worshipped you in a dream," he said. "A naked goddess shining in the night."

Bonne said, "It was not a dream. Was that you looking in the window? I wish I'd known. I was bored, naked in the candlelight with nothing to do."

"Well," Caesar said, "since my armour is ready. God will *tell* us something, after all. That's the thing, isn't it? I mean, something will come of it!"

"God will tell *you* something, Caesar," she said, and added, "at last! Afterwards, we shall converse with each other."

Roger, whose subtle but governmental intelligence had been doing its best to latch on to the meeting of those arcane minds, demanded noisily, "What are you two saying? What does he mean?"

Bonne regarded him with scorn, as if he were sadly out of touch with current dialectic fashion. "He means that he will fight the German knight," she said. "Caesar will be the young man's champion."

# Chapter 34

# DEATH AND GLORY

BONNE was putting Caesar into his old armour as if she had done it every day for years, which she had, once upon a time. Caesar pranced a little like a horse feeling his oats.

"Keep still," Bonne said.

"That's too tight," Caesar said.

"No it's not," she said. "Not if you want it to stay on."

Vigorce was hefting, not Caesar's ordinary sword, but the great two-handed sword that had hidden many years in the dark, the sword with which the father had killed the son.

"Let me get the feel of it," Caesar said, and took it from the captain and passed it lightly through the air. "It feels like a feather, as light as a feather," he said.

"I sharpened it," Bonne said. "It sang to me. It's as good a sword as ever was."

Caesar balanced it and poised himself for the telling blow. "Do you think it will open that helmet of his?"

"Oh, yes," Bonne said. "He has a foot on you in the way of height, but you have those long arms. If you get the distance right and can bring it down on him, he'll split like an orange."

Flore could hardly believe her ears. The two of them sounded as if they were preparing for a wedding. At first she had been beside herself, thinking that the German giant would kill her father, and the Viscount would then hang Amanieu. Now she was bewildered. Random pulses of fear and hope, of grief and love, beat in her and pushed her sometimes to tears, sometimes to high and hectic laughter.

"Will my father win?" she asked Amanieu.

"I begin to think he might. He thinks he will win, and that's one half of the battle—so he might do it," Amanieu said.

That mortified gallant was settled against the wall, keeping his arm still until after the fight—when either he would be hanged, or his arm splinted. If he was fated to die, at least he would be spared the bone-setting. "Also," he had explained to Flore, "Roger knows that if I ran, I wouldn't get far with my arm still loose."

"Would you?" Flore had asked. "Would you run away if you could?"

"Sweetheart," he had answered, "you would not see my heels for the dust."

Now Flore said, "It is odd that my father should be fighting your battle for you, isn't it?"

"It doesn't seem odd to me," Amanieu said. "He dropped the poet on me and broke my arm."

"That was an accident."

"I don't say it wasn't."

"All the same," Flore said, "it is not what I expected, that my father would fight our battles instead of you."

"A great deal of life is not what one expects," Amanieu said. "I have never expected that a poet would drop on me out of the sky," (his arm was hurting him) "or I should have spitted him on my sword, and preserved you from these irritations."

Flore wept, and pulled her fingers with the other fingers—"I am wringing my hands," she thought—and walked up and down looking at nothing everywhere she could find it to look at. She stopped near Amanieu again, for he might be hanged in an hour, but kept her face to the sky and her eye on the void.

"Your father is fighting this for his own sake," Amanieu said to her, "because he wants to. He's not fighting for you or me, but for himself and Bonne. He's bursting at the chance. You only have to look at him."

Flore glowered at Caesar, who carved great fillets from the air with his sword. He looked as if it was his birthday, and someone had come up with the right present. Flore was distracted with fear and beside herself with rage. The words she had just said to Amanieu, were surely not what she had wished to say? She must try to say something nice to him.

"I think that's very selfish of Father," she said.

Caesar was on top of the Mecklenburg horse. It was in good fettle and a bad temper, just the beast you wanted for a killing match. Caesar had the big sword bare on his back and his old round shield on his arm. At the entrance to the bridge Vigorce was waiting for him with the lance. He gave his naked sword to the captain to lean it against the end of the bridge.

"If it comes to sword-strokes," he said, "I'll have been knocked this far anyway."

He took the lance and trotted the horse about on the grass till they were both handy with the extra weight, for this was no light jousting weapon but a heavy shaft of oak, twice as high as he was. Mosquito had joined Vigorce at the foot of the hill and they waved their bonnets as he passed them—loyal fellows!—on his way back to the bridge. There, beside the blue silk pavilion splashed with red teardrops, Bonne waited for the onfall.

There was no one else on this side of the bridge. On the far side a green hillock overlooked the gorge, and up there was the Viscount, with his sword wrapped in a white cloth to act as a marshal's baton. The men behind him would be Roger's own following. Caesar looked to his front. The German knight loomed above the swarming peasantry to a height that—even at this distance—alarmed the eye. Now that Caesar had taken his place the serfs drew back from the black knight to make room, leaving a space like a broad arrowhead with the German at its point.

A miracle poured into Caesar. Inside him, his spirit shone. He felt the bones gleam in his blood, and the blood sparkle against his skin. He was filled with delight to be himself, to be who he was, and not to be that powerful, pompous figure—sworn to keep itself encased in the stale stink of its giant's body, and its face in that closed helmet darkened from the day.

Caesar was flushed with hilarity. He was rapturous and debonair and his madness was in its prime. I have stood by willow-trees under the full moon, he said to the black knight. Now you will see! Here was Bonne at his left hand, in her beauty and her pride. Bonne in her yellow dress framed by the opening of the blue tent, silk on silk and colour against colour! The sun frolicked in her blowing skirts and her wind-thrown hair. Her eyes were flames of gold.

"I rejoice!" he cried out.

His horse jumped forward at the sound and he pulled it in. He laughed. He spurred the horse and reined in again, to make it angry. It sprang off on its hind legs and came to a stop and nearly threw them both over. It smelled its blood running from his heels and neighed and danced.

"Come up!" he shouted to it. "Come up!" It settled on all fours, but stamped and snorted, eager to charge.

Roger waved the white-wrapped sword to catch his eye. Caesar made ready. He set the heavy lance in rest. Its long steel spear-point glinted before the horse's eye. The horse stamped and quivered and tossed spittle from its mouth. "Yes," Caesar said to it, but held it in, "yes, yes!"

Roger let fall the whitened sword.

"Hi-hi-hi!" Caesar shouted as he kicked in the spurs and brought the lance point to the level. The horse squealed and threw itself into the charge. Caesar's bright bones were jarred and battered as the iron hooves thumped the hard and stony ground.

Into the narrow passage of the bridge the black knight on his black horse flew to meet them. For the battle black plumes had sprouted from his helmet, and from its sides black feathers grew and flapped like wings. These additions to his size made so much darkness that under the high noonday sun the giant rose like fear on his own shadow. His shield was kite-shaped, black and dull, nothing on him shone. He will make black wounds, Caesar said: and saw that he was Death.

"On, on!" Caesar cried, for his own shadow had touched his heart. His blood paled and the bones weighed like lead in him. His spurs spiked the warhorse till it screamed and bit the air. It flung itself at the enemy horse. Caesar saw the leaf-blade of black steel a moment from his eyes, from his soul.

They struck with a shock that sprang the marrow from Caesar's bones. He felt the blood spurt from his face, from ears and nose and mouth. He made his arm of stone, for the lance it held was thrusting its way into the black knight's head.

The warhorses were stopped dead, hurled back onto their haunches. They staggered to their feet, too stunned to bite and kick each other. The black knight, with the lance through his face and stretching out from the back of his head, screeched and clutched the blood-spouting broken helmet with his mailed fists. Caesar's arm let go the lance and the giant fell over the bridge.

Caesar looked down into the abyss and watched him fall, his black wings flapping, squawking like a raven. "Speak!" Caesar heard himself shout to the spirit flying through the air.

The black giant dropped to the rocks beside the river, to end with his arms spread out and the pierced head laid sideways by the lance. It looked like a bird shot by an arrow.

"Not the phoenix," Caesar noticed, "but a crow."

*          *          *

He turned the dazed and wander-footed horse back over the bridge, and rode to the blue silk tent where Bonne waited. She gave him a cup of wine, and he drank it, and another one. After that he came down slowly from the saddle.

"Oho!" he said. "My back!"

He lay flat on the ground, stretching his limbs and his spine slowly to their extremities. Nothing parted. With great care he sat up again. Bonne washed the blood from his face with wine.

"I've never seen so much blood from your ears," Bonne said. "Can you hear?"

"Yes. They're hardly ringing at all now. You'll have to keep talking loud, though." He gave a laugh. "I'll tell you a funny thing. As he fell through the air, I asked him to speak. 'Speak!' I shouted. That was an odd thing to do, wasn't it?"

Bonne smiled, slightly. "Did he answer?"

"No!"

"You can't have everything," she said.

"That stroke!" he said. "Right through the face! That was a fluke, if you like—the horse did it! I was lucky there."

"You were a champion, Caesar," she said.

He laughed for joy. His eyes lit on the motto embroidered in gold thread above the entrance to the tent. "*Pour mon désir*," he read it out.

"That's northern French," Bonne said, and turned to look. She faced him again. "Shall I tell you my translation?"

Caesar nodded.

She kissed his lips, and opened his mouth with her tongue, while she undid the lacing of his helmet. She drew the helmet off and pulled back the mailed hood, and washed the blood from his ears.

"*Amor vincit omnia*," she whispered.

*Chapter 35*

# DEPARTURES

ROGER'S horse was at the door. His couch and his cooks, his hangman and his hangers-on, were already winding down the valley road. The Viscount was taking his stirrup-cup, but in comfort, seated in Roger's great chair. Round Roger's neck was a noose of wild flowers, an ironic tribute from Flore. He was much taken with her.

"If I catch that girl on her own, I'll fall upon her," he said. "So beware!"

Bonne reminded him that she and he were of an age. "You were always a tom-cat, Cousin Roger," she said.

"I always will be," he said, "when I can get the time. On that score, I've filched your troubadour. He's keen to be out of here, and promises to sing lewd songs of you, my fair cousin, round our winter fires."

He sat back and grinned at her—tit-for-tat. Bonne made a grimace, and sighed, and dropped her eyes, and smoothed her green housekeeping dress: Roger's lustre was rather dimmed by such coarseness.

To Caesar, who stood gathering dust among the sunbeams, Roger said, "He'll make you famous for that exploit on the bridge."

Caesar's smile, that was today less manic than usual, became caustic. "He has little cause to sing well of me."

"He will have," Roger said. "If I pay the piper, I call the tune."

Caesar laughed crisply, hardily. "Well, I daresay he did not fall as heavy as the other."

Roger laughed. "That was a rare lance-thrust," he said.

"The horse helped," Caesar said.

"The horse did what you made it do," Roger said. "You made it jump at the perfect moment. You're a cool hand, Grailly."

Caesar, all dust and sunbeams, bowed a gentle bow.

Roger watched him. The Viscount's face became curious and hard, a little crafty. "How's the boy's arm? My hangman tells me it will mend well; a clean break, he says." It was Roger's hangman, enjoying complementary skills, who had set the broken bone.

Caesar, still looking out of the door, shrugged a shoulder and turned a hand.

When the silence ran on, Bonne spoke. "The boy seems well enough. He's outside somewhere, with Flore."

The Viscount said, "My hangman thought it was not the break you'd expect from a horse's kick."

Bonne answered, "Then the arm must have broken when he fell off the horse, when it hit the ground."

"Not that either, apparently," Roger said.

"It's not a thing that interests me," Caesar said. He turned his deep smile on Bonne's cousin. "Besides, we are all content, unless you hoped to hang the boy."

"No, no," Roger said. "You're quite right. I am content, you are content, they—the boy and the girl—they are content! It was only something in my mind, itching in my mind, you know?"

"I know," Caesar said.

The mastiff offered itself at Roger's knee, a cheerful diversion, and he scratched its neck heartily. "Good old dog, ain't you? There's one thing, Grailly. His armour's yours, all his gear is yours, it's worth a pretty penny."

Caesar's smile froze and fell on Roger with a perceptible thud. "I don't want his armour. He's being buried in it, and all his stench with him, at this moment. They've dug a pit for him in the graveyard. I've just been down to see it."

The display of personality irritated Roger. "It's a waste to throw away good armour like that. I would have bought it off you. I can't help a man who won't help himself!"

"Help?" Caesar said, lost.

"Help!" Bonne said, cut to the quick. "We need no help. Besides, I have taken the man's horses, and the money from his tent. Gold as well as silver. Caesar is entitled to these."

"Have you, by God!" Roger stood up. "I can see I'm outclassed here." He laughed with vexation. "I know what's wrong with you, Bonne, and I'm sorry we can't build your house up into a castle. You'll get over it. A castle's not the way to make your place in the world, not these days. It's a money economy we live in now. I told you Adelaide wants to see you. I'm going to tell her you'll spend the winter with us. I'll tell her you've lost none of your spark. Maybe you'll like it there. Half the gentry live in the towns now. And you, Caesar, you won't find many opponents worth your steel, up on this hilltop! See me off. I'm for the road. Where's that daughter of yours?"

They found the young people outside. "Walk me on my way," Roger said to them. He took the reins of his horse from the iron ring on the wall. "Your parents have gone all hoity-toity on me," he grumbled to Flore. "Here, take this creature on while I say good-bye to them."

Bonne and Caesar, indeed, held themselves like two beings in a myth. Remotely from Hymettic peaks, their blue and golden eyes stared down on the unhoneyed folk beneath, whose world had no place in their own private and mysterious history.

The Viscount did his whole duty. "Bonne," he said, "your beauty irradiates the hour. Even so ferocious a champion as Caesar Grailly is honoured by such a prize."

All bowed.

Bonne saluted him politely on both cheeks. "Cousin!" she said, floating more inflections on the word than you might think it could embark, without sinking.

Roger bore it out to the bitter end. "Good-bye, Grailly!" he said, and Caesar allowed him to grasp a long handful of fingers.

"You're for off, then, Trencavel," he said, speaking as if he were perfectly human. "A good road to you!"

Roger turned from the amazed blue eyes and the endless smile that had no meaning, and left them to their exalted fate.

*     *     *

At the top of the track Flore sat on the grass with the horse snuffling at her ear, and Amanieu stood with an arm in a sling and the other impatiently knocking flies from round his head. Roger lifted the reins from Flore's lap.

"Your man's disgruntled," he said to her.

She jumped up. "He's alive!" she said.

"Your father stole his thunder," Roger said.

"Oh, that!" she said. "It was a great thing for Father, but Amanieu could do that any day of the week."

"Ha!" Envy (an unwelcome stranger) and chagrin clogged Amanieu's voice. "No I could not, by God! No one could. Could you?" he demanded of Roger.

Roger shook his head. "No. He was a freak. He was too big to be fought."

"Exactly!" Amanieu said. "I wasn't going to fight him. I was going to cheat, kill the horse and knife the man. Your father beat him on his own terms. He tore into him like a hero!"

"Well," Roger said. "He wanted to, and you didn't, so there's no harm done."

"He might have got me hanged!" Amanieu said.

"You might have earned it," Roger said.

"If *you* haven't hanged him," Flore said, "you don't think he needs hanging."

The two men looked at her. "How do you like that?" Roger said.

Amanieu's face unclouded. "I like the sound of it," he said.

Roger said, "I like the sense," and he climbed onto his horse, which was restive. "Will you stay or leave, you two?"

Amanieu said, "We won't be here tomorrow."

"Good," Roger said. "This is no place for you." He turned on Flore a quick passionless look, hiding emotion. He leaned down and touched a hair of her head. "Good luck to you," he said, and let the horse go.

*    *    *

When the Viscount had crossed the bridge and waved, and cantered off, Flore set about striking the silk tent.

"We have three horses and a tent," she said. "That's not a bad start. Where shall we go first?"

"Catalonia," Amanieu said. "The Count of Barcelona won this war, if anyone did. Let's go where the winners are."

"Oh, good," Flore said. "I thought you might want to visit your home at Noé."

"And count my brothers!" He laughed, hardly sarcastic at all.

Flore sat on the folded tent. She gazed south at the Pyrenees and a doubt came to her about their journey. "What about the robber-bands," she said, and pointed to the country below, "all living on human flesh?"

Amanieu tossed the purse of German gold in his good hand. "We'll go to the coast," he said, "and take ship."

"Ship!" Flore hid her face in her skirt for excitement. She sat up again—she must not be childish—and became serious. "What if we are taken by pirates?" she said.

"Then I'll go for a pirate," Amanieu said. "What do you think?" He nodded at the pile of silk she sat on. "Can you put the tentpole on top of that? We'll go and tell the priest he's got a wedding."

*    *    *

Vigorce was packing his bags. His face was cunning and his eyes flinched when Mosquito came in the door. The captain became still.

Mosquito said, "I've got the horses behind the keep."

"Good. Thanks for that. I'm going out that side, over the desert." Vigorce went on with his packing.

"I thought you'd go that way," Mosquito said.

In a moment Vigorce spoke again. "Horses, you say? I've only one horse."

"I'm going that way too," Mosquito said.

Vigorce said, "I don't need your company."

"I'm not giving it," Mosquito said. "It just happens, that's the way I want to go."

Vigorce tied up one of his bags. "I'm going home," he said, "to Burgundy."

"There you are," Mosquito said. "I don't know where I'm going. All I'm doing is leaving."

They did not speak, riding up the meadow past the goats. They went by the old woman in the Spanish hat, leaning with folded hands on top of her stick, and staring blindly at the stone cliff. She made no sign and they exchanged no greeting. When they came to the rocky plateau they dismounted and began the arduous crossing, leading the horses over the shifting stones. At a wild olive tree, they stopped to settle their minds on the hard travelling before them.

"She made me come away," Vigorce said. "She told me to leave. She offered me her jewel to leave—to leave them alone!" He sounded, not heart-broken: heart-cracked. "I took the jewel. I took it, Mosquito. I had to, or I'd not have gone. I'd have stayed up in that keep, looking at them." He shook his head. "I thought I'd have done anything for her, and I took her jewel. It was the most precious thing she had, and I took it from her!"

"Cheer up," Mosquito said callously. "You could say, that she bought herself from you. How does that feel?"

Vigorce sat on the ground and laid his jaw sideways on his hand. At first Mosquito took him to be in deep thought, but then he saw old seams on that ill-used face crack open. Vigorce was ready to laugh.

"I have a story too," Mosquito said, "so save your laughter, if you can. I followed the young lad through the arch, and I had his head on my knee the moment he fell off his horse. Then I looked up, and there was my old lord. 'How is he?' asks Caesar. 'Stunned,' says I, 'banged his head.' 'Is that all?' asks Caesar. 'Yes,' I say. 'Mosquito,' he says to me, 'break his arm, quick!' ''

Vigorce exclaimed. "Break his arm! What for?"

"Why? So that Caesar could fight the giant!"

"You did it!"

"Yes. All these stones lying about—I propped his arm on one, and cracked it with another."

Vigorce asked, "Did you get paid?"

"No," Mosquito said. He burst out laughing. "They must have meant the jewel for both of us."

"They?" Vigorce said. "It was hers!" He looked in dismay at the sky, and said, "Them!" Soon, he asked Mosquito, "Did you know the jewel was her talisman against madness?"

Mosquito said, "Maybe that's why she gave it to you."

"You're laughing at me," Vigorce said, with his face turned sideways to the small man, and looking at him out of one eye.

"Sure," Mosquito said. "Let's see the jewel!"

Vigorce took the jewel from his saddle-bag and looped the silk cord onto the wild olive tree. The stones, green and yellow and blue, took the sunlight to their hearts, while the gold accepted its caress. It made them quiet for some moments, to look at it. Then Mosquito held it on his hand, and afterwards Vigorce put it back carefully among his belongings.

They woke their horses, and set out for the mountains to the north. Behind them the keep of the unfinished castle sank slowly out of sight.

# Harvill Paperbacks are published by
# The Harvill Press

For the full list of titles please write to:

**The Harvill Press,**
84 Thornhill Road, London N1 1RD
*enclosing a stamped self-addressed envelope*